Champagne Book Group Presents

Albion Moon

Albion Moon Chronicles, Book 1

By

M. L. Mastran

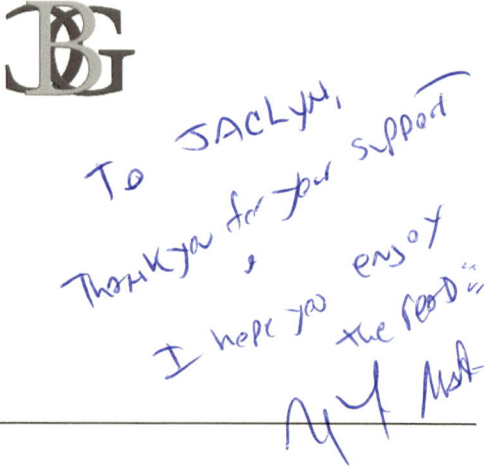

This is a work of fiction. The characters, incidents and dialogues in this book are of the author's imagination and are not to be construed as real. Any resemblance to actual events or persons, living or dead, is completely coincidental.

No part of this book may be reproduced or transmitted in any form or by any means, electronic or mechanical, including photocopying, recording, or by any information storage and retrieval system, without permission in writing from the publisher.

Champagne Book Group
www.champagnebooks.com
Copyright 2018 by M. L. Mastran
ISBN 978-1-947128-37-8
August 2018
Cover Art by Creative Paramita
Produced in the United States of America

Champagne Book Group
2373 NE Evergreen Avenue
Albany OR 97321
USA

Introduction

16 Decembre 1899

My dearest Madelena:
I trust your visit to your family in Spain goes well. Unfortunately, I must advise you of something before you return to our home in Albion in Aprile. Centuseeries ago, mayhem amongst the clans bloomed. This turmoil raged in the Highlands over land, honor, and principles. Each clan believed they had the right to fight.

English reports came in saying my own Mac Griogair clan, being vicious and bloody, were amongst the most prominent of them all. As the battles raged on, the English Queen Elizabeth sent troops to quell the uprisings but stories of the Mac Griogair, being unnaturale strong and not men but beasts, swirled. Before her death, she deemed my own Mac Griogair uncontrollable, and so, our own James, King of England, issued a decree, proclaiming the name Mac Griogair "altogidder abolisheed." Those of us who bore the name had to renounce it... or be executed.

Several of our leaders, including my uncle and our chieftain, were captured and sentenced to death. This was when we Mac Griogair took different names and dispersed into five different families until the day we could be whole again. One hundred and seventy years passed before the English decreed we could reestablish.

In 1774, the time came to reunite the clan, and word was sent out, calling those who had left to come back home. Two of the five families returned to the Mac Griogair, and we searched for the remaining three. It was learned they fled to the New World, and I was named to go with other conscripts to search for, find, and bring our brethren back to Albion.

We found the Granndach, the first of the lost families, not long after our arrival. And when they did not want to come back, I sent word to Albion. We were ordered to finish it and find the other two families. With a heavy heart, I had to destroy my own blood. The battle lasted days and was both bloody and violent—just as all our battles were. Just *like before, stories of us being beasts and cursed circled once again. Shortly after, war broke out between the colonists and the English. I was relieved of my command, so I could return home, and it was upon this visit that I met you and your father. My brethren still in the New World found the second lost family during this time. They too refused to come back to Albion. Are we Mac Griogair so intolerable that our kin wish to not return to their family? It is my hope that when we find the remaining family, they will come home to Albion and no more of our blood will be lost. But we shall see. Oh, Madelena, I long so to see your lovely Spanish face just as I remember it.*

    Your loving husband,
    L.M.

One

Sacramento, California
Present Day

A chill went right through Jimmy as he walked down the cold, damp steps of the parking garage to the lower level. He glanced at his phone to check the time as most of his colleagues had already left. Quickly looking under 'favorites', he clicked Evaline's icon and put the phone to his ear.

"Hey, big brother!"

"Happy birthday, sis!"

"Thank you, thank you. Are you still at work?"

"Yeah, I had court, plus I have this new client, and he's pretty demanding."

"Is he a criminal like most of the clients at your firm?" Evaline asked in a sarcastic tone.

"Ha, ha very funny. Anyway, there's a lot of properties and paperwork I have to look into for him; it's just time consuming, that's all." He hastily opened the door to the parking garage. "I'm coming to pick you up and take you out for your birthday, okay?"

"But Jimmy, it's late, and I know you're probably wiped. We can do it over the weekend."

"Nope. I always take my sister out on her birthday; it's tradition," he said, smiling.

"Okay. Okay, I'll be ready. Just be careful?"

Before he could answer, a strange scratching sound broke through the eerie quiet and stopped him in his tracks. The strong scent of pine and earth surrounded him. Shadows moved.

"Okay, Eva, gotta go," he said as he listened to what was making the strange sound. "Love you, sis."

"Jimmy is everything okay? Why do you sound weird?" Evaline asked.

He peered directly into the shadows but saw nothing. "I'm fine. I'm coming now, all right?"

"All right, love you too."

With that, they hung up.

His heel thuds echoed across the concrete, only interrupted by an occasional water drip from somewhere or an engine starting from a level above. An unsettling sensation came over him as he hastened to his car, unlocking it with the remote. Before he reached it, something hit him hard, and he tumbled through the air then slammed back to the ground; his briefcase skidded across the pavement.

Frantically, he got to his feet in time to see a large figure coming right for him. He moved swiftly, and it missed. The figure stood on two legs and wicked smile on his face as Jimmy anticipated a move.

"What, you trying to rob me, you piece of shit? Come on then!" he yelled.

The man lunged toward him and pushed him into the wall. At that moment, more figures appeared and jumped Jimmy from behind. He swung at one of them, and the guy stepped back. The other two grabbed ahold of him firmly.

"What do you want?" he shouted.

The one he hit stood in front of him, and in a thick Scottish accent, said, "Been looking a long time for you, Jimmy. Now we get the other and put this search to an end."

"What are you talking about? Who the hell are you?" Jimmy struggled.

"Don't struggle, little wolf. It will be over soon. We need to make one more stop." With this, the man held up a picture of Jimmy and three other people smiling from a trip last summer. One of the girls in the photo was circled.

Looking at the man holding the photo, he exclaimed anxiously. "No! No! You stay away from my sister, or I'll kill you! Do you understand? I will kill you!"

"Jimmy, Jimmy, you think we want to hurt her? Well, if she doesn't cooperate maybe, but..."

Managing to twist from the grip of the two holding him, Jimmy shoved the guy holding the picture. Loping as fast as he could with the three men in pursuit, he managed make it to the street and sprint to the front of the building. The pit of his stomach churned as he anxiously reached for his cell phone in his pocket. The street was empty as only the distant car horns and police sirens echoed in-between the buildings.

He tried in vain to open the doors. Still holding onto his phone, he pounded on the glass doors as loud as he could. The guard normally at the front security desk was absent, and papers lay scattered across the lobby floor.

The words the man spoke to Jimmy kept playing over and over *if she doesn't cooperate, maybe*. Frantically, he swiped the screen on his phone and quickly punched the unlock code. Despite only one bar of service, he hoped the call would go through. A bottle rolled somewhere close on the ground as he looked up and saw the same group of men approaching him. He started backing up as he clicked Evaline's icon; he had to warn her.

Before it rang, something hit him hard, slamming him against the front of the building, his phone next to him in pieces. He struggled to see what hit him as the force of the blow knocked the wind out of him. He made out several large, dark figures in the shadows that moved with an uneasy speed. The silhouettes he could see didn't appear to be human as they were far too large and bulky.

He finally managed to stand, leaning heavily against the building façade.

"Jimmy, Jimmy why are you being so difficult?" a voice asked. A different voice; no accent.

"What do you want with me?" Jimmy asked while wincing at the throbbing pain in his shoulder.

His gaze finally focused on a figure standing several feet away from him with a couple of the other men from the garage next to him. The man wore a police uniform. Behind the men, and around them, the shadows moved as if alive. Everything in his head screamed to run as fast as he could.

A car passed by the side street less than a city block away. He eyed the street then the police officer, who hadn't moved. Jimmy shifted and managed to pull away from the building. Holding his knee briefly, he stumbled for the side street. With every painful stride, he got closer.

At that instance, the shadows closed in. Nails scraped on the pavement, low growls echoing around him. He glanced behind him. The sounds got closer as the shadows gave way to giant black and gray figures that stood on two legs but were far larger than any man. Each of their glowing eyes penetrated the darkness and eyed him as if he were prey.

~ * ~

Officer Marcus Campbell had no intention of allowing this one to get away; too much was at stake. Jimmy was but a few feet away from the curb when, like a rogue wave from the sea, the darkness completely encompassed him. A single scream escaped him and then, like the wave that took him, he was gone.

Marcus Campbell stood motionless before peering at Patrick, the Scottish man from the garage, who reached into his jacket pocket at the buzzing sound of his cell phone.

"We have him, sir. He is at the site, and we are waiting for Leathan." Patrick paused as he glanced at Marcus. "I see. Unexpected, but welcomed. I understand." He clicked end call.

Marcus eyed him. "Who was that?"

"Management. Just checking on progress," Patrick answered.

"Fine, let's get this over with then."

Both men walked away as the street filled with silence.

~ * ~

Three weeks later
One hundred and twenty miles north of Sacramento, California

I turned up the radio as the wind blew through my hair: a perfect day to put the top down. Rounding each bend as the engine screamed, I stepped on the gas harder. I headed home to Dunsmuir, my hometown. Due to the construction on I-5, I decided to go the back way.

The engine roared as I drove under the canopy of trees on either side of route 89, sunlight shimmering through the ceiling. Stopping at one of the general stores along the road, I picked up lunch and supplies. The parking lot teemed with people in RVs, campers, and other vehicles. I usually ignored their stares but sometimes it was because of my car. My 1973 Cougar with the fading red paint job and the cracking black vinyl seats was my dad's and hardly was car-show worthy. Nevertheless, it's still a classic and folks loved to look at it.

After grabbing some snacks and getting back on the road, I turned east and entered Dunsmuir, a quaint town of one thousand six hundred and thirty-three souls and a perfect little place with perfect little shops and stores.

"A great place to raise a family" was its motto. They were right, of course. Big city crime didn't find its way here. There was a three-hour buffer zone between Dunsmuir and Sacramento, and no other major city around, so Dunsmuir was spared from major illegal activities. Nestled on the edge of the mountains and national forest, if serenity and quiet was what one wanted, this was the place. Tourists would flood the streets and shops during the summer months on their way to camp in the mountains, so tourism provided a nice income for the town.

I followed the river to Clark Street and turned. There were eight houses on the street, my aunt's house being the last one on the left. It was an old house with wood siding, and the white, faded paint was chipping off. The porch showed its age. Despite the repair needs, I loved the house and the memories it held. I pulled into the drive, and before I could turn the car off, Kristy was outside.

Hugging me, she said, "Oh, Evaline, I'm so glad you're here. You have no idea how much. I can't—I just can't..." Tears welled in her eyes.

I looked at her, hoping to offer some reassurance. "It's okay. We'll do this together. You're not alone?"

Her saddened expression eased into enthusiasm. "I can't believe how good you look and how long your hair is. Just like Aunt Lillian!"

I laughed, grabbing a piece of my hair and inspecting it. My brownish-red hair hung to my mid-lower back, and I usually had it tied back. "Yeah, well, I just haven't gotten around to cutting it, and I think Mom wore hers longer."

She smiled and hugged me again.

Kristy was twenty-two and had made the decision to not attend college because she hadn't decided what she wanted to do. She had shoulder-length black hair and dark eyes. She was pretty, but she didn't date much, preferring seclusion to a group, and she usually only hung out with one or two friends. The desire for solitude ran in our family.

She smiled as Laine came out of the house.

My cousin Laine was rougher around the edges. He was twenty-one and seemed like he should be on a beach surfing instead of in a forest town. He hugged me tight.

"It's great to see you, Eva. We missed you." He pulled away as grinned at me. "Damn, girl, looking good."

We grinned at each other for a moment, and then his amusement faded. "Any word on Jimmy?"

I shook my head.

We started walking, with him and Kristy on either side of me. Kristy asked, "You mean the police haven't found anything?"

I didn't want to tell them what I suspected. "No, they haven't found a thing. They aren't presuming anything, and since there is no evidence of foul play, they're treating it as a missing person." I stopped for a moment. "He's never missed my birthday. Not ever."

Her expression changed to sadness, and we entered the house.

My stomach churned nervously as I knew in my gut Jimmy was gone, but my heart didn't want to believe it. The roadblocks in the investigation prompted me to investigate on my own. The three of us sat at the kitchen table, and I told them of what I knew up to that point, but not all.

"So you know Jimmy still worked at the law firm he signed with directly after law school?" They nodded as I continued, "Well, they are one of the biggest law firms in Sacramento. He loved it. You know Jimmy got the fast car, big office, and he was so good at it. Well, Jimmy told me this firm handled clients with money and criminal problems. I guess a specific client requested him a few weeks ago. He was so excited."

"Did you talk to his boss? Maybe this person had something to do with him disappearing?" Kristy asked.

I winced at the thought. "Yes, but he was little help. Therefore, I contacted Kenny, Jimmy's friend from the police department and tracked the name of Jimmy's last client. Apparently, Kenny found out this client was involved in shady dealings. I tried to get answers from the firm, but I was referred to Jimmy's boss, who seemed sympathetic to my plight…but that didn't stop him from avoiding my questions about Jimmy's last client."

"Sounds like they know something, Eva," Laine said.

"Well, the case is still ongoing as far as I know. The police said they are looking into all leads."

What I couldn't tell them was, in actuality, no leads presented themselves, and the search went nowhere. Seemed like a dead end popped up whenever a supposed lead rose. I convinced myself someone was deliberately blocking the investigation, so I decided to take matters into my own hands.

Figured I must have stumbled onto something, as that's the time the threatening phone calls and e-mails started. I convinced myself Jimmy must have seen something he shouldn't have. I didn't want to tell them whenever I spoke to Jimmy's boss, it felt as if he tried to deter me with something to the effect of "these types of people" don't like to be bothered, and it would be in my best interest to drop the case and let the police handle it. All that did was fuel me even more to find out what happened to my brother.

The more I searched and uncovered, the more feathers ruffled. Things started getting scary when my investigation started to point to a cop named Marcus Campbell being dirty. It wasn't long before threats came in the mail, on the phone, and even suspicious knocks at my door.

However, every time I heard a knock at the door or heard my phone ring, despite the awful feeling in the pit of my stomach, I vowed not to give up. Even the complete fear of being hurt or worse did not quench my drive to find my brother. The police took me into custody for bogus tickets they claimed I never paid and another time for making false reports about Jimmy. All harassment.

Officer Campbell apparently was into much more than I'd imagined. His list of indiscretions included drug trafficking and using his job as a police officer to run the merchandise. I observed it myself one afternoon when I decided to tail him. I suspected, based on his demeanor, he'd have no problems with murder, racketeering, and who knew what else. I had contemplated what to do when I'd gotten the call from Kristy.

I sat back. "So, tell me what happened with Aunt Deb?"

"She was on her way to the grocery store after work, and they told me her car gone off the road. I guess she died instantly when she hit the tree." Tears filled her eyes.

I gently touched her shoulder. "We can get through this, okay?"

She wiped the few tears that streamed down her face as the three of us gazed at the mess of papers on the kitchen table. Laine rubbed the back of his neck. So much disorganization surrounding Aunt Deb's funeral.

I quickly scanned the papers. "Kristy, have you contacted the funeral home or picked out a casket yet?"

"Yeah, we did that yesterday morning. They gave us this." She indicated the bill. "They said it would be due before burial. Um, Evaline, I don't think Mom had the cash. I mean, we looked at her checkbook and confirmed with the bank, but they said they needed a death certificate to give us any information."

"How much was in there? I mean, would it be enough to bury her?"

She shrugged as Laine spoke up. "This is a crock. We can't even bury our mom because of this bullshit."

A bit of shock raised my eyebrow until I remembered how blunt Laine could be. "Laine, we'll figure it out? I'll go to the bank tomorrow and make some calls—just calm down. Right now, you both need to relax and concentrate on what we need to do over the next few days. The funeral is the day after tomorrow, right?"

"Yeah," he murmured.

"Kristy, you need to pick out something for Aunt Deb to wear, a favorite dress maybe and jewelry you want her to be buried with." I eyed Laine. "You can help get things ready for the wake. People will come over afterward with food and cards. The house needs to be cleaned, especially the kitchen which I'll help with. Do you both work? Did you call off?"

He winced. "Yeah, I'm in-between jobs right now."

I wasn't surprised.

He stepped back. "Hey, I had an interview the other day."

Kristy said, "Yeah, I told them I wouldn't be in for a few days."

"Okay, the next couple days will be tough, but we'll get through them. Is there food for tonight?"

She shook her head slightly. "There's nothing here. We've been living off the casseroles the neighbors made for us when it happened. I haven't gone to the store yet."

"Okay. How about pizza? Is there a good pizza place nearby, or do you want to go out?"

Laine pipped in, "Well, there's Papa Pepper's that delivers."

My stomach rumbled with hunger at the thought. "Cool. Can you order us food and get pop to drink while you're at it? I'll go to the store tomorrow when I'm out."

We dispersed, and I stepped into the quiet hallway, peering into the living room and dining room. A family portrait hung in the living room, which drew my attention. I gazed at it with love and sadness at the same time. My family—my father, Jimmy, my mom, and me.

I took a closer look at my mom. She was the heart of our family. Beautiful with long brown hair and bright hazel eyes; the very same hazel eyes I had. I remember she was protective of us as any mother would be, but I had the distinctive impression she would defend us, whatever the cost.

I pulled away from the picture and walked upstairs to my room. Each room appeared darker than the next; the good times I had in this house were gone: no smiles, no happiness. Coming home to Dunsmuir under these circumstances was harder than I'd thought.

That night, I lay in bed wanting to cry. I stared at the ceiling with a thousand thoughts rushing through my mind. Memories mixed with anxiety and emptiness surrounding Jimmy's disappearance screamed in my head. It was in times of despair or tension that I found comfort in my grandmother's pendant. She'd passed it on to my mother and Mom had passed it to me.

Whenever I needed guidance or comfort, I gripped the pendant. Jimmy got the ring that matched it. They both had a dragon with a sword in a shield, which represented a coat of arms, and below it, there were words in a lost language. I'd asked my mom what it meant once, but all she would say was that it had to do with our heritage.

I held it tightly, as I knew I needed to be strong for Kristy and Laine, but it was tough. Thoughts of Jimmy had been plaguing my sleep since he disappeared. It was like he was trying to tell me something but yet he was pissed off. The dreams were never clear as to why he was angry.

I sighed. Financially, I could keep us above water for a short while, but eventually I would need to find work. There were a couple banks in town, one being the same branch that I worked in Sacramento, so I kept those in mind. Tomorrow would be another day. Maybe a better day.

Two

Marcus casually walked toward the darkened limo behind the Sacramento Police Station. He glanced around the stillness of the night, a half-moon partially illuminating the sky. In the distance, he heard sirens and cars on the nearby expressway. He stopped in front of the rear door, seconds passing before the door finally opened. Taking one last look around, he stepped into the car, closing the door behind him.

Patrick, clad in a black leather jacket, sat quietly in the corner next to Leathan, who worked on a laptop across from Marcus. Leathan was muscular beneath his suit. He had shoulder length brown hair, which was pulled back in a ponytail. He merely glanced with his dark eyes at Marcus and handed him an envelope, which he looked inside then smiled briefly at the contents.

Leathan leaned in. "They want her followed. If it's found that she hasn't let this thing with Jimmy be, then you need to persuade her, but don't touch her."

"Why not just take her out of the equation? It would be better for all of us if she were no longer a threat."

Disgust tinted his expression. "Officer Campbell, you do what you're told as per our agreement," he said in a thick Scottish accent. "You were sloppy, and now this is the bloody fallout. The agreement is that she is not to be touched yet, but it's still up for debate. We may just take her back by force, but until then, you keep yourself and your boys in line."

Marcus sat back. His lips twisted. "I will, but what about the sheriff?"

"Taken care of. The paperwork is prepared, and you should be set. I'm sure you remember Patrick? You can use him however you need to get the job done, and as you well know, he is quite good at persuasion." Leathan sat back.

He agreed as Leathan picked up his cell phone and clicked a button. He eyed Marcus again. "Don't fuck this up."

Marcus and Patrick exited the limo, leaving Leathan to answer his phone.

Marcus heard him say, "I need to speak with Kamden." He paused, then said, "They sent the order. Yes, I sent Patrick with him. She went back home to be with her family. I understand. We shall see."

Leathan ended the call, put his phone down, then picked up the car phone, ringing the limo driver. "I'm feeling a wee bit hungry. Head up to the mountains."

Reaching over he pulled the car door in front of Marcus's face but not before he said the end of the e-mail Leathan had been typing: "Your Loving Husband, L.M."

~ * ~

Funerals are always tough. In some cultures, death was celebrated because it was believed the soul went to paradise. Not so much in American culture, although I have viewed death differently from others. The day of my aunt's funeral was filled with sorrow, and I did my best to keep Kristy and Laine from losing it. I knew exactly how they felt as I had been there not so long ago.

The cemetery was probably the toughest for me. After the service, I walked over to my parents' and my grandma's graves. They were all there together, beneath the giant oak—and now Aunt Deb was as well. At least now that I was home, I could visit them more often. I missed them terribly, and with Jimmy gone, I was completely and utterly alone.

After the funeral and service, everyone filed back to the house for the wake. Food covered every open counter space and the dining room table. Some of the people there were ones I remembered from my youth and grade school, but many were new. Flowers and cards piled up in the breezeway and in the back sitting room. In a town with so few people, you were bound to know at least half of the population, and it seemed like the entire town was there.

By the end of the first hour and a half, I was tired of smiling and crying. I was tired of hugging people, so I went to the kitchen and put on my iPod for a moment before I had to get back to the living room. I was putting water in one of the vases when Kristy came up behind me.

"Eva, this is my best friend, Elizabeth."

Elizabeth was a pretty girl with long, dark hair and piercing eyes that had a strange shimmer to them. She was around Kristy's age, and she smiled as she extended her hand. There was another, older girl standing quietly behind her.

"It's nice meet you, Elizabeth. Kristy talks a lot about you."

Elizabeth winced. "Good things, I hope, and please call me Lizzy." She glanced at Kristy who rolled her eyes. Lizzy eyed my iPod on the counter as heavy guitar riffs blared from the earbuds. "Great song."

I turned it off. "Yeah, sorry about that. I needed a break."

Kristy and Lizzy exchanged knowing glances as Kristy stepped aside to introduce the girl standing behind her.

"This is Lizzy's sister, Lucy." She was closer to my age, maybe a little older, and very pretty, with dark hair just below the shoulder and blue-green eyes that had the same slight shimmer as Lizzy's. I took notice of her necklace, which was strangely like mine but with a different design. It was clearly a coat of arms.

"Hi." She appeared standoffish, but she still managed to extend her hand.

"Did you guys eat? We have plenty."

"No, we're good thanks," Lucy said.

Kristy pointed to the corner. "That's from them." It was a meat tray with cheese and crackers. "Do you remember where I told you I work?"

"That place right outside of town, right?" I asked.

"Yes, well, their family owns it. The tray is from all of them."

"Thank you for this. It really does help." I leaned up against the counter as Kristy and Lizzy moved off.

Lucy eyed me. "She's happy you're here."

I took the vase out of the sink and placed it on the counter. "Well, it's what family is for. She's the closest thing I have to a sister, and Laine, well, Laine is Laine. He handles things very differently."

"I know what you mean. I have a younger brother who does that," she indicated with a chuckle. I smiled in agreement, as she continued, "Kristy said you have a brother?"

I winced. "Yeah, I do." I paused briefly. "Jimmy. He's my older brother."

"Is he here as well?"

I did not want to have this conversation. "No."

"I understand. Brothers can be tough to deal with sometimes."

"How many brothers do you have?"

"Four."

"What fun! Good luck with that." We laughed as Kristy and Lizzy turned back toward us.

"We need to get back," Lucy said to Lizzy.

Lizzy hugged Kristy and me as well. As they turned to leave, Lucy turned to Kristy. "Isaac said you don't need to be back to work until Tuesday, okay?"

Kristy heaved a sigh of relief as she waved bye. "I'll text you later."

As they exited, the people in the living room seemed to make room for them as they passed. There'd been a strange uneasiness when they'd been there, like what prey must feel like when being stalking or when you know something is watching you, but you can't see it.

After everyone finally left, Laine disappeared on his bike somewhere, and Kristy helped me clean up. I asked her about Lizzy's family.

"They moved here about six years ago. They keep to themselves. There are four brothers, Lucy, and Lizzy. They run the Blue Dawn. It's a restaurant and bar right outside town."

"They live in town?" I asked.

"No. They have a place outside town. You can't really see it from the road, but I guess there's a lot of property. Except for Jonas, they're all pretty quiet."

"Jonas?"

Kristy smiled briefly as she explained, "He's the youngest brother and is best friends with Laine. They're always getting into trouble. Used to drive Mom crazy."

I couldn't help but smile at her blushing. "You like him?"

We moved to the kitchen table and began drying off the glasses.

Kristy laughed. "Um, yeah. I'm crushing on him big time."

"You'll have to introduce me." I waited a moment. "Kristy, we're going to have to start cleaning out your mom's stuff. I'm thinking sooner is better than later. You and Laine need to think about what you want keep and what you want to get rid of."

She lowered her head. "Yeah, I didn't want to deal with that."

I touched her hand. "I'll be here. I had to help Dad and Jimmy when my mom died too." I pulled away as I continued, "It's not easy, but believe it or not, it helps. It's kinda therapeutic in a way. It helps us move on."

"Are you going to go through Jimmy's stuff?" Kristy asked.

I hadn't even thought about it. Since it was a current investigation, I couldn't take anything from his apartment let alone go through it. "I don't want to just yet. I don't want to think that he's gone. I still have that tiny glimmer of hope maybe he fell and doesn't know who he is or something."

"Yeah, maybe. Hope is a good thing to have nowadays."

I sighed as I thought of the loss. "Our family has been through so much over the last several years. We've lost so many."

Kristy said nothing more. We finished up cleaning and ended a very exhausting day. I was out as soon as I hit the pillow.

~ * ~

Over the next couple of days, we put everything away and began to clean out Aunt Deb's stuff. It had to be Laine and Kristy who did it, but I helped as much as I could. Leaving them alone to look through Aunt Deb's closet, thoughts of Jimmy raced through my mind. I could have used him over the last few days—how much we all could have used him.

Plopping down on the floor, I reached for the box underneath my bed. Placing it on the bed, I opened it then peered into it. Painful memories vied in my mind at the sight of newspaper articles, files, photos, and reports; the pages of harassment from my phone, answering machine and emails warning me to back off—it was all here. After getting nowhere with Sacramento PD soon after Jimmy disappeared, his friend Kenny started helping me out. Kenny had called me one afternoon and said he had found something big about Jimmy's disappearance and needed to meet me. I had gone to meet him, but he never came.

I glanced at the newspaper clipping of a car being pulled out of the river. After Kenny hadn't showed, the very next day I'd gone to the department—he'd never arrived for work, and they were trying to call him. I knew something had happened.

They'd found Kenny's car a week later in the Sacramento River, but they never found him. That's when the harassment intensified. Because I wanted my harassers to think I gave up, other than the post office, I left without a word or forwarding address. The information in the box was why Jimmy and Kenny had both disappeared. I needed to collect a few more bits of information before I approached the authorities with it.

There were a few cold cases connected with one particular officer. I had suspicions about Sergeant Marcus Campbell, who appeared to be into everything for which he had sworn to fight. Officer Campbell called the shots, and I was sure he knew what happened to Jimmy. I looked through the articles, and my gaze fell on the picture of him I had given the police. It was a picture he'd taken at his firm, when he first got hired. As I gaze at his picture, I made him a promise.

"I'll find out, Jimmy, and they'll pay. I promise they'll pay... I miss you so much." Tears welled in my eyes, and I wiped them away.

I sat at the computer and searched the last place Officer Campbell had worked before Sacramento. He'd toiled with several cases in Redding the year before he arrived. Kenny had highlighted several of these that were deemed suspicious by Internal Affairs but nothing had been done due to lack of evidence. There had to be something I could use against him, something I could follow up on—something they wouldn't see coming. I would continue to search until I found just the right lead. I placed everything back in the box and slipped it back under my bed. Engrossed in what to do next, I lay back on my bed and closed my eyes.

There was a slight knock at my door, and it opened as Kristy peeked in. "Evaline, I think the bathroom faucet just broke," she said as she held a broken knob in her hand.

"Okay, well, I gotta run some errands. Why don't you take a break and come with me, and we'll stop at the hardware store?"

She agreed, and we drove into town. The bathroom faucet knob had not only broken, but it had decided to snap off completely. So, we brought the old faucet to the store and showed it to a clerk who then indicated where the new faucets were. Kristy was looking at something up front, and when I came back, she was talking to Lizzy. I was annoyed at how much the faucet cost as I was keeping a close eye on finances. We'd found a stash or two among Aunt Deb's things. I walked up to where they were talking as Kristy turned to me.

"You found it," she said.

I grinned at Lizzy. "Hey, Lizzy. How are ya?"

She smiled back, and I took notice of her charm bracelet which had a similar design to Lucy's necklace.

"I'm good." A horn sounded as she was talking. "Um, that's Jonas. I have to go. Bye, Evaline. See you at work Tuesday, Kristy." She left and got into a souped-up Jeep with big tires.

We checked out and got back into the car. At first, my car didn't start.

"That's the third time it hasn't started for you," Kristy indicated with a concerning look.

I waited a moment and tried again. It started up after some difficulty. "It's the starter. I have to call around and see if I can get another one."

Kristy leaned over and turned on the radio. "You need to be careful. It's gonna get you stranded somewhere."

As we pulled out, a man appeared out of nowhere in front of us, and I slammed on the brakes to avoid hitting him. As I observed through the windshield, my heart sank. The figure standing in front of my hood and wearing the Dunsmuir Sheriff uniform was someone very familiar. Speechless, all I could do was stare as a sneering Campbell turned and walked toward the courthouse.

Three

Jimmy held my hand, and we were running through the woods. I couldn't see what was behind us, but something was there—something was after us.

He kept encouraging me. "Don't stop, Evaline! Keep running! He'll get you!"

As we fled, every time we were almost out of the woods, it got darker. I could hear growls and heavy breathing behind us. We finally reached the edge of the woods. Jimmy came to an abrupt halt.

Puzzled, I held his hand and eyed him. "Jimmy, come on! It's him! Please come with me!"

He stared at me but didn't move. He seemed sad as his dark eyes peered behind us and then back to me. "You need to leave me, Evaline. Don't stay. This is all I can do now to protect you from him. Stay away."

I wouldn't let him go. "Jimmy, no! I found you. Please come home."

Again, he looked behind us and then back to me. I closed my eyes for a moment, squeezing his hand tightly and praying it wasn't a dream. When I opened my eyes, he was gone. I looked down at the hand he had held, and it was now full of dirt.

I let the dirt fall through my fingers, and the growling and breathing was now directly in front of me. I stared into the fog and saw a man's silhouette. He started walking toward me, but a sound behind me made me turn around. There, a beautiful white-and-gray wolf stood. It didn't move or growl. It just stood there. I didn't feel threatened, so I turned back to the man, whose face was now illuminated by the moonlight. It was Campbell, and he grinned at me as I stood mortified.

He was in uniform, and he leaned toward me and whispered, "Found ya."

Dripping with sweat, I woke up and bolted upright. A dream. I put my hand to my forehead as tears streamed down my cheeks. "Jimmy. Jimmy," I kept saying. I wanted to go back and find him despite the danger coming from Campbell.

Trying to figure out the dream, I laid back. I knew in my heart what the dirt meant, but I still did not want to believe it. It wasn't the only time I had a dream like it. My father's mother had similar dreams as well. She called them premonitions. Grandma said that not everyone in the family had "the gift," as she liked to call it. I tried not to put too much weight into the dreams, but sometimes they came true—other times, they warned me. Either way, when I had them, they appeared so real. This one filled me with sadness and fear at the same time. All I could do was cry myself back to sleep.

The next morning, I went downstairs to the kitchen and got cereal. Laine was up and had already made coffee. I sat with a cup and glanced at the newspaper on the table. The headline read *No Details on Missing Dunsmuir Sheriff*. It was too much of a coincidence that the sheriff disappeared just as Campbell had shown up.

Laine leaned against the kitchen counter, drinking his coffee. "Mom paid the paper subscription for a year, so we have it for another five months." His voice broke into my thoughts. My mind wandered to the dream with Jimmy as Laine continued, "Evaline, you okay?"

"I'm good. Just tired."

He sat next to me and leaned in. "You had a bad dream last night, didn't you?"

I sipped my coffee but didn't say anything.

"Was it about Mom or Jimmy?"

I nervously bit at my lower lip. "Jimmy, he's always trying to tell me something in the dreams, but he just can't say it."

In a cautious tone, Laine asked, "You think… you think he's dead?"

Remembering the dirt in my dream, I hesitated for a moment. I glanced at Laine and was sure he could see the pain on my face. "Yeah, I do. I think he was killed because he found out something he wasn't supposed to."

I couldn't tell him what I suspected about Campbell and my investigation or the harassment. I didn't know whom I could tell without endangering them. Campbell or whoever it was hadn't hesitated when making a cop disappear; a nobody from a small town wouldn't be a big deal.

I changed the subject. "Did you check on the place that Mr. Givens said was hiring?"

"Yeah, I start in an hour."

I smiled. "You need a ride?"

He shook his head. "I'll take my bike."

Kristy came in, saying, "Yeah, well, you need to be careful or the rent-a-sheriff will give you a ticket."

Laine rolled his eyes. "Hey, I have turn signals and legal plates. He can't do squat."

A spark of anxiety came over me. Campbell had undoubtedly come to Dunsmuir because of me. I looked at Kristy. "Rent-a-sheriff?"

She poured a bowl of cereal as she answered, "I've never seen him before, and he's only been here for a few days, but I guess he's something else from what's being said in town. He's only temporary until the council can elect a new one."

I couldn't believe he was in Dunsmuir. "Do they know what happened to the old sheriff?"

Coming to the table, she sat with a spoon and her cereal. "Sheriff Peters disappeared the day we buried Mom. It's like he vanished completely." She continued as she eyed Laine. "Well, one thing is for sure; this one will hate Laine too." Laughing, Kristy punched Laine in the arm as he stuck his tongue out at her. "Maybe you and Jonas can stay out of trouble?"

He took one last sip of his coffee and put his mug into the sink. "Fat chance. The law hates bikes, four wheelers, snowmobiles, and anything else they can't catch." He got up and headed for the door. "See you guys later."

I chuckled to myself as he left and eyed Kristy. "What about where you work? Didn't they have any openings for Laine?"

"Nah, we tried that. He and Jonas were constantly screwing around, and they pissed off Isaac, so he got fired."

"Is Isaac your boss?"

"Isaac is the oldest of the brothers. He oversees everything. Mason's my boss. He oversees the employees, and Aaron and Jonas handle the grill and security. Lucy works the bar sometimes, and Lizzy works the floor with me. Personally, I think all four of the brothers could handle security solo."

"Why do you say that?"

She leaned in. "Well, they're huge, like linebackers. Plus, they're hot."

I laughed. "And Jonas?"

She smiled. "Yeah, I've liked Jonas for a while, but he's so… harsh I guess I would say."

"Is he mean to you?"

"No. He just doesn't care. Like if you're making him mad, he won't be polite about it. He'll just tell you, 'You're pissing me off.' You know, kinda like you do when you get mad enough."

I grinned as I finished my coffee. "Sometimes things just need to be said. What time do you work today?"

"Four this afternoon to two in the morning. What are you doing?"

I got up and put my cup into the sink. "I have to go pay the cemetery today for Aunt Deb's plot and then I'm heading to the library to do some research."

"You writing a book or something?"

"No, I'm just working on a project. I may be in bed when you get home so I guess I'll see you in the A.M."

With that, I left and headed to the library, which proved grueling. I found countless newspaper articles and made copies of anything pertaining to any of the cases Kenny had highlighted in the files. Some items were names and places. Particularly where Campbell was the investigating officer, nearly every one of the cases he worked on in the last year, before he transferred to Sacramento, concerned an "accident" or "missing persons" case. A pattern began to emerge, and it started with Campbell.

Most of the cases were resolved, but a few remained open. In all the cases, the missing and murdered were from all lifestyles: petty thieves to doctors. I ran the victim names through Google and came across the family of one of the missing people who still resided in Redding. I wrote down their names, address, and phone. I planned to call them the next morning. Didn't know what I would say, but knew I needed to talk to them. After several hours, I went home with heavy thoughts.

As I walked up to the front door, I noticed a white envelope jutting out from the screen door's frame. Kristy and Laine were both working, so it wasn't from them. Grabbing the envelope and going inside, I flicked on the kitchen lights and opened the envelope. A gasp left my lips at what was inside. All it said was, *"Found you, sweetness. Back off or else."*

Something dropped from the envelope, and a lump formed in my throat as I recognized Jimmy's driver's license. I grabbed it and studied it. There were smudges that could only be one thing: blood. I put the letter and license back into the envelope and headed upstairs. Pulling out the box of evidence, I added the envelope as well as my findings from the library. Despite the threat, I was determined to not back down.

The next day, I got up earlier than the previous morning from a dream-free sleep. I had heard Laine come in right before sunrise, so I knew he wouldn't be up for a while. Kristy had worked until two in the morning, so she didn't often get up before eleven.

I had my usual cup of coffee as I looked at my finances. I was facing the realization I would soon need to get a job—part-time until I was done investigating. I needed time to follow up and research.

Kristy had urged me to go see Mr. Parker at the bank, but I think I was more worried that I would get the job than that I wouldn't. The position was a full-time job, and I would be stuck in an office. Where was the happy medium? I just didn't want to think about it at that point.

Kristy and Laine had absolutely no interest in rummaging through files and papers, so I decided to take on the task of going through Aunt Deb's office stuff and passing along anything I thought they should have. By the time I got through the bottom drawer, Kristy had woken up, gotten her coffee, come into the living room, then sat on the couch.

I smiled at her. "Hey, how was work last night?"

She still appeared tired. "Long. This group of creeps came in last night, and they were so rude. Jonas almost had to kick them out. They were saying stuff to me, Lizzy, and the other girls. It was just ignorant." She shook her head.

"I know what you mean. You're always going to have ignorance, and trash is in nearly every town. We just have to know how to deal with it."

She took a sip of her coffee. "I know. They were drunk too, but it doesn't make it any better."

"Have you thought about maybe looking at college again? Maybe pick up a few classes?"

"I don't know, Evaline. I'm not as smart as you or Jimmy. Plus, I have no idea what to do. I mean, you have a degree, and you're not working."

"I'm not working because that's a choice I made. Right now, I have other things going on. It doesn't mean I'm never going back to work. I just need to straighten things out first. Do you want to wait on ignorant assholes forever, or do you want to do something else?"

She sat up and put her cup on the table. She drummed her fingers for a moment. "Well, I know I don't want to do this forever, but what would I do?"

"Well, what do you enjoy doing? What are you interested in?"

"I love to draw, but how can I make a living at that?"

"That's something. Maybe graphic design with some business classes. Not only could you do your art, but it would also give you some computer and business knowledge."

"I guess I didn't think about that. I'll look online later and check out Shasta College and maybe Simpson University. Thanks, Eva."

"Not a problem. Wanna help me with the top drawer?"

An expression of relief came over her as she sat next to me, and we started going through the drawer. "Mom sure had a lot of crap in this desk."

We laughed.

"Oh," she said suddenly. "I think my car is broken. It was making a weird noise when I pulled in the drive after work. I turned it off, and when I tried to start it again, it wouldn't."

"I'll look later, but I can take you to work."

She nodded, and we continued to clean out the desk drawers. Shortly after one thirty, Laine came downstairs and got what was left of the coffee. He joined us and sat on the couch.

Kristy looked up from sorting paper. "What time did you get home?"

"I think it was five thirty." The corners of his eyes crinkled. "It was a good night."

"What did you do? Were you with Jonas?" she asked.

His eyes narrowed. "Spanish inquisition, Kristy, but yeah, we went out after work. Why?"

She rolled her eyes. "Okay, bite my head off, Laine. I was just asking. Mom used to hate it when you didn't come home, that's all."

"Yeah, well, you're not bailing me out of jail this morning, so don't worry about it."

She shook her head and continued to rummage through the drawer.

"So how was work?" I asked, trying to break the tension.

"Good. Should get my first paycheck next week."

I guess now was as good a time as any. "Well, I wanted to tell you something while you're both here. Our finances are dwindling. The money in your mom's account is almost depleted, and so is what we found to pay the car payments for the next month. I've dipped into my savings to keep us ahead, but it's not going to last forever. I will need to get a job very soon, but we all need to pitch in. Luckily, Aunt Deb paid the house off two years ago, so we don't have to worry about a house payment, but there are utilities and other living expenses we'll need to split. I need you guys to start putting cash in the jar to help pay for things."

They stared at each other.

Laine was the first to speak. "So, what I make, I have to give to you?"

I knew this wasn't going to be an easy discussion. "No, but I'll need a percentage to pay for stuff, otherwise we will end up living at a local hotel. It's up to you. I put an old coffee can up in the cupboard. Just put the cash in there."

Kristy flashed him a look. "Yes, that makes sense. Can you come up with how much, so we can start preparing?"

I nodded, focusing on Laine. "Laine, it is what it is. If all three of us pitch in, you'll still have spending money after you help. Just don't lose this job, okay? We need you."

He seemed to back off as he got up. "Just let me know how much."

After he left, Kristy was apologetic. "Sorry. He would do that when Mom asked him too. He just gets weird with money."

"It's fine. He'll come around. We'll make it work. I promise."

We talked for a while about when we were younger and family stuff. Before we knew it, it was four o'clock.

"Oh man, I'm so late!" she suddenly yelped.

I moved quickly. "Okay, go get dressed, and I'll check your car."

I threw on a jacket and drew my hair back. I tried to get it to turn over, but her car was dead. She came out on the porch as I was getting out of her car. "Dead as a door nail," I said. "I'll look at it later. Come on. I'll take you to work."

We got in my Cougar and dropped the top as we headed down Old River road. I glanced over at Kristy. "I'll come in with you. Maybe they'll cut you some slack."

She smiled. "Yeah, maybe. You should come in and eat though. They have the best burgers."

That sounded good. We entered the parking lot of the Blue Dawn bar and grill. Despite opening at four, the lot only had a few cars in it. I parked up by the door, and we got out. The bar had a rustic, old-time feel to it. To the far left, was a stage and a dance floor; there were booths and tables scattered throughout. On the opposite side was a smaller version of the main bar, which stretched the entire length of the main room. I received a few glances by a couple of patrons seated at the bar as I followed Kristy to the far end of it. A guy with muscle and tattoos on his upper arms was standing there, writing on a clipboard.

Without looking up, he said, "You're late, Kristy." As she scrambled to put her apron on, Lizzy joined her and smiled at me.

"That's my fault," I said. "Sorry."

The guy's head jerked up. He was unbelievably good-looking,

with a partially unshaven face, dark hair, and bright green eyes that had a strange glimmer to them. The blue muscle shirt clung to his body and the sleeves hugged his broad arms. He didn't say a thing—just eyed me with a gleam in his eyes.

After a moment, I spoke again with an apologetic smile. "We were, um, reminiscing and lost track of time. It won't happen again."

"It's not the first time and won't be the last," he said finally, his tone amused, without taking his gaze off me. "You must be the cousin."

I was still smiling. "And you must be the boss."

"Does the cousin have a name?"

"It's Evaline."

He extended his hand, and I reached out mine, and we shook hands. "That's a nice name, Evaline. Mine's Mason."

I glanced over at the kitchen window to see two cooks and a waitress watching the conversation. "So, Mason, is the kitchen open?"

His eyes lit up. "You want to eat?"

"Well, I heard your burgers are pretty good." A strange sensation came over me as his gaze penetrated right through me—I wanted to tell him everything. It was intriguing and exciting. He smelled amazing, like pine. I wanted to just look at him all afternoon, and the weird thing was, I sensed he felt the same.

"You heard right," he replied. "They're the best burgers in the area. How did you want that?"

"Medium well, cheese, tomato, lettuce, and onion. Thanks."

He grinned again. "Coming right up."

Lizzy and Kristy had watched our conversation like it was a tennis match, and neither said anything but were both wide-eyed. I gave one last grin at Mason before turning and heading for a booth.

Kristy was next to me in a flash. "Oh. My. God," was all she could get out.

"Diet Coke Kristy, please?"

She turned to the bar. My phone beeped, indicating I had an email. I had placed a call earlier that morning to the Collins family in Redding about Harvey Collins, who was one of the missing people in Campbell's past. I'd left a message and provided my cell number and email address, briefly explaining I was a student studying unsolved cases and was given Harvey's case. The email was from Amanda Collins, Harvey's wife. She said she was willing to talk to me, but she wouldn't be back in town for a few days. She'd contact me when she returned to Redding.

I put my phone away as Kristy approached with my Diet Coke. "Lizzy is going to bring me home after work, so you don't have to come get me."

"Okay," I said.

She smiled, and I knew she wanted to talk about the Mason thing. I noticed a poster on the far wall indicating a live band on Friday night. I then glanced up to see Mason walking toward me with my food. He placed my burger in front of me. "Thank you. Looks awesome."

He leaned near me. "Did you want ketchup or mustard?"

"No thanks. This is good."

He straightened. "There's a good band this Friday. You should come," he said, indicating the poster I'd been looking at.

"Yeah maybe. Thanks for the invite."

My face got very warm as he tilted his head. "Talk to you soon," he said calmly.

Butterflies in my stomach fluttered like crazy. With a slight smile I answered, "Yes."

Kristy had been right. The burger was amazing.

After I left the Blue Dawn, I headed home, my mind flooded with thoughts of meeting the Collins's and, surprisingly, also of Mason. I didn't understand why I couldn't stop thinking about him. I had only spoken to him for a total of maybe six minutes. Nevertheless, those bright green eyes and that pine smell… Both had a strange familiarity for which I couldn't explain.

~ * ~

Over the next couple days, I picked up applications from the couple of banks and other places in town as well as in Shasta, the next town over. On Thursday, Kristy, Lizzy, and I hung out and went for ice cream downtown. We hit a couple of stores as Kristy wanted to get some clothes. I loathed clothes shopping. I peeked at the racks while Kristy tried stuff on and Lizzy weighed in. She got a text. One of the other servers had called off, and Mason needed her to come in.

"I have to get to work. Sorry, Kristy," Lizzy said.

"That's fine," Kristy said. "Can we get some lunch there when we take you in?"

I shook my head slightly at her scheming.

"Absolutely," Lizzy said, looking at me. "Let's go."

We piled into my car and headed out onto Old River Road. It was a great day for a convertible ride. The late summer sun beamed on us as we drove down the road. I had AC/DC blaring, and as we rounded a curve, I heard a siren. Peering into my rearview mirror, I eyed the red flashing police lights atop one of the town's two SUV police units.

Kristy glanced back. "What the fuck? You weren't speeding."

I looked down. I was just below the speed limit. After I pulled over, I got out my registration and insurance. The cop approached my door, and what I saw caused a huge lump to form in my throat.

Campbell had a smug look on his face as he spoke. "License, registration, and proof of insurance please."

I handed them over without making eye contact.

He examined my license, which still had my Sacramento address on it. "A little way from Sacramento, Miss Bennett, aren't we?"

"Yeah, I guess I am."

"Where are you headed right now?" His tone turned from mocking to icy.

"I need to get her to work," I said, indicating Lizzy.

He eyed Lizzy, who appeared annoyed by his questions. "Oh, a Cowan sister. How fitting. Tell your brother I got a nice cell waiting for him." She didn't say anything as his attention moved back to me. "So, are you here on vacation?"

My blood boiled as the dream I had with Jimmy came back to me. I glared at Campbell. "I'm visiting family for a while."

"So, what is the address you're staying at in town?"

"What does that matter?" Kristy interrupted any response I was about to make. "What the f—?"

"Smart ass like your brother," he said, cutting her off. "He's a great bunk mate for Jonas."

Now speechless, she sat there.

After opening my door, he indicated for me to move. "Please step out of the vehicle."

Not wishing to cause a scene, I complied and stood by my car.

He turned me around. "Face your car, hands on the hood."

Kristy found her voice again. "Are you fucking kidding me? We weren't doing anything!"

Campbell flashed her a look. "Shut up and don't move." He then patted me down. "Do you have any weapons or drug paraphernalia I need to be aware of?" He spun me back to him.

Looking at him dead in the eye, I answered, "No."

Holding my elbow, he walked me toward his vehicle as he eyed Kristy and Lizzy, who were clearly uncomfortable with what was happening. Despite my apprehension, I followed him. He took me behind his patrol truck and returned my license.

"I suggest you watch yourself, Miss Bennett. These back roads are dangerous, and if something were to happen, it could be quite a while until you'd be found." My stomach churned as he leaned into me and whispered, "A woman like yourself, all alone, might entice trouble." He reached for my breast, and I reacted quickly.

Shoving the bottom of my palm up into his lip, I knocked him back but didn't wait to see his reaction. I returned to my car, got in, then took off. I was sure he was going to follow, but he didn't.

Kristy turned to me. "We need to report him, Evaline. That was wrong in so many ways."

Shaking my head, I said, "It will make things worse, trust me. Just forget it, okay?"

She gave Lizzy a concerned look, who then asked, "Why did he take you back there?"

I didn't say anything as we drove into the parking lot, parked, then got out.

Kristy was still fired up. "This is such bullshit. He made a move on you, didn't he?"

"Just drop it, Kristy, okay? It's over. I wanna forget it."

The dust kicked up in the parking lot as we made our way through the front doors. A few patrons were seated at the bar, and several booths and tables were occupied. We headed to an open booth as Lizzy returned to the back.

While still a bit shaken from the encounter, I pondered what had just happened. A knot was in the pit of my stomach as thoughts raced through my mind.

Does he know I know what he is? Will he try to hurt what family I have left? Will he hurt me to find out what I know? I thought of my dream again—Jimmy had warned me. *Or will he kill me?*

Lizzy broke into my thoughts as she said, "What did you guys want to eat?"

Beyond her was Mason and another brother perhaps, standing at the corner of the bar, observing us and talking.

I squinted at Lizzy. "Who did you tell about our little adventure?"

She shrugged. "It was wrong, Evaline. I'm just pissed off, that's all. Anyway, what did you want to eat?"

I sighed. "Diet Coke, buffalo burger with fries." She jotted my order down as I looked at Kristy. "I'm going to the restroom. I'll be back."

I got up and strolled by Mason and the other guy. He was almost as big as Mason and had tattoos on his arms and his neck. He had unkempt dark hair, a baby face, dark eyebrows, and piercing, light brown eyes that had the same odd flicker as all the Cowans, making me assume he was a brother.

Mason kept his attention on me, and I flashed him a quick smile. He met my gaze and returned the smile. I walked into the bathroom, splashed cold water on my face, and beheld myself in the mirror.

Taking in a deep breath, I headed back out and was immediately slammed against the wall, cold hands grasping my neck. I couldn't see who it was at first.

He slipped his hand to my rear end to attempt to hold my arms behind my back and, instinctively, I elbowed him in the eye. He fell back as I turned to face him then tried to knee him in the balls. He countered my knee, but I punched him hard enough it made my hand numb. He shoved back, and I fell onto my ass. I didn't recognize him.

He stood over me, holding his jaw. "I'm here to deliver a message." He threw a piece of paper at me.

Still whirling with anxiety from my earlier confrontation with Campbell, I braced myself to hit the jerk again. Clenching my fist in preparation, I glared up at him, ready for an attack, but I was still reeling from being jumped.

His eyes glinted as he stepped forward. A big hand shoved him, sending him against the wall. Standing there was Lizzy and another guy. He was younger than Mason and had longer hair, which was tied back. However, he had muscles and tattoos like Mason as well as the peculiar shimmer in his eyes that seemed to be becoming more common with the family.

Lizzy knelt. "Are you okay? This is my brother Jonas."

My assailant looked up at Jonas but didn't move.

As if his hard look said it all, Jonas never took his eyes off the guy when he finally got up. He spoke slowly and firmly. "You've got less than thirty seconds to find the door and exit before I show you where it is."

The man said nothing, flashing me a quick look as he exited. I swiped the note and stuffed it into my pocket before Lizzy helped me up.

"Was his nose bloody from you?" she asked.

I smiled in acknowledgement and considered Jonas. "Thanks. I thought you were Mason for a second."

He tilted his head. "He just left. Did you know that guy?"

"No. I think he thought I was someone else, but I'm fine. Thanks, Jonas." I faced Lizzy. "Don't say anything to Kristy, okay? She'll freak out and worry."

She agreed, and I returned to the booth. I sat, joining Kristy and Lucy. As soon as settled, I grabbed a French fry off my plate as my food had shown up while I was gone.

Lucy leaned in. "I heard you met the new sheriff."

I sighed and glanced at Lizzy. "Yeah, he wasn't very nice, kind of creep."

Two attacks in one day—I spent a good part of the evening weighing my options. Since I knew I could not trust the local authorities, I would need to go to the Federal level.

But if I decided to go to the Feds now, it may not be enough for them to follow through on. On the other hand, I may not live long enough to see this through if I didn't go.

I reached into my pocket to get the note. After I unfolded it, a small lock of hair fell out. *"Back off or suffer your sibling's fate."*

In horror, I stared at the piece of dark hair I held in my hand. A few loose stands tickled my palm as in my heart, I knew they belonged to Jimmy.

Four

It was Friday. I had every intention of going to the Blue Dawn and listening to the band Mason had mentioned earlier in the week. Kristy was working, and I thought even Laine was going later. My car was still acting up, so I had to let it sit a bit before trying again.

Throughout the day, I received a couple strange e-mails and hang ups on my cell. Sacramento all over again. Not that I was that surprised, with Campbell in town and the mystery attacker from the Blue Dawn. Obviously, I was a threat, just as Jimmy had been.

Disgusted with the whole Campbell situation, I decided to stay home despite the texts from Kristy. I needed to think about the evidence I'd collected so far. Two things came to mind: First, the following morning I would go to the post office and acquire a P.O. box. Second, I had to stay my course and get everything on Campbell I could before I turned anything in to the Feds.

For that, I had it all planned in my head. How I would gather enough evidence on Campbell, turn it in and it would be enough for the Feds to do something. However, in nearly every version, I got hurt. It was a risk I was willing to take to bring those responsible for my brother's disappearance to justice. I was going to find out what happened to Jimmy if it killed me.

That night, as I lay in bed thinking, I finally drifted off to sleep.

My heart was pounding as I stood in the woods facing a small, dark building with no door I could see. The moon was full, and it was a cool night. I wanted to look for a way in, but Jimmy's voice kept saying no. I couldn't see him, but I could hear him clearly.

"Evaline, don't. Please don't."

"Jimmy, please help me," I called out to him.

Then I heard the growling and snarling—the sounds surrounded me. I peered into the trees and saw nothing, but on a nearby hill was the white and gray wolf again. Just like before, he wasn't the one growling. Now the snarls came from inside the building.

I took a step, and the wolf, now at my side, made a noise. The growling stopped, and I looked up to see the man who had attacked me standing with Campbell in the doorway of the building. The man held a shovel in one hand as he shook Campbell's hand with the other. They smiled at each other and seemed to move aside to look at me. Looming directly behind them was a dark figure. It did not have a face, no distinguishing characteristics, nor did it make a sound. Didn't need to.

My stomach churned nervously as fear overcame me. I was terrified of this figure, and I didn't understand why. I cringed as the man with the shovel was suddenly in front of me now, as if he moved like lightning. He didn't move, just silently stared at me. When he breathed, it sounded like a low, animalistic growl. Then he raised the shovel to strike me, and the white and gray wolf leaped at him.

My phone started ringing, and it woke me. I glanced at the clock: 6:37 a.m. When I answered, I heard Laine on the other end. "Evaline, are you there?"

Blinking the sleep away, I said, "Laine? Where are you? It's six thirty."

"Evaline, I need you to please come get me. I'm at the sheriff's department." He sounded exhausted.

As I rubbed my eyes, I let out a sigh. "How much is your bail?"

He paused a moment before answering, "A thousand."

I almost dropped the receiver. "Goddamn it, Laine. What did you do?"

"It's stupid. Please, just come get me."

Pissed off, I hung up. This meant I would have to fork over cash we didn't have. I rolled over to get up. This was because of Campbell. Had to be. Heading for the kitchen to make coffee, I started to pass Kristy, who moved in the direction of the bathroom.

She stopped me in the hall. "Evaline, what happened to you last night?"

"Sorry, but there was a lot of crap, Kristy, and it continues. Laine got himself arrested, and I have to go get him."

Her mouth dropped open before she said, "Are you fucking kidding me?"

I started down the stairs.

She yelled, "Don't go alone! I'll come with you. Let me pee."

The coffee tasted so good. I was pondering my dream when Kristy joined me and got a cup of her own. "I have to wait until the bank opens to get the cash. It's too much to pull out through the ATM."

She sipped her coffee. "How are we on cash in that account?"

"Well, we will only have enough for a few months of bills after

I take out this thousand."

"A thousand dollars for bail? What the hell did he do? What an idiot!"

I let her vent before replying. "I guess we'll find out."

"Do you think it has to do with that cop the other day?" she asked.

"I don't know. Maybe." I paused before I said, "So how did last night go? Were they packed?"

"Super busy. I had a good tip night. I started putting cash away, so tell me how much I need to give." She tilted her head. "Soooo, Mason was there last night."

"Well, rightfully so. They own it, don't they?"

She smiled. "Yeah, well, I think he likes you."

Shaking my head, I took a drink of my coffee. "Kristy, we've seen each other twice. Just stop."

She leaned in. "Evaline, you used to be the biggest romantic, and yet you never care enough about it to discuss it."

"I'm sorry, Kristy. I just have a lot on my plate right now."

She was right about one thing: I didn't like to discuss romance, but not because I didn't care about it. Love was something I wanted, but given everything that was happening, it seemed like more of a liability. It occurred to me at that moment that perhaps Kristy's constant focus on my love life may be serving as a distraction to the loss of Aunt Deb. She had barely even discussed her mom since the funeral, but it seemed every time an opportunity concerning Mason and myself came up, she was on it. If that's what she needed, I don't mind supporting her. We put the cups in the sink and headed out.

Of course, this time my car wouldn't start, so we took Kristy's. The police station was a small one that probably saw the same offenders doing the same things repeatedly. The front reception area was tiny, and a security door and counter separated the waiting/reception area from everything else. Just inside the doors, Mason was standing with the guy I'd seen him with at the bar the other day and another man I'd never seen before. I presumed both were his brothers. Laine and Jonas must have been arrested together.

Mason and his two brothers were intimidating standing there. All three were big and muscular. They all had one large tattoo on their upper right arms which was the same, and as the three turned to watch us walk in, I noticed their eyes—despite them being different colors—had the same eerie definition to them which made their eyes crystal clear. As Mason's gaze fell on me, his eyes softened a bit as I approached.

37

I stopped and smiled. "Must have been a hell of a night."

His expression warmed with a smile. "Yeah, looks that way."

"So, they were together?"

He shrugged, telling me I was right. I sighed.

"Miss Bennett." An officer had come up to me, and Campbell stood directly behind him. I nodded to Mason and went to the counter. The officer handed me some papers. "Please fill these out, and what is your method of payment today?"

I started filling out the forms as I answered, "Cash."

He nodded and walked away.

Campbell stepped up to the counter. "I told you they would be bunkmates soon enough. I kept that cell ready for him. It was just a matter of time with that kid."

I didn't acknowledge him and continued to fill out the forms.

"These kids these days, always doing something they're not supposed to do and then they wind up getting hurt." He paused before finishing his sentence, "Or worse."

His clipped tone told me he was annoyed I had nothing to say. The tension resonated from Mason and his brothers.

"What's wrong? You don't like cops?" Campbell continued his attempt to rattle me as I filled out the second form.

"I like the honest ones," I couldn't help but mutter.

He stepped closer to the counter. "What was that? You got something to say?" The Cowans tensed up, and Campbell took notice and eyed them. "You Cowans need to stand back. I'm having a conversation that doesn't concern you."

Mason and his brothers stayed silent but watched the sheriff with undisguised contempt. The tautness in the air made it reminiscent of a room after a fight. They seemed to be getting angrier by the minute. The other officer returned with a receipt book and counted the money I handed him as Campbell kept his attention on me. I wanted to put him through the wall. The officer handed me a receipt and indicated where I needed to sign.

When I was done, I looked Campbell directly in the eye. "I'd like to see my cousin now."

He was aggravated, but the funny thing was, I'd heard fear in his voice as he spoke to Mason and his brothers. Campbell motioned for another officer and ordered him to bring out "the Bennett kid and Jonas Cowan."

My gaze never left Campbell as he stepped back with a smug look on his face. I was nauseated by his very presence and felt nothing but contempt for him. Anger welled within as he didn't move his focus from me. He finally turned around as another officer handed him something to sign.

Kristy leaned closer to me. "What a complete dick."

I couldn't help but chuckle.

Laine was escorted out through the security door, and he regarded me with an "I'm sorry but this sucks" look on his face.

Kristy, Laine, and I went to leave, and I nodded to Mason. "See you around."

"Definitely."

Campbell came from behind the counter. "Must run in the family," he said.

Kristy and Laine looked over their shoulders at him as I tried to usher them out without giving him attention.

Neither Laine nor Kristy said anything as Campbell continued, "You know, getting into things that don't concern you."

I froze. At this point, I was past nausea and nervousness. My blood boiled at the sound of his voice. I wanted to scream.

Kristy, knowing I wasn't afraid to say what I thought, leaned into me. "Evaline, no. Don't. He's an ass, just…"

I jerked my chin at her. "You two wait in the car, okay? I'll just be a minute." I turned to Campbell with an icy smile. "A word, Sheriff?"

He lifted a brow as curiosity filled his face. He met me by the security door while Jonas was being brought through.

I smiled at Jonas when he saw me. "Hi, Jonas."

He gave me a toothy grin but seemed a bit confused to see me there. "Hey, Evaline."

I walked by him and met Campbell in the doorway. I knew why he was there so why pretend? I leaned toward him. "I want you to know that I know what you are. I know who you are. I know what you did, and I know you know what happened to my brother. The evidence is in a safe place, and it continues to pile up. Rest assured, Campbell, I'm going to bury you with it." I stepped back and smiled. "You have yourself a great day, Sheriff."

At first, he just gaped at her with his eyes wide as if in shock. Then he mumbled, "Yeah, you too."

As I spun to leave, I met Mason's gaze, flashed him a quick smile, then left. I should have not said anything, but Campbell was one of those people who could get under your skin.

As we drove home, Laine told us what happened. He and Jonas were in the backwoods on the jeep trail with Jonas's truck. They came up on a deep pit behind the fence and noticed it had been newly dug out on the one side. The other side was filled with junk, such as desks, chairs, paper, boxes, and everything else, all piled up. A trail coming from the pit went off into a fenced-in wooded area.

As they peered into the pit, Laine said the smile disappeared from Jonas's face, and his demeanor changed. He closed his eyes as if smelling the air near the pit. At that moment, he seemed focused and said they needed to check it out. They'd started to climb into the pit when Campbell showed up. Laine and Jonas never made it to the bottom, but when they were in their cells, Laine asked Jonas what he'd been looking for.

All Jonas said was, "There's something down there."

They were booked for trespassing. One peculiar thing, though. Laine said Campbell was insistent on no one checking out the pit. He ordered the other cops to leave and said he would take care of the situation personally. That was the conversation, which Laine and Jonas first thought, was suspicious.

Of course, I was intrigued. I knew there had to be a connection between whatever was in that mysterious pit and Campbell. Another piece to a very large puzzle.

~ * ~

That night, I got an e-mail from Amanda Collins asking if I wanted to meet on Monday. It was what I'd been waiting for. I told her I would be there in the afternoon, and I would call her before arriving.

Sunday morning, I got up and came downstairs for our coffee-and-cereal ritual. There was a note on the table from Kristy that she had plans, and Laine was working. This made it was a good day to figure out the starting issue with my car since I needed it to go to Redding the next day. I had some car knowledge, but I didn't know everything. I had a set checklist of items which it could be, and if it wasn't any of those, I would call Petrolli's, the local salvage yard.

As I was removing the carburetor to clean it, I heard a truck pull up and glanced up to see Mason walking toward me. "Hey."

He grinned. "Hey, how you doing?"

"I'm good. So, what brings you here?"

He handed me an envelope. "Kristy's paycheck. They were supposed to have it yesterday, but the situation with Jonas kinda screwed everything up."

"I know what you mean. It was kind of peculiar charge."

"Yeah." He paused for a moment then said, "That new sheriff is relentless."

"Yeah, I'm a big fan," I said, heavy on the sarcasm.

"Something my brother said the other day... some guy

attacking you at our place?"

I shook my head. "It was, um, random. He put his hands on me, and I reacted. Creep."

For a moment, I sensed a wave of anger from him, and then it was gone. He had a look of concern on his face. Just as before, he stirred that yearning desire inside me. This strange craving and power infused with a primal passion for which I hadn't felt with anyone else before. The pit of my stomach clenched, and my heart fluttered from the warmth of his skin emanating from him. My own skin tingled at the unusual body heat washing over me, despite the fact he wasn't touching me. I had to turn away for a moment.

"It should have never happened, and I'm sorry about that."

Shrugging, I smiled. "It wasn't your fault, Mason. You can't control what every jerk is going to do."

"Point taken." He examined my pendant. "Nice necklace."

I glanced at it then back at him. "Ah thanks. It was my mom's, a family heirloom or something."

"Scottish," he muttered.

"Yes, it is but ancient."

His lips twitched briefly, then he regarded my car. "What happened?"

"A starting issue. I was thinking maybe the carburetor needed to be cleaned or it's my starter, but I may need to call Petrolli's for parts."

He reached in to peek at the motor. "Yeah, I agree it's likely your starter."

"I thought that may be a possibility too, but I guess I'll find out."

He reached in and fiddled with some wires. I tried not to gawk at the tattoo on his massive arm. The tattoo all the brothers had that resembled something Celtic or Gaelic. I couldn't help but notice it matched my necklace though it was of a different design. Above the tattoo were the words: *Sic itur in altum*.

I recognized at least one of the words from stories my mom told me when I was young and heard myself whisper it: "Heaven." His eye brows raised at my comment. "Sorry, I was looking at your tattoo. Is that your family crest?"

"More like a variation of it."

"What does the rest say?"

"This way to Heaven."

He studied me for a long moment—and I just wanted to fall into his arms. His green eyes pierced right through me. I was enveloped by his enticing smell, and I knew I was safe—and wanted him even more.

Once again, I had to look away. "Um, I wanted to ask you, are you familiar at all with the Redding area?"

He nodded. "Yeah, we go there sometimes to get supplies. Why?"

"I need to go there tomorrow for something. The southeast side."

"There are a couple rough areas around Redding." He straightened. "I could take you if you'd like."

My heart skipped a beat. "Um, wouldn't want to put you out—"

"You're not. I want to take you. It'll… make me feel better."

I wondered if he experienced the same strange sensation I did when he was near: my heart skipping, the strong desires, and now the sweaty palms. Did I want this conversation to really end? I finally nodded. "Okay. I need to be there by one in the afternoon if that works for you."

He nodded. "I'll pick you up at eleven thirty." He regarded my engine again. "And you may need to call Petrolli's."

"Thanks."

He grinned as he started back toward his car, then he stopped. "I'll see you in the morning." Then he was gone.

The strange magnetism lingered for a few minutes, but I would not let myself forget what it felt like so quickly.

~ * ~

The next morning, I finished my coffee and straightened up the kitchen before Mason got there. When he honked his horn, I was out the door. I had my questions about Harvey's disappearance in a folder, ready for the Collins'. The folder laid on the seat between Mason and me as we headed down the highway. A country song played softly on the radio, and I looked at him, surprised.

He winked. "It's a good break from the heavy stuff sometimes. Do you like country?"

It was intriguing that he would be into anything but metal, given his rough look and tattoos. "Yes, and you're right, it's a good break from rock."

During our conversation, my stomach fluttered again, and the strange attraction toward him returned even more intense than yesterday's encounter. An exciting sensation, like when you're near a wild animal at the zoo and you think if the fence weren't there, you would be lunch—but I felt a sense of security I couldn't describe.

We pulled off the interstate and headed toward Redding, and as we turned, he glanced at me. "So what do you need to get in Redding?"

I winced. "It's nothing I'm getting but rather I'm going to see someone. This person can help me for some research I'm doing." I motioned to make a right at the next street.

We stopped in front of the house, and he twisted to me. "Call me when you're finished, and I'll come get you."

"What are you going to do? I mean, I don't want you to be bored."

"I won't get bored. Don't worry. Just holler when you're done, okay?"

I grabbed my folder and flashed him a look as he smiled at me. Like a gentleman, he waited until Amanda came to the door before he left. After we introduced ourselves, she led me to the front room and indicated that I should sit on the couch.

"I'll be right back," she said as she whisked out of the room, only to return a moment later with cookies and coffee. Her voice had a hint of a southern drawl.

"Amanda, if you don't mind me asking, where are you originally from?"

She smiled as she set out the cookies. "Lived in West Virginia twenty-some years. Decided about ten years ago that we'd move out here. We always loved the west. Kids were grown, and it was a good time to come."

I eyed the gold couch and bright red shag carpet with giant flowers on it—she had terrible taste, but there was also a cluster of pictures on the mantel and end tables of what seemed like a happy family: Amanda with three children and a man I assumed was Harvey.

She sat back. "So, tell me about your assignment."

"Well, it's concerning strange disappearances. I did some reading on Harvey's case. He was your husband, right?" Sadness filled her eyes if only for a moment as I continued, trying to be gentle and not too inquisitive. "What can you tell me about him?"

She stared at the ceiling a moment as if remembering. "He was a good man, a good father. There was nothin' that man could have been into to cause his leavin'. Police got no leads either. They said there was no sign of foul play, so you tell me what you think happened."

Pain and anguish came from her trembling words. "If you don't mind me asking, what did your husband do?"

She took a sip of her coffee. "He sold real estate round here and regionally. Some of those are in thick woods and not many people."

I winced at her indication. "You think he might have been showing a property and something happened?"

She rolled her eyes, shaking her head. "I told the police that. Oh, 'We'll get right on that, ma'am.' The little prick never followed up, and then I called the station to get an update, and they said he'd left and my case had been handed over to another detective."

I put my cup down. "Was it an Officer Campbell?"

Her mouth gaped for a moment. "You sure did your homework. You should get an *A* on this assignment. You probably could solve the case better than what we got here on the case in Redding."

I smiled as I continued, "Mrs. Collins, what did the police say they think happened to Harvey?"

Her smile faded. "Nothin, that's the problem. They think he left me, but I know better. They don't know what Harv and I had." Tears welled in her eyes, and she picked up one of the framed pictures. "If you believe in that sort of thing, he was my… soulmate. I knew it when I first saw him. It's utter completeness—like two pieces that belong together but got lost and now we're together again. I knew something bad happened to him when he didn't call or come home. There are some things you just know in your heart, and if you listen hard enough, you'll learn what you need to know, not necessarily what you want to know. It's because of this, I know he's dead. I just want to know what happened." She clutched a small silver dove pendant that hung around her neck as she looked at his picture.

He wore one just like it. She told me Harvey had gotten those doves for their first Christmas, and they'd never taken them off—never in thirty-eight years of marriage. My mind raced. Was it possible to love someone else so much you would know they were in peril? I did believe this much: I was connected to Jimmy in a similar way. Nothing had been found, but I knew he was gone. Amanda said it right when she said, "There are some things you just know in your heart."

I admired her strength. "Did the police consider his clients?"

She nodded as she wiped away tears. "Yes, they checked his client book and calendars, but something was weird."

I waited while she pulled herself together.

"He mentioned another name to me days before he disappeared, and when I told the police, they said there was no one by that name in his book or calendar, so they dropped it."

"Do you remember the name?"

She gazed at the ceiling again, then shook her head. I was sure the name was the key to the mystery, perhaps the central figure to a long line of disappearances. Figured the only lead was a name she couldn't remember. I sent Mason a text to come get me as I leafed through Harvey's datebook.

Mason's truck rumbled as he arrived.

I turned to Amanda and rose. "Amanda, if you think of that name, please let me know. It may be more important than you know. Thank you so much for talking to me, and I am so sorry for Harvey. He sounds like a really good guy."

She smiled as her eyes seemed lost in a distant memory. She walked with me as I headed for the door. I turned to hug her briefly, and she stopped me as I reached for the door.

"Spend… no… Spanditto. Charles Spanditto. That was it." She nodded.

A tiny victory. I had another piece of the puzzle. Hopefully it was a big piece. As I walked to Mason's truck, I repeated the name over and over, trying to remember if I had seen it in any of Jimmy's things. I'd heard the name before but where?

Mason smiled as he opened the door and helped me climb into the truck. He closed my door and came back to the driver's side door then got in. "Did you get what you needed?" He started us moving.

I nodded. "How about you?"

He indicated the two large boxes in the bed of his truck.

I pursed my lips before I said, "Do you know where the library is by chance?"

His beautiful eyes gleamed with delight. Clearly, he was entertained. Why, I had no idea. "Yeah, it's right up the street. So now you need a book?"

I shook my head. "I'm sorry. I just—"

"Evaline," he said. "It's not a problem." We drove toward the library.

Once at the library, Mason came in with me. I would check Jimmy's appointment book for Charles Spanditto, but for now, I went to the computers and typed his name into the news database. Nothing came up. Then I Googled his name, and a list of items scrolled down the page.

I sat for a moment, thinking and looking at the list. My gaze fell on a result toward the end of the list. "Span Enterprises" was a company I didn't recognize, but I clicked on it anyway. It was a manufacturing company for holding tanks and storage containers. They appeared to be small and had a few offices, all of which were in the Pacific Northwest. A strange nervousness twitched through me as I felt eyes on me, so I turned. Mason stood directly behind me, looking at the screen. He tilted his head at me but said nothing as he drew a chair next to me.

He leaned in to see what I was reading. "Are you looking for a storage container?"

I sat back. "No, not exactly. I'm just checking out this company."

"Well, it must be something real specific you are looking for. You look so serious." Deep green eyes remained locked on me.

I had to tell him something, but I didn't want to say too much for fear it could get him hurt. I wouldn't be able to live with myself if something happened to him because of me.

I took in a deep breath then said, "This is about my brother, Mason. He's been missing for some time, and I've got a lot of suspicions. That lady's house you dropped me off at earlier—her husband disappeared in the same manner…"

"And you want to see if they are connected," he said, finishing my sentence.

"Yeah, something like that." I focused on the screen and continued to search Span Enterprises.

His chair creaked, and his body heat reached out to me. "So, you have a brother. Is he like you?"

He was close enough to me that when I looked over my shoulder at him, his face was mere inches away. My heart skipped as it always seemed to do when he was near. "In some ways, he was just awesome. He could do anything. He was a lawyer in Sacramento."

"Was? You think he's dead?"

I took a moment before answering. I didn't want to give too much away. Turning away, I tried to restrain my emotions. The thought was horrible, but I knew what the dreams meant. "I don't know, but I guess there's always hope."

"So, you two are close. That's cool. Family is important."

I scrolled down the screen and found a tab for staff listings but didn't recognize any names. I glanced at my cell and noticed the time. "I'm sorry. I shouldn't have asked you to come. I'm sure you had stuff to do."

"Nah, I was coming to Redding anyway, remember? Would you like to go get something to eat?"

"That sounds really good right now." I gathered my things.

We walked to the local diner and sat in the corner booth by the window. The place was half-filled with locals and a couple tourists. Mason's very presence drew women's gazes, but he didn't seem to be fazed. Despite the flirty waitress and occasional stares, his focus was on me.

"So, you didn't say: Did you find what you needed for now? I mean, for your investigation?"

I smiled. "Not quite, but I'm getting there. I mean, it definitely helped."

The waitress brought our drinks and got our order. He took a drink. "Did you ever give Petrolli a call about your car?"

"Yeah, in fact, he came to get it before we left. I should have it back by tomorrow. Whatever was causing it to not start sometimes has been bad for a while. I just never took it to get fixed."

"Your car is pretty nice."

"Thank you. It was Dad's baby. We had a special bond over cars. I remember sitting in the garage and helping him work on engines. I can still smell the oil and gas as he worked underneath the hood. I would hand him the tools, as he would explain what he was doing. We were supposed to restore it together, a father-daughter project you know, but he died before we could. I swore I would restore it myself."

Sadness touched his face. "I'm sorry about your dad and brother."

"Thank you."

"So, you grew up with Laine and Kristy here in Dunsmuir?"

"My Aunt Deb, their mom, was my dad's sister. Jimmy and I consider them our siblings." Lost in a memory, I fell silent for a moment then said, "I remember Sundays the best. It was dinner at Grandma's house, which was a family tradition. She was my father's mother. Grandma Pauline and I had a special bond. She always knew when I was troubled. I really loved her."

Mason's expression was both sympathetic and concerned. "I'm sorry; I didn't mean to bring up any painful memories."

"No, I like to think of them. It keeps them alive."

His perfect features illustrated complete understanding as I continued, "Anyway, Grandma Pauline died on a Friday. Everything changed that Friday. They said her heart gave out, but thankfully, she went peacefully. My dad was devastated of course, and at eleven years of age, it was my first experience with death, or at least one I could remember. I recall asking my parents what happens when you die and why Grandma had to go. My mother explained it by saying, 'When it's time, God calls you and you go.' I have never forgotten those words, and they never rang truer than when my mom got sick."

"What was it?" he asked.

"You know thinking back on it now; it was so odd how fast it happened. One day she wasn't feeling well, and the next, the doctors said it was cancer, and she would be gone within the month. Every day, she withered away as the cancer ate away at her insides. It was two weeks of watching the light in her eyes—which had always been so bright—decrease more each day until there was no light left. She died at home on a Tuesday, three days after my high school graduation."

"Oh Eveline, I'm so sorry."

"It's surreal, you know. My dad followed shortly afterward. The doctors said it was a heart attack. Thinking back on it now, I was sure it was a broken heart that killed him. With my parents, it wasn't just till death do us part; it was more till after death and never do us part. They never left each other's sides."

"You admire that?" Lifting his brow, he stared at me intently.

"Yes, I guess I do. To have someone love you that much—not many of us can say we've had that. Most of us probably won't ever."

He took a drink of his water before he said, "Why would you say that? You don't believe it could happen to you?"

I smiled and shook my head slightly. "I don't know. I haven't thought about much lately. What about you? Do you believe in love like that?"

As he smiled, I could clearly see that deep glimmer in his eyes. "Definitely."

"So, you have been in love before?"

"Yes, I have, and I would have stayed with her until the end if she hadn't died. Love is the most powerful emotion next to hate, and just like hate, it can consume you."

I was nearly speechless. I was surprised to hear his words about love and how powerful it is. Mason was apparently a closet philosopher. "I'm sorry. I didn't mean to—"

He hitched one shoulder. "No, you're fine. It was a long time ago."

The waitress set our food down. I glanced at the steak he ordered, which was still bloody as he had ordered it rare. I peppered my chicken and continued our conversation. "So enough about me, what about you? Where are you from originally?"

He answered me as he knifed into his steak. "Pennsylvania. We moved out here a few years back."

"So, I've met Elizabeth, Lucy, and Jonas. What are your other two brothers' names?"

"Aaron and Isaac."

I took a bite of my chicken. "They seem nice."

He smiled. He'd nearly finished half his steak. "They were curious about you."

"Ah, I'll bet. Probably think I'm a crazy chick asking their brother, whom I barely know, to drive me to a town one and a half hours away."

He chuckled. "I don't think you have to worry about that. I said they were curious, not shocked. Actually, they think you're okay, and Lizzy talks about you a lot because she's with Kristy all the time. They were intrigued about your little private meeting with the new sheriff when you went to get Laine at the police station."

"Ah, I see. Well, Campbell is a creep, and he knows it. I'm tired of him riding Laine all the time. He shouldn't even have a badge, you know?"

"Yeah, well, he must have pissed you off early on since he hasn't been here that long."

I continued to chew as I needed to watch what I said. I didn't want Mason involved. "Yeah, you could say that. I wanted to ask you, do you know about the pit where Laine and Jonas got picked up that night?"

"I've never seen it, but Jonas mentioned it before. Why?"

"I think they got arrested because there's stuff in that pit no one is supposed to see."

"Evaline, they got picked up because it was on private property."

Frowning, I sat back. "That's a minor infraction—a warning to never come back, not a night in jail. They didn't even enter a building."

Mason's expression went from amused to serious. "Why? Do you want to go check it out?"

I eyed him. "Don't tempt me. I just think it's weird they were hauled out of there so quickly, that's all."

"Maybe the owner just doesn't want people on his property."

"Or maybe he has something he's hiding at the bottom of that pit."

I smiled at his concerned look as I bit the last chunk of my chicken. "Don't worry. I'm not feeling adventurous today."

He grinned.

~ * ~

Later that night, after Mason dropped me off, I lugged out my evidence box from under my bed. I then pulled out the datebook Jimmy had kept in his car. I perused the pages for the weeks leading up to his disappearance, and there it was: "Charles Spanditto 9:00 a.m." There were similar entries which spanned the last two months before Jimmy disappeared.

He wasn't in the client log Jimmy's firm gave me and the

police. I placed what I collected from Amanda and the Redding library in the box and put the box back under the bed. Might need to get that safe deposit box in the morning until I could hand it over to someone. I would not stop until I knew what had happened to Jimmy and those responsible paid for it.

As I sat at the desk in my room pondering my conversation with Amanda, the neighbor's dog barked. After rising, I peered out the window. The dog yapped and growled at the bushes across from my bedroom window. My stomach tingled as a sense of uneasiness came over me. The longer I stood there, the more I felt eyes on me but could see nothing. The same uncomfortable twinge I experienced in Sacramento when the harassment occurred.

I stepped back and slipped to the floor with my back leaned against my bed. I did not want to give into fear and have a freak out. I was not one to back down even if it meant getting hurt. The barking almost became deafening. My heart beat fast and hard. The anxiety was so intense, the room seemed to spin. A moment later, there was a high-pitched yelp and then silence. I got up and went to the window again, and there was nothing. Perhaps the dog went back home. Perhaps.

Five

My own scream woke me. Sweat coated my skin and tingled at the breeze from the ceiling fan. Another dream with Jimmy trying to get me to leave the woods. The same growl, the same hot breath, the same dark figure was always there. Jimmy pleaded with me, and his tear-filled eyes were trained on the ground. Then I was in a box, buried, screaming, but I knew no one could hear me. When I turned my head, lying next to me was Jimmy. That's when I'd woken.

This time it had almost been too real. I sat up in bed for a minute, catching my breath. At that moment I knew I was getting close. The growl was much more intense this time. Then there was the white and gray wolf. Ironically the fierce growls never came from him, but the something in the woods—the something Jimmy and I were running from. This time, as the growling moved closer, the wolf stood by my side, ready to pounce. The wolf gave me a feeling of protection and warmth—I never wanted that sensation to go away. Not as long as I was in danger.

But I needed to see this through.

I went downstairs where Laine and Kristy were drinking coffee and arguing.

Kristy spoke up first. "Hey, Evaline, um, Petrolli called. Your car is done."

"Thanks. Can you take me to get it?"

"I can take you after my doctor's appointment, which is," she glanced at her cell phone, "now. I need to go." She whisked upstairs to change as Laine pipped in.

"I can take you if you don't mind the bike."

I smiled as I poured coffee. "That's fine. Thanks, Laine." I sat across from him. "So how are things with the job?"

"Good. I put my share in the coffee can for the house, okay?"

"Yeah that's fine." I thought about the mysterious pit where he and Jonas were arrested. "Laine, the pit where you and Jonas were picked up—did they say who owned it?"

He shook his head. "We just got close enough so we could start climbing in when four four-wheelers, two security trucks, and two cop cars showed up. They gotta have cameras or something watching that place."

I frowned. "So, you didn't see what was there? Did it look like they were digging something?"

He shrugged. "Not exactly. It kinda looked like they had dug the pit out and were slowly refilling it. Jonas said he smelled something bad, but I didn't smell anything. The one security guy was a real dick though."

"Do you remember his name?" He shook his head again. I couldn't help thinking it was tied to Campbell and the creepy guy who had attacked me at the Blue Dawn.

"Oh yeah, did you go out with Mason?"

"Well, it was more of an information quest for me rather than a date, so don't get excited. We were at the library."

Laine grinned. "Libraries are perfect…"

"Laine!"

Now he chuckled. "What? It's true. Anyway, why did you go all the way to Redding when we have a library right here in town?"

"There was something else I needed to see."

He was silent a moment then asked, "Is it about Jimmy?" I didn't say anything as he continued, "I heard you last night. You've been having dreams about Jimmy. Doesn't that mean something?"

I searched for the right words. "Laine, something bad happened to Jimmy, I know it, and yes, I'm having dreams about him; he keeps trying to get me away from something."

"Did you find something? I mean, do you know what happened to him?"

I so didn't want to have this conversation. "Look, I can't right now. It's a bad enough situation that I don't want to get you or Kristy involved. I'm not sure what everything I've collected means, but I do know I'm getting closer because things are getting unnerving. When I know for sure, I promise I will tell you both, but not now, okay?"

He seemed a bit unnerved by this information and got up to put his cup in the sink. He turned back to me. "Okay. Do I need to be alert about anything?"

"Just be careful."

We moved swiftly down the road on Laine's bike. Petrolli's Auto and Scrap Service was located outside town. We pulled in and walked into the garage. A few of the workers eyed me as I approached the front desk. Laine was clearly annoyed by their stares as I could hear him mumbling.

I turned to him and whispered, "Shh. It's not their fault they've never seen a woman before."

He laughed.

At the front desk, I asked the guy if Tony was around.

"He had to run into town. Is there something I can help you with?"

"Yes, he finished my car. It's the 72 Cougar."

"Oh yeah, yeah, nice car. You wouldn't wanna sell it, would ya?"

I shook my head with a slight smile. "No, sorry. Sentimental value. So what was wrong with it?"

"It was a bad starter, but we did check everything." He furnished me the bill to check over, and I handed over my Visa. He continued as he ran my card, "Tony thinks it'll need a tune-up pretty soon. You may wanna think about getting it done before the winter. You don't wanna be stranded somewhere if it dies on you."

I agreed at the possibility. "How much does a tune-up cost?"

"Well, given the year of your car, you're probably looking between five and seven hundred bucks to do it right. Some of them wires and sensors are original, which means some are corroded."

"Okay. I'll have to see." I signed my card slip, and Laine and I turned and left.

As we walked to my car, he said. "What a rip-off. Seven hundred? Is he nuts?"

I chuckled. "It's the price I have to pay for a classic, I guess. I'll see you later? I'm headed back home."

"Be careful." He returned to his bike.

At home, I sat in the living room with my laptop on the coffee table and a notebook next to it. I wanted to see what I could find out about the property Laine had been arrested on. I knew the county auditor's page could give me information, but I didn't have an address. I typed in "Charles Spanditto", the very name that kept coming up in my investigation. Clicking search, I was hoping there would be something but then "not found" came up. Next, I tried "Span Enterprises." Bingo. A property appeared under the Commercial Property tab under that name.

I jotted down the address and glanced at the building layout; it was a large building with several outbuildings. The area was a parcel right outside of town, which was near the state park. The last thing I saw on the page was the date of purchase, January of this year.

I exited the page, sat back on the couch, and closed my eyes.

My mind raced about the missing people and this mysterious Span Enterprises company connection. Couldn't have been a coincidence that both Harvey and my brother had a secret appointment with the same person, and then they both went missing. Couldn't be a coincidence Campbell seemed to be everywhere in this whole thing, and now the connection with this property.

Next thing I knew, it was late afternoon. Rats. I had fallen asleep on the couch. Getting up, I went to the front door to check the mail. I grabbed the mail from the mailbox and headed for the kitchen. Kristy left a note: *Eva, I didn't want to wake you. I'm at movies with Lizzy. I got the stuff on the counter and fridge—pleeeeease make your famous spaghetti!!!! Love you, be home late. xoxoxox*

I smiled and glanced over at the counter and at the pasta, tomato cans, garlic, onions, and spices lined up neatly. I needed a break.

I made my sauce the same way Grams had done it, the same way Mom had done it, and the same way Aunt Deb had done it. The house filled with the sweet aroma of fresh garlic and onions. It was relaxing, cooking in an empty house with only the soft jazz coming from the satellite station. I even had a glass of wine. I was pouring myself another as I glanced at the mail I brought in earlier. One of the envelopes was forwarded from my Sacramento address and was from the Sacramento Police Department. My heart sank as I read the first sentence.

Ms. Bennett,

This letter is to inform you that the missing person (s) case involving, Mr. James Christoff Bennett, has been moved to the Cold Case division. Since there is no new evidence over the last two months, it does not warrant an active investigation. Should new evidence come forth, you will be contacted and an active investigation will resume.

Sincerely, Detective Neal Roberts, SPD

Sadness welled in me as I refolded the letter, placed it in the envelope, and then stashed it in my back pocket. My last conversation with this Roberts was about my suspicions concerning Kenny's disappearance. Of course, nothing came of it. I wasn't sure what happened to his case after that.

I gave my sauce a quick stir. I leaned against the counter and examined the local newspaper laying there. *Missing Pets and Local*

Animal Attacks Have Residents Worried. It was a stretch from the big city headlines.

I was giving my sauce another stir when there was a knock at the door. I walked down the hall and peeked through the glass—nothing. No one. The phone rang, and I hurried to pick it up. "Hello?"

Nothing. A dead line. At that moment, I had that same uneasy sensation from the night before and right before I left Sacramento. I knew the only reason I was still breathing was because they didn't know what I knew or who I'd told. Of course, I wouldn't endanger anyone else by telling them about my suspicions. I needed to be sure about Campbell before I showed anyone anything.

There was another knock at the door. I grabbed the knife I had been cutting the garlic and onions with from the counter. I peered through the glass door, and this time, someone was there. I sighed with relief to see Mason smiling and holding up an envelope.

I smiled back as I opened the door. "Hi."

"As promised, here is Kristy's tip money. We had a register issue, so I couldn't give it to her before she left."

"Thanks, I'll give it to her later. She's out with Lizzy."

His expression was casual, and his eyes seemed to penetrate my soul, but it gave me a very different experience as opposed to the ominous feeling I had a moment ago. He made me feel comfortable—safe even. The scent of a pine forest was familiar and intoxicating. He smelled wonderful. I really didn't want him to leave.

Raising his chin, he regarded the air behind me. "Something smells really good."

I grinned. "Did you want to come in?" I blurted out, "I'm just cooking."

"Are you sure? I mean if you're in the middle of something, I can go."

I shook my head and stepped back so he could enter. He followed me into the kitchen as I went over to the stove where water boiled for the pasta. I glanced over at him, leaning against the counter and peering into the pot.

"Wow, garlic, onions, and a slight pinch of fresh parsley—nice."

My mouth opened slightly. "How did you know about the parsley? I didn't even put in more than two small leaves."

He shrugged. "I have a nose for food, and this smells awesome."

I put the pasta in the water and leaned back up against the counter. "Thanks."

We both stood there for a moment, and his eyes seemed to see right through me. "Are you okay?"

"I'm fine." I reached for the wooden spoon then dipped the spoon into the pot. Spooning up some sauce, I tried it. Yummy. After getting some more, I held the spoon out to him. "Try some and tell me what you think."

His chest gently touched mine. He opened his mouth as I maneuvered the spoon to his lips, and he took a taste. I was trying to keep my cool on the outside, but inside I was screaming with delight. The strong desires I had when it came to Mason exploded in me. My heart thudded a rapid beat against my chest as my breathing deepened. Again, the pit of my stomach fluttered. I wanted him. At that moment, I wanted him like no other. To me, he was perfect in every way.

The corners of his eyes crinkled. "The best I've ever had. May have to have you show Isaac. He can't make sauce for the life of him."

We both laughed, and when Mason looked at me, once again, it was like he could see right through me. I was usually in control in these types of situations, but at that moment, I could've fallen in his arms. I fought the feeling with every fiber of my being. I couldn't deal with something like that with everything else going on.

Finally, I tore my gaze from him. "Um, they're... gonna be home soon."

He smiled and took a step back. "Okay. I have to get back to work, anyway. Well, um, I wanted to... ask you to... I mean if you want... maybe we can go out or something this weekend."

Without hesitation I answered, "That sounds good, yeah."

He smirked. "But no libraries or investigative work this time, okay?"

Giggling, I nodded. "Agreed, no investigative stuff."

He turned and strode for the door. I followed. At the front door, before he opened it to leave, there was a peculiar moment when he faced me that something familiar flashed in my mind. Only for a second did I feel it. I tried to place it and failed. He didn't say anything, but his expression was one of certainty. A long moment I wished I could freeze.

I finally said, "What are you looking at?"

He lowered his head slightly. "I'm looking at you." A smile twitched on his lips as he reached for the door knob. "I'll call you Thursday night or Friday morning, okay?"

I nodded, and he was gone.

~ * ~

The next morning, I lay in bed for a short while, thinking about

Mason from the evening before, but my mind soon wandered to the letter from the Sacramento PD. I had to step it up. I glanced out the window at the turning leaves. It was a cool, cloudy day outside. A good day to go to that pit. I needed to see why it was such a secret. After dressing, I headed downstairs. Kristy was laying on the couch and texting. Laine was, presumably, still sleeping.

I stood in the kitchen doorway. "Hey, did you get the envelope I left for you under your door?"

"Yeah thanks," she said, not looking up.

I went straight for the coffeepot and poured some. "As requested, I made the famously delicious family recipe for spaghetti last night. It's in the fridge," I yelled to Kristy while leaning against the counter.

She came into the kitchen, smiling in delight. "Yummy. I'm gonna have some for lunch." She sat at the kitchen table and put her phone down. "I got a text from Lizzy." She examined me for a moment and a smirk crossed her lips. "So how long was Mason here?"

Surprised, I raised a brow. "How did Lizzy know he was here?"

"Well in case you haven't noticed, the Cowans are very close. Anyway, she knows he's totally hot for you."

I shook my head. She was relentless.

"He *is*! This is so perfect. So, did you guys…"

"Don't be ridiculous," I said, frowning at her.

"I was going to say, 'Did you guys talk at all?'"

"Yes, we talked. We're going out this weekend, okay?"

Since I tended to keep my love life to myself, my acknowledgment of a date caused her to almost jump for joy. Once again, I chalked her interest in my love life to the needed distraction from Aunt Deb. Perhaps it was a good distraction. She got up and hugged me. "Oh, Eva! You guys will be so good together."

I couldn't help smiling about it as well. "It's only a date."

Her eyes were wide with excitement. "I know, but he is so unbelievably hot. Where are you guys going?"

"I don't know, but I was thinking of dropping spaghetti off to him, and then I was going for a drive, check out this one place outside town. What time do they usually get to work?"

"Not until eleven."

"Do you know where they live?"

She simpered and tilted her head a bit.

"Okay, Kristy, wanna come?"

"Um, let me think… Yes!" She ran upstairs to change.

~ * ~

We headed far from town, but Kristy had told me before the Cowans lived way out. We turned onto a long and curvy dirt road that twisted along and revolved into the driveway. After a few minutes, we saw the house, which resembled a rustic, two-story log home—simple but big. There were chairs and couches set around a fire pit and a truck, a car, and other mechanical parts scattered around. The remnants of a small garden were on the opposite side of the house. Then there was an open area about the size of a football field on the other side and to the rear of the house, which was a muddy mess as if someone had a wrestling match in the rain the night before. Mason's truck, along with several others, were parked all around as though there was no specific place for the cars and you just parked where you had room.

I got behind Mason's truck and jumped out, grabbing the container of food while Kristy followed. "Did you tell Lizzy we were coming?"

"Yes, she said someone should be here."

We walked up the steps to the front door then knocked. I could hear footsteps as the door opened, and one of Mason's brothers stood there.

"Hey, AJ," Kristy said in greeting.

He leered, nodded, and was eyeing us up and down.

"Hi, is um… Mason here?" I asked.

AJ shook his head. "Nope."

I handed him the container. "Okay. Can you please give this to him?"

He took the container. I smiled, said a quick thanks, and Kristy and I turned to leave.

As we got back into the car, she said, "He was being weird."

I glanced at her as I started the car. "Why was he being weird?"

"Their cars are here. So, where are they?"

I shrugged. "Who knows? Maybe they're in someone else's car. It's not a big deal."

As soon as we headed back toward the dirt road, Kristy pipped up. "I'm a little surprised we didn't hear Oasis or Nirvana booming from the stereo."

"Why would you say that?"

"Well, Aaron has this weird thing about the music from the nineties. Lizzy says they tease him about it, and I remember Isaac put him in charge of situating the music for the jukebox. When he realized Aaron filled it with all nineties stuff, Isaac made him redo it."

I chuckled at the thought. We pulled down the drive and out. I headed in the direction of the pit. Kristy, unaware of why I wanted to take a ride, turned on the radio. About five minutes later we came upon a fence along the roadside indicating private property. Searching for a driveway, I drove on. As we approached an entrance, I slowed. There was a warehouse of sorts and several small buildings behind it. No movement.

"What's this place?" Kristy asked. "Why're we slowing down?"

"I'm not sure. It's curious though."

She shrugged. "I guess."

We passed the fence on the other side and the sign for the state forest. We came to a trailhead, and I pulled in.

As she glanced at the outhouse facilities, she frowned. "Do you seriously have to pee here?"

I grinned. "Let's take a walk. It's a great day—not too hot, not too cold."

She was speechless for a moment then she said, "But… what about bears and stuff? We don't have a gun."

"Meh." I got out and went to my trunk as Kristy followed.

I loved the outdoors and had done enough camping and hiking to always be prepared. Opening my trunk, I removed the backpack I always kept in the trunk that had a flashlight, granola bars, water, road flares, first aid kit, etc. I also kept a can with tiny stones in it. It was a trick my father had shown me that whenever you walked on a trail where there was wildlife nearby, you needed to announce your presence, so they'll shy away. You never want to startle them, so you can tape, carry, or place on the end of a stick a can filled with pebbles and give it a shake now and then. When I reached in and withdrew the can, I noticed my dad's pocketknife and grabbed it too.

"But what if we get lost? Or something wants to eat us?" Kristy asked, still clearly concerned.

I laughed as I noted her reluctance. "Why are you being a wuss? Look, there are several other cars. It's a trailhead. We'll just walk a bit and come back okay?"

She finally agreed as we started on the trail. I kept track of our direction as I needed to know where the warehouse was. The forest was beautiful; the coolness of the trees, the sounds, and the serenity were awesome, not to mention the irresistible aroma of fresh pine, which reminded me of Mason. Perhaps that was what attracted me to him. Being around him recalled the forest. Despite my best efforts, it was difficult to keep him out of my thoughts for long. Believe me I did try.

When we reached the part of the trail where we needed to head in the opposite direction of the normal path to check out the warehouse and pit, I paused before forging toward it.

Kristy stayed with me, but she figured out where we were headed. "You wanna see that warehouse, don't you?"

"Yes. I'm just curious," I quickly answered.

Not very long after we walked the trail, we came up to a fence which was like the one along the roadway. I stopped and peered into the yard but couldn't see much. I glanced around, looking for cameras, but didn't note any. One building resembled an office, and the others seemed like smaller versions of the main warehouse. As we followed the fence, I noticed a clearing behind it and what I presumed to be the pit Laine and Jonas mentioned.

We stopped when I could get a clear view of the pit edges but still couldn't see much of what was inside it. There were tire marks indicating an off-road trail of sorts. I assumed this was what Laine had described the morning I picked him up from the jail. We inched closer, still along the fence line. Again, I checked for surveillance cameras. Nothing.

Kristy turned to me as she gripped the fence. "This is kinda creepy. What do you think they use it for?"

I shook my head. "I'm not sure. This is where Laine and Jonas were when they got arrested." I rotated back to the pit but couldn't see much except for a mass of boxes and broken furniture.

"What is this place? I think you know, but you won't say."

"I'm just curious," I said, trying to be nonchalant.

"Hey, I'm just as adventurous as the next person. But why this place?" She pointed to the top of the fence. "It doesn't appear electric, but there is barbed wire on the top."

Instead of looking, I indicated a large tree. "Look there." Directly below a hanging branch was a small storage shed of sorts with a rusted door falling off its hinges. No doubt, the small shed had been there before the current owners.

"Damn, Eva, that branch is super high."

I headed right for it. "Think of it as a nice climb. Come on. It's not that bad." I grabbed one of the branches and pulled myself up. Reaching down, I helped Kristy until we were both up on the first two pretty thick branches.

"Kristy, you don't have to come further if you don't want to. You can wait here. I won't be long."

"No, no. I'm all about the mission; although I have no idea what we are looking for."

I was amused as I moved up to the next branch up, which was

at least two feet above the branch I stood on. Kristy followed as I inched around directly below the branch above the small shed.

She clasped onto the trunk of the tree as she peered down onto the shed. "Do you think the roof will hold us? It looks old."

I examined the roof with some doubt as I turned to her. "I know but it's our only way in, save going over the barbed wire." I reached for the branch as I pulled myself up.

The branch still hung a good four feet above the roof. Kristy came up behind me but stayed low on the branch.

"Kristy, just inch yourself down and stay close to the edge. That's where it will have the most strength."

She nervously agreed, and I sat, holding the branch and twisting myself so I could hang from the branch. Touching the roof with my feet, I sidestepped to the edge. Once I was steady, I let go of the branch and gently let the roof take all my weight. The wood creaked and seemed as if it would buckle, but it didn't.

Jumping off on the side closest to the fence, I watched Kristy, who was preparing to do the same. Moving closer to the shed as she dropped on the ground, I stared toward what I assumed was the office. Behind one of the buildings, there was a small pond several feet away. At the sight of three people near the trunk of one of the two cars there, we scrambled behind the shed. One guy I immediately recognized as the one who attacked me at the Blue Dawn.

They tugged out a long object rolled up in a rug and loaded it on to the security vehicle, then went inside the office. When I glanced up, I saw a surveillance camera atop the side of the building next to the office facing the warehouse entrance.

"What the hell is that they just loaded?" Kristy whispered.

I shook my head.

"It looked like a body," she continued. "I feel like I'm in one of those creepy movies where the main people do something stupid and get killed—like jumping the fence onto private property and observing something they aren't supposed to."

I didn't take my gaze off the office as I answered her, "Okay, okay, we'll go. You're right. This is creepy, but I want to peek in the pit before we leave."

She reluctantly agreed, and we stepped toward the pit.

There are moments in our lives when we think we know what we're doing, but then when we think back on it, we don't understand our own decisions and actions. This was undeniably one of those moments. We sneaked to the edge of the pit and peered down. It was filled with broken chairs and desks, empty boxes, pieces of what appeared to be old carts, paper, car parts—you name it, it was there. The collection of junk was like a giant garbage heap.

Uneasiness came over me. My heart ached with utter sadness and pain as I stared into the pit. I couldn't describe it in words. I was drawn to the pit and could not understand why sadness and pain flooded my system. Kristy agreed to stand watch while I descended. As I climbed down, the ache in my heart got stronger, as did the smell. I got a whiff of something horrid, an odor I had only scented when I drove by something dead on the side of the road—a dank, decay smell.

Kristy whisper shouted, "What's wrong?"

Looking up at her, I put my hand over my mouth and nose. I tried to pinpoint the origin of the smell, but it wasn't long before she signaled for me to come up. Her sense of urgency indicated someone was coming. Abandoning my search, I planned to come back another time. I started up and was almost to the top when I slipped on a slick of mud. My face crashed into the side. The rumble of a motor echoed in between the buildings.

I motioned for Kristy to get behind the shed as I dove into a box close to hide. The box was large, like it once held a refrigerator. One side was partially crushed but was still together enough to offer a hiding place. A small tear in the box enabled me to see the rear lights of a security vehicle back up to the edge of the pit. The truck turned off, and two doors slammed. I lay completely still for fear any movement would alert whoever they were. My stomach churned nervously as I made every effort to take in short breaths and tried to see through the small tear at the top of the box. As I strained, I was able to see two men from the waist up chatting by the edge. After a moment, one disappeared from my sight, but I could still hear them talking. Something on the vehicle slammed, and the other one re-appeared as they dropped the tailgate. They slid a rolled up carpet to the gate's edge.

"O'Dell didn't say how long."

"Did he say when they're filling this in?"

The other man shook his head and glanced around. "Ask him. He's on his way." They set the carpet on the edge of the truck bed and waited.

One pulled out a cigarette, and I could hear them whispering to each other. My stomach churned again from the mysterious but nauseating smell. I panted, so I didn't throw up, and pulled my shirt over my mouth so I could attempt to breathe without puking. The strange sadness and pain sensation wouldn't go away either. I chalked it up to me being anxious, but that wasn't all. It was something else.

For what seemed like an eternity, I lay there quietly, trying to stay calm. Peering through the tear I could see the two men were still standing by the edge of the pit. Finally, I heard a car pull up, and the door slam. The man who left earlier joined the other two at the edge.

"O'Dell, do you know when they're filling it?" one of the men asked.

"The trucks are bringing in the fill dirt this week. Everything will be buried."

"Shouldn't we burn the pile first?"

"No, you idiot. The smell would bring too much attention, and we don't need any unscheduled visits from any state troopers or unwanted cops like last time."

One man agreed, and the other turned to O'Dell as he indicated the carpet. "What about this one?"

I didn't dare breathe as I watched him eye everything in the pit.

He glanced at my hiding place briefly before answering. "It goes with the rest. These little reminders of sloppy work don't go unnoticed. This is why he brought in Campbell, so don't fuck up, either of you."

They both nodded and one asked, "And the problem? Do you need that handled?"

"Not yet. He has something real special planned for her."

They both were in agreement, and I couldn't help wondering if it was me he was talking about. It crossed my mind there was a possibility that absolutely nothing was going on here but illegal dumping, but my gut told me differently. My nausea from inside the pit told me differently as did the weird feeling I kept having. My cell phone vibrated. I didn't dare move for fear they would see the box wiggle.

The afternoon seemed to drag on as I continued to lay there quietly, unmoving. Why were they still there? Finally, I heard a few grunts and saw them hurling the rolled carpet into the pit, I prayed it didn't hit the box. It didn't, instead landing about two feet from me on a heap of broken chairs, then sliding down and resting against the box. My gaze settled on the edge of the carpet which was at the opening of my box. The color of the carpet was bright red—so vibrant, so gaudy, so… familiar.

Car doors slammed following by the rumble of the car pulling away from the pit. I finally breathed. Checking my phone, I saw several texts from Kristy and Mason. Hoping she was still right outside, I texted her and told her to let me know when the men were gone. Mason, I would text back later.

I inched toward the box opening and stared at the edge of that rug, trying to place where I had seen it before. My heart sank as I realized it was the same carpet from Amanda Collins's house when I visited her in Redding.

I unraveled the corner of the carpet as I heard Kristy, in a very loud whisper, say, "Evaline! What are you doing? Come on! Let's get out of here."

I stopped when I eyed a very large lump in the center. Ice rushed through me, and my stomach twisted again with anxiety. I knew what was in the carpet. Finally leaving the box, I hurried toward Kristy, who was on her knees, reaching out to get me. As I crawled up and over the debris, tears filled my eyes. I had gotten someone killed. Amanda was dead because of me.

Kristy grabbed my hand, and we jumped behind the shed, resting against the wall briefly. I was breathing loudly, trying to keep from screaming—trying to get myself together.

"Eva, what's wrong? What happened?"

I shook my head. I needed a moment. Finally, catching my breath, I said, "Something horrible." My voice barely came out on a whisper.

Details would come later. For now, we had to get out of there. We climbed onto the shed roof, over the branch, and down to the other side. As we dropped from the tree, I heard a noise. I could see a little way down the fence. One of the men was unlocking a gate as he eyed us. I grabbed Kristy, and we ran into the thicket and hid behind a tree.

"I saw you, little mice! Come out, come out, wherever you are!" he yelled after us.

"I need you to get back to the car," I whispered to Kristy. "Do you remember where it is?"

Her worried expression was evident as she wiped the sweat from her brow. "What about you?"

Taking in a deep breath, I urged her. "I need to lead him away from you. Here are the keys. Just follow the fence line, and you'll be fine."

She immediately turned and ran along the fence but still under the cover of the trees. Knowing he would hear her running, I picked up a large branch and waited.

Rustling leaves and twigs crunched. He came closer and closer so I waited for my moment. My heart pounded with fear and excitement as he finally neared. He reached the tree, and before he had a chance to respond, I slammed the stick into him. He went down, and I took off, careful not to lose the fence line for fear of getting lost. The sun had almost set, and as I headed for the car, something hit me, and I fell. I looked up to see one of the men staring at me with disbelief.

"You don't know when to quit, do you? You're dead, bitch." He pulled out a large knife. "You should have just left it alone."

He lunged at me. I kicked him in the face and down he went but not for long. As I scrambled to my feet, he turned back to me, his face twisted in rage. With a grunt, he sprang at me again but missed, and when he did, I swung my fist and punched him across the cheek. A low groan escaped him as I turned to run, but he grabbed my hair, yanking me back then hurling me against a tree. I crashed to the ground, clutching my wrist. It throbbed with pain as I looked frantically around for something to defend myself. He advanced on me, and I was suddenly overcome with the intense sentiment this was it—he was going to kill me.

Nevertheless, no sooner had he taken a step than I heard it—a growl that seemed to surround us. The man scanned the area, but I didn't move. He hesitated with the knife held high as if to come down on me with it. I closed my eyes, but as soon as I did, I heard a yelp and a hot wind blew by me. I opened my eyes and could hear him screaming as I focused my gaze on the large mass of fur mauling the man on the ground. I should have run, but I couldn't. I was frozen in place.

The man's screams ceased, and silence reigned in the forest once again. The mass of fur turned to me but didn't advance. A wolf. More specifically, the biggest wolf I had ever seen. At least the size of a tiger. It watched me while I watched him. I should have been terrified, but the truth was, I wasn't. There was a certain ease about this wolf, a sense of safety. The shape and look in its eyes were familiar but that was impossible. Then, just as quickly as it appeared, the wolf ran back into the woods.

I sat there for a moment longer until I heard the other security guy calling out a name. Realizing he was looking for the dead man, I forced myself to get up and dart toward the fence. I followed it back to the main trail, then to the trailhead. Kristy was in the car when I got there, and before I knew it, we were out of the parking lot and headed home.

I didn't tell her about the wolf though—not yet.

Six

Rain pelted the window. It was morning, but dark due to the cloud cover. I lay in bed, thinking about what happened the night before. How was I going to deal with this? The scenes from the pit, and how I could keep my family safe? Then there was the wolf—his scent, his fur, the familiarity of his eyes. How peculiar all of that was. There was a knock at my door. "Come in."

Kristy placed my coffee cup on my nightstand and sat on the edge of the bed. "Are you okay?" she asked gently. "I don't even know what that was last night."

I sat up, taking the cup she had brought and took a drink. "I'm sorry, Kristy. I shouldn't have taken you. I wasn't thinking."

"No, I wanted to go. Wasn't your fault, but I still don't understand why we were there."

There it was—the conversation I didn't want to have. I finally answered, "Has to do with Jimmy. He met with a client outside his law firm a few weeks before he disappeared. This client was into some pretty bad stuff, and I think Jimmy found out about it."

She blinked as she took everything in. "So, you don't think he's still missing?"

"I don't know what I believe. This is still so surreal. The thing is, I wasn't satisfied with what the police were doing to find Jimmy, so I started investigating, and I guess I ruffled a few feathers because I got threats. I knew I had to leave Sacramento when you called, and it seemed like the perfect way out. I could still try to find out what happened to Jimmy and not be in the city. But I never wanted to bring this on you and Laine. You two are all I have left."

She took my hand. "And the warehouse from last night?"

"I think it's owned by the same person Jimmy was meeting with, and I think it's a dummy corporation. This is bad stuff, and I don't know what do. I don't think I have enough to go to the state police or the feds for that matter."

She sat back. "Well, what about the local—"

"They're in on it," I said, cutting her off. "The new sheriff—

Campbell—he's from Sacramento and before that Redding. It seems like wherever this corporation moves, Campbell is there."

She got up and walked over to the window. After a moment, she turned back to me. "Well, we have to do something. Those guys saw us last night."

"No, one guy saw us. The other one didn't come until later. And the guy who did see us won't be talking anytime soon."

Her head tilted, a puzzled expression on her face. I couldn't tell her it was a giant wolf. She would either freak out or think I hit my head. "Something—something attacked him last night when he was chasing me. It was big, probably a bear. I didn't stay to find out."

She put her hand to her mouth. "Eva, what are we going to do? I mean, what did you see in that pit? You were kind of freaked."

"We need to be cautious. These people are dangerous, and two little girls from a small forest town aren't going to stand in their way. Just don't say anything to anyone, not even Laine or Lizzy—at least not until I can figure this out, okay?"

She shrugged as if defeated. I put my coffee down and got out of bed as she walked to the door. "Oh," she added, "we better go to the Blue Dawn. Your phone is lit up with about a hundred texts from Mason."

I lifted a brow.

"You left your phone on the kitchen counter last night."

I let out a long sigh. "Where's Laine?"

"He left for work. See you downstairs."

~ * ~

Campbell sat on a picnic table outside the warehouse. He was on his cell phone and smoking a cigarette. His expression was troubled as he waited for a response from the other end of the phone.

A voice came across after a moment, "Yeah?"

"I need to speak with Leathan. It's important."

A moment went by as Campbell observed a bulldozer entering the parking lot on the bed of a truck. He motioned the driver to the pit and returned his attention to the phone.

"Yeah, things took a bad turn last night. She was here, at the warehouse, and I don't know what she saw. One of my guys is dead. I'm almost positive it was a wolf." He listened intently for a moment. "I understand, but that's going to be a problem because she's so close to the Cowans... I can do that. They'll be a lot easier than her. I think I know where they are." He rolled his hand over and eyed the bracelet he held. "No problem. I'll call when it's done."

He hung up and strode to a police car.

~ * ~

Kristy and I sped down the road as the rain pelted my windshield. It was a warm day, and the wind was blowing as well. We pulled into the Blue Dawn parking lot, and there were only a couple cars in the lot since they didn't open for another few hours. Inside, one of the servers was filling the salt and pepper shakers, and Lucy was doing inventory by the bar. We sat near her.

Kristy whispered, "Uh-oh."

I glanced up to see Mason coming from the kitchen over to us.

He gave me a quick smile, and then turned his attention to Kristy. "Just called your cell. I need to know if you can work a double tonight."

"Sure, but I don't have a car to get home."

I sat up straighter. "I can come get you."

He shook his head. "No, it'll be late. One of us can bring her home. I appreciate it."

"Is Lizzy back there?" she asked. He indicated the kitchen, and she went to see Lizzy.

Mason sat on the stool next to me. A tinge of guilt overcame me for a moment as I realized I hadn't gotten back to him.

"I'm sorry I didn't call. It was… kind of a weird night."

"I know what those are like." His gaze fell on the scratches on my hands and wrists from climbing out of the pit and then running.

"Like I said, weird night."

I could see his concern as he inclined a bit toward me. "You okay?"

"I'm fine, really. Nothing a little Neosporin can't handle."

He smiled, but that seemed to satisfy him. He placed my Tupperware on the table.

Recognizing it as mine, I asked, a bit nervously, "Well, did you like it?"

"What little I had of it. My asshole of a brother AJ ate almost the whole thing."

I couldn't help but laugh. "Oh, sorry. Do you want me to bring you some more?"

"You don't have to, but next time, text me you're stopping by."

The butterflies in my stomach were working overtime. As much as I tried to seem not so willing, I felt myself answer, "Deal."

He glanced from me to the menu lying on the counter. "So, are you hungry? I can have Jonas throw something on for you."

Opening the menu, I eyed the list of burger names. "The wolf burger looks good. Is it big?"

His eyes twinkled with amusement. "It is, but I can have Jonas make a small one for you."

"Thank you."

Mason rose, then he leaned down so his face was near mine. My insides fluttered. I never wanted him to move away—his amazing aroma enveloped me, and his piercing eyes made me warm. "I'll pick you up at seven. Movie and dinner sound good?"

Sounded like heaven. "Yeah, sounds fun. What are we going to see?"

"I'll let you pick," he said, before turning and heading back to the kitchen.

Kristy returned a moment later. "Pamela called off again. Isaac is pissed."

"Does she call off a lot?"

"Yup. Anyway, how is Mason?" She grinned.

I shook my head ruefully. "You need to stop worrying."

She rested her arm across the table and lowered her voice. "So, Lizzy said you were *the* topic of discussion yesterday. I guess Mason has been acting weird, and they think it's because of you."

"Don't be ridiculous. We haven't even known each other that long."

I knew what she meant though. The strange urge I had with him was like he and I had known each other in another life. The fact I'd only seen him less than a half-dozen times wasn't a factor. Every time he was near, that sense of an inexplicable connection wouldn't go away. Perhaps he felt the same.

"Evaline, you light up when he's around," Kristy said.

Satisfaction brightened her eyes as she sat back. One of the waitresses brought us two Cokes.

"What about you?" I asked, changing the subject. "Still crushing on Jonas?"

"Shhhhh!" Her eyes got big. "He can hear you."

I laughed. "You should just tell him how you feel."

She shook her head. "He knows, but I don't think he feels the same. There's lightning when Mason looks at you. When Jonas looks at me, there's not even as much as a spark."

We quieted as Mason came out with our food, Isaac right behind him. Mason placed my burger in front of me.

We started to eat, and Kristy turned toward Isaac. "How come this tastes different?"

He winced. "We switched distributors. It's not good?"

"I didn't say it was bad. Just said different."

Isaac seemed entranced as he watched me take a bite of my burger. I nearly moaned it was so wonderful trying to ignore the long moment, he studied me. He was as good-looking as the entire family and as the oldest, he seemed to be in charge.

A grin stretched his mouth. "Your spaghetti sauce was unbelievable. Any chance of you giving me the recipe?"

Mason raised his brows. I tried not to laugh as I swallowed and shook my head. "Sorry, family recipe. Maybe we can work it out, and I will make a batch for you."

He acquiesced with a nod. "Fair enough."

"How is the burger?" Mason asked me.

"Amazing," I said, taking another bite. "Tell Jonas he's awesome."

Lizzy and Lucy came over to say hello and sat on the stools next to Kristy as we ate. It was nice, everyone enjoying themselves and laughing—at least for a short while.

Then, just like any moment you can't hold on to, the happiness was fleeting as Campbell entered. Everyone went quiet except for Isaac. "Hi there, Sheriff Campbell. What can we do for you?"

Campbell came over and eyed all of us.

"Jonas was home last night," Isaac offered.

He was quick to answer. "I'm not here for your brother. I need to talk to Kristy."

My gaze wasn't the only one to focus on Kristy who was, at the moment, eating a French fry. She froze for a second upon hearing her name but tried to cover as she finished chewing. "I was home too."

I glanced from her to Campbell. "There was an animal attack yesterday at a warehouse outside of town. Security guard was mauled. Likely a bear attack but we need to investigate further."

Isaac's gaze never left him. "Sorry to hear that. We'll have to be careful."

Campbell's expression turned inquisitive as he continued, "Sure thing, but I still need to see Kristy now."

She hopped off her stool and followed him. My gaze tracked them as they halted a short way away for privacy.

Lizzy leaned over Mason to say to me, "Notice he stayed away from you."

I shook my head and flashed her a quick glance.

Isaac caught the look. "Why?"

"A few weeks back, Campbell stopped us and—"

"Lizzy," I said, as I glanced at Isaac and Mason. "It was a minor traffic stop. Not a big deal." Campbell and Kristy came back to where we all were. He stood behind her as she grabbed her purse. "Where are you going?" I asked her.

"I guess... paperwork?" she said, her tone incredulous.

I frowned. "She's not going anywhere with you." He seemed bemused as I continued, "You talk to me."

He took a moment before saying, "This particular issue has nothing to do with you—yet."

I wasn't backing down. "You can talk to her here."

Mason sat back, watching him with suspicious eyes.

"You're firecracker, aren't you?" Campbell said, glaring at me.

"What do you want?" I asked, ignoring the comment.

He stilled as his radio squawked, and then he considered me as he answered his dispatcher. "Okay, Jess, I'll head over there now." He sighed. "I suggest you, Miss Bennett, and both Kristy and Laine stay close to home. I'll be in touch." He left, and we sighed in relief.

I turned to Kristy. "What did he say to you?"

"He said my bracelet was found in the woods last night where the security guard was killed," she said, as she returned to her stool.

I thought I caught Mason flash Isaac a look before he turned to me. "Were you two somewhere you shouldn't have been?" Mason asked.

"No." His jaw clenched briefly but I noted the movement. "What?" I asked in response.

He just chuckled. "You're quite the mystery."

I sighed.

Isaac asked, "Everything okay?"

I kept a cool expression to not let him suspect anything. "Really, we're fine."

No one said much else. We finished our lunch, and everyone went back to what they had to do. I left and headed home thinking it would only be a few hours before I would see Mason for our first official date—with no library involved.

~ * ~

Mason showed up promptly at seven and soon we were racing in his truck down route 5 toward Shasta Springs. Rain pelted the windshield on and off but the air was still warm.

It had been a while since I'd been on a date, and it wasn't something I thought much about since Jimmy had disappeared. In addition, what had happened with Kristy and me the other night was still fresh in my mind. So was the fact that the beast from my dreams had come out of nowhere and saved my life, even though I hadn't accepted it yet. A memory flashed of a distant wish of a little girl so very long ago. The fact was fairy tales with princes, castles, and dwarves were just that—tales. On the flip-side, real life did possess at least one attribute of fairy tales—monsters, but these fiends weren't ogres or orcs. They were human, and they tended to be much more terrifying.

I was pulled out of my reverie as Mason wheeled the truck into a movie plex and turned to me. "Anything in particular you'd like to see?"

I glanced over at the list of movies and their times.

"I'll even go see a chick flick if you want," he said, grinning.

I laughed. "I didn't think Bruce Campbell did chick flicks."

His eyes widened. "You like Bruce Campbell movies?"

"They are having a Bruce Campbell festival. Let's go see *Return of the Evil Dead*; it looks pretty good."

He sat motionless for a moment as he studied me. Finally, he got out, opening his door as he turned to me. "Don't move, okay?"

I didn't realize why until he came to my door and opened it. He held out his hand. I was stunned for a moment, and then reluctantly took his hand and slid out of the truck. "Wow. I guess chivalry isn't dead after all," I said, taken aback. "Are you from this century?"

"Not really." He chuckled.

We walked to the ticket booth holding hands, but we didn't say another word. Another perfect moment. We sat through the movie without a word, only smiling occasionally at each other when a good scene came on.

The movie let out, and we decided to go eat at the local pub. When the waitress came to the table to see what we wanted, she stuttered through the specials—it was the effect Mason had on many women.

He leaned back. "So, did you like it?"

I had this thing for scary movies. It had driven Jimmy crazy when we were kids. "Yes. It wasn't bad. Not as good as the original, of course, but good nevertheless." I eyed him with a smirk. "What about you? Do you like scary movies?"

"Hell yeah. I thought it was good, but I agree—nothing beats the original."

I was so into him, and I wanted to tell him what happened but how could I involve him? How could I risk putting him in jeopardy? It was a delicate balance of keeping those I cared about safe, but still available in case.

He seemed to examine me before asking, "What's wrong?"

I paused a moment, thinking about telling him everything. He patiently waited as I struggled internally. "Mason, this will sound weird, but I need to know if you're my friend."

He didn't even blink as he answered me, gently, "I think it's more than that. You can tell me what's wrong."

His expression, the tone of his voice, how he was looking at me—they all told me he saw me as something far more. Perhaps he was as drawn to me as I was to him?

"They called off the search for my brother." Tears yearned to fall, but I fought them with everything I had.

"I'm sorry. I can tell you loved him very much." He gave me a moment before continuing, "I lost two brothers and a sister, so I understand."

I was astonished as he proceeded to tell me he thought of them often and time didn't necessarily heal the wounds. "At least you have your other brothers and sisters. You all seem like you're close."

His lips softened. "That we are."

After toasting his obvious love for his family, I decided to tell him. "We were there that night the guard was killed—Kristy and I were, I mean."

The waitress brought our food. Mason's eyes darkened as he patiently waited for the waitress to leave. Finally she left, and he asked, "Why were you there?"

I told him what I found out about Campbell, Charles Spanditto, and the Span Enterprise Corporation. He sat quietly until I was done, when he finally asked, "You went to check out that pit, didn't you?"

"Jonas was right. Mason, there's something at the bottom of that pit. Something is dead down there. And someone needs to know."

"Hmm. That explains it."

"What?"

As he explained, apparently, Jonas had been riding his bike along the park road, not far from that property, and he'd seen a truck with two bulldozers pulling into the driveway through the gate. Mason thought I'd gotten too close, and they had to cover up the evidence.

"I want you to stay away from all of it, Evaline," he said. "You don't know anything about these people, and who knows, they could hurt you."

"I know, Mason, but I need to discern if they killed Jimmy. The thing is, I think they did but I must confirm what happened, and when I do, I'm going to bring them all down."

"Maybe you should contact the state police now, before it gets out of control."

I shook my head. "Well, I did make a call, but I don't know

how far I'll get since I don't have a smoking gun. Right now, I just have a lot of indirect evidence. I wanted to have everything before I made the call, but things are getting scary. I didn't tell you this so you would worry or try to stop me from finding out the truth."

He slanted his head. "Then why did you tell me?"

"Because I needed to tell someone, and I know I can trust you."

Not saying much, we left the diner and headed home. He was quiet, and his expression seemed troubled. When we entered my driveway, Mason turned off the truck, and we sat in silence for a long moment before he jumped out of his truck and strolled to my side then opened my door. We walked up to the dark porch.

"Why don't you come to the Dawn tomorrow night?" he asked, turning to face me as we reached the door. "There's a live band. Come and hang out."

My face heated as he took a step toward me. His chest touched mine as he backed me up against the door gently and bent his head. You only see the kiss in the movies, the kiss you only read about—the kiss that sealed the deal. That was this one. Just as quick as it started though, he stopped and turned his head to look across the street. His body went rigid, his attention fully on whatever was over there. His expression was both suspicious and angry.

I glanced across the street but saw nothing. "What's wrong?"

He said nothing, lifting his head slightly, as if he could smell something. A long moment later, he turned back to me, and his expression softened. "Sorry, thought I heard something."

I kept quiet for a minute and then blurted out, "Did you want to come in and watch TV?"

The corners of his eyes crinkled; the look of concern disappeared. "I'd love to."

We sat on the couch and watched a late-night movie, him holding me close. I must have drifted off at some point because I woke to the front door slamming and still in Mason's arms.

I sat up and eyed Laine, who strolled down the hall and up the stairs, smiling briefly before he was gone. Mason's gaze was on me as he brushed the hair from my face.

"I think I need to go to bed," I mumbled.

He smiled. "I think I should probably head out anyway." He stood and followed me to the door. "See you tomorrow?" He waited for me to nod, kissed me, then was gone.

~ * ~

The darkness was complete, but I could hear the ferocious growls getting louder. I was being chased through a swamp, the smell of decay and dampness overwhelming me. I saw a light and started running toward it. When I reached it, I stopped dead in my tracks.

The giant wolf stood there in the light. He reared in a defensive stance, and I could hear more growls and realized he wasn't alone. Three more wolves, just as large, raised up behind him. To my right were two more, smaller but just as ferocious, ready in what appeared to be an attack formation. The wolf had never attacked me before. Had always given me a sense of safety.

I turned and saw Campbell standing less than ten feet away. His expression was one of anger, rage even. He stood on graves, and the longer I watched him, the more graves there were until there were hundreds. Screams erupted from the graves as he advanced toward me, a machete in hand. The wolves came closer, preparing to attack, when Jimmy appeared behind Campbell, grabbing him from behind.

Jimmy's eyes fixed on me. "Run, Evaline!" he shouted. "Run and don't stop! The others are coming!"

I saw beyond him where two more dark figures were. I turned to run, but a vine wrapped around my leg, knocking me down in front of the white and gray wolf. I expected to feel teeth, but instead, a warm hand helped me up. There, just where the wolf was, was Mason.

Gasping, I woke. The dreams were getting more intense, and sometimes I could hear his whispers, even when I was awake. They were so faint at times, I couldn't make out what he was saying, but I knew he was telling me to stay away or get away.

Thinking of the wolf and Mason, I rolled over. When he grabbed me from the ground, the wolves had been gone. The thing was, he was familiar to me in the same way the wolf was—as if… as if they were the same.

I made my way downstairs and found Kristy on the couch with a book. As we did every morning, I headed for the kitchen for some coffee. With a quick stir for the cream, I went back into the living room and sat next to her. She was reading a class catalog for the local college. "You're going?"

She rolled her eyes but smiled. "Maybe. I'm just looking to see what they have."

I beamed with the thought as I had tried for a while to get her to go to college. Now she was actually thinking about it. I was happy for her, but my focus was still on my intense dream. She took notice.

"Eva, what's wrong?" Kristy asked, stopping my train of thought.

She was the only one I could talk to about it, so I dove in. "Do you remember those dreams I would have when we were kids? The really intense ones?"

"How can I forget? Jimmy and I had to calm you down that one night when it got to be too much."

I got anxious as the memory flashed. "I remember. You guys called it my psychic link."

"Are you having those kinds of dreams again?"

"Jimmy is trying to tell me something. They are so extreme, Kristy. In the one last night, Campbell was coming to kill me, and Jimmy and some wolves stopped him."

She blinked. "Wolves? Jesus, Eva, I remember those dreams. Some of them were so unbelievably real and worse, some even came true."

She was right. "I have a call in to the state police. Hopefully, someone calls me back. However, you know if we say what we think we saw, they're gonna want to know why we were there. It's trespassing. Although at this point, I guess that part wouldn't be a huge deal. I just… don't know what to do."

"You called the police?" she asked a bit bewildered.

"Well, just know, the dreams are related to what's really happening with the warehouse, the sheriff and Jimmy."

Kristy looked at me, puzzled. "But how?"

"Well, Jonas was riding near the warehouse a couple days ago and said he saw a truck with bulldozers pulling in by the gate. They probably filled it in. Who knows?"

Disbelief widened her eyes as she sat back. "And all the evidence."

I continued as she eyed me with a concerned look. "I think… I think someone has been watching the house. Whenever I'm home alone or even just gotten home, I can sense someone. It happened last night with Mason, and I'm thinking that is why he stayed."

She smirked. "Mason stayed because he likes you, not because someone is watching the house."

I smiled and shrugged it off. Yes, I knew Mason and I had a strong connection, but I was uneasy when we were on the porch last night, and it wasn't from him. I shook my head ruefully. "Just the same, please don't go anywhere alone, okay?"

She agreed, and we hugged for a moment. She pulled back. "What are you going to tell the police if they call?"

I didn't answer. In truth, I had no idea what I was going to say.

Seven

The parking lot was busy as cars and trucks pulled in and out. Music filled the air, pouring onto the back patio. I pulled my car underneath the huge pine and made my way inside.

"Hey, Eva!" Lizzy said, catching my eye as I walked in. "Glad you're here."

I smiled as I stood next to her. Kristy and Lucy came out from the back.

"I'm so happy you came," Kristy whispered. "Mason was wondering where you were."

I looked around but didn't see him. "Where is he?"

Lucy grabbed a tray of beers. "He went out to his truck. He should be back in a minute. Did you want a beer or something?"

"Sure, I'll have a Bud Lime. Thanks."

She let the bartender know, then headed off to one of her tables.

"You guys are slamming tonight," I observed of Kristy.

She glanced over at Lizzy, who was heading out with another tray of beer. "An understatement."

Hands were on my back, and I turned to see Laine smiling at me. "You finally came out."

I shrugged. "Yeah, well, I needed some time out."

He smiled as he sat next to me. "Does this mean I can have a beer with my favorite cousin?"

"Definitely."

The bartender placed my beer in front of me. I picked it up and clanked Laine's bottle.

"Hey, wait for us," Jonas yelled as he, Mason, Isaac, and Aaron were walking toward them.

Mason saw me. "Starting without us?"

"See what happens when you leave to go to your truck?"

He laughed, and they raised their beers.

"May the trails be clear for riding," Laine said.

Jonas piped in, "And the trucks are ready."

I couldn't help but laugh as Aaron continued, "To good friends."

Everyone nodded as Isaac spoke. "To good times."

I held up my beer and said, "To family." I glanced at Laine, who smiled.

Mason smiled. "Well said."

Isaac watched me and Mason with curiosity. "Amen to that."

We drank as the place surged with bodies. The jukebox changed to the next track as the band prepared to take the stage. In an instant, there it was playing over the speakers, the undeniable guitar riffs and unmistakable vocals of the Generation X mantra of *Lithium*. I remembered what Kristy told me about Aaron and his nineties obsession. I glanced at him as did everyone else around me. I didn't think anyone could help but laugh as he grinned from ear to ear.

Isaac just shook his head.

The dance floor was steaming with people anxiously waiting for the band to start, and it wasn't long before one of the security guys approached us. "Isaac, we're officially at capacity."

Isaac took a quick look at the door and then whispered instructions, "Put Big Mike and Richey at the door. Do a count for admission—if three leave, then three can be admitted."

The guy nodded and left.

Isaac turned to me. "How's the car running?"

"So far so good. Knock on wood."

Aaron grabbed a basket of peanuts from under the bar and placed them in front of us. "Yeah, that's a real nice ride you have."

"Thank you."

I glanced at Mason who was fixated on something across the bar. He had the same look he had last night on my porch. Isaac, Aaron, and Jonas followed his gaze. Soon they all had the same focused look.

"What's wrong?" I asked, wondering if it was related to the previous night.

Isaac and the others looked from me to Mason, whose gaze fell on me. His face softened, and he paused a moment before he answered me, "Nothing to worry about."

But I knew it was something. I was also having the same weird feeling I was being watched. I tried not to let it look like it was bothering me, but it was. The slight glimmer of danger was around us, but I had a sense of safety standing with Mason and his brothers.

"I'd like to show you something," he said suddenly. "Let's go for a ride."

I was intrigued. Kristy and Lizzy gave me big smiles and

thumbs-ups as we strolled out of the Blue Dawn, and soon we were in Mason's truck, heading down the road.

"Where are we going?" I asked.

He smiled. "You'll see."

I recognized the turn as we drove his long and curvy driveway. "You taking me to your house?" Not that I minded.

He smirked but said nothing. We went past his house, to a path at the rear of the property. Into the woods we went. It was a ways in, but his truck chugged along, through the trees and mud to a clearing, and that was when I saw it. The three-quarter moon bathed the entire clearing in moonlight, revealing a small lake surrounded by trees and bushes. It was like something out of a dream. The water resembled glass, the weeping willows on the water's edge giving it a jungle feel.

Mason pulled up by the water, and I jumped out. The shore was small pebbles and sand. Across the water, there was another clearing set close enough to the woods where there was a carpet of moss leading to the water. He stood next to me as I sighed with pleasure and in awe. This was a bit of paradise in the mountains, completely secluded and apparently owned by the Cowans.

"Oh, Mason. This is so amazing." When I caught his gaze, I realized he wasn't looking at the scene but rather at me.

A soft smile curled his lips before he finally gazed at the water. "It's our lake. I figured we would go for a swim. It's pretty warm tonight."

He began taking off his clothes, and I immediately became awkward. I never seemed to know the right thing to say in this type of situation. A secluded lake, a warm night, a hot guy undressing and wanting to go for a swim with me—what could I say? I kicked my shoes off as he made his way to a rock overhanging the water just enough. I stood in pleasure over his perfect naked silhouette as the moonlight embraced him. He was absolutely beautiful in every way.

Moonlight glistened off his skin, and my heart fluttered. The pit of my stomach trembled with eagerness, and anxiety built as my breathing deepened. He jumped into the water, and I continued to undress, nervously removing my underwear. I made my way up the same rock overhang and stood looking down at him in the water. He gazed up at me, smiling.

"How cold is the water?" I asked.

He laughed a little. "It's nice. Trust me."

I was still nervous to jump, and he must have seen my hesitation because he said, "Evaline, I would never steer you wrong."

I took a few steps back and launched myself into the water—

and toward a waiting Mason.

Warm water rushed over me as I swam up to the surface. I wiped the water from my face, and he came to me as he tugged me closer, and I couldn't help but giggle. Anything I was thinking prior to then—about Campbell, the weird sensation of being watched, what I had seen in the pit, and even Jimmy—was temporarily suspended as if it would all work out—or as if I didn't care, at least for that moment.

"Why do I feel so safe with you?" I asked.

Without hesitation, he said, "Because you *are* safe with me, and you always will be."

"You can't be everywhere, Mason. Sooner or later the demons catch up."

"That's true, but I can be there along the way. I said it before, and I'll say it again. These are potentially dangerous people, Evaline."

"I want you stay out of this, Mason Cowan. I mean it. I can't lose anyone else. I don't think I could take it."

His expression didn't change. "You're in it deeper than you think."

"I know, trust me, but it's my problem. I can handle it."

His mood was unwavering as he answered without a pause, "Rest assured, baby, when you can't handle it anymore, I will be there."

Gently, I put my hands behind his neck as I really didn't want to talk about this anymore. Just by his tone and words, I knew he would absolutely, without a doubt, be there for me if I asked him. And I knew, at that moment, I was absolutely and irrefutably in love with him.

"So, tell me about this place." I glanced at the serene water and its surroundings.

"We like seclusion, in case you haven't noticed. Isaac saw this place and knew we had to have it. We call it Alban Loch, which literally means 'Scottish lake.' It's something our father used to call a similar place on our property back east when we were growing up."

I could see the name had special meaning to him. As I rolled my hand over the tattoo of his family's crest on his massive arm, I glanced up at him with a smirk. "Ah, a loch, eh? You wouldn't be Scottish by chance, would you?" I couldn't keep a straight face as I asked in my best impression of an accent.

"Oh no, of course not," he answered playfully as he fixated on my necklace. "You're Scottish."

I touched the necklace around my neck. "Yes. This was my grandmother's. When she died, my mother wore it. When my mom got sick, she gave it to me. So now it's mine, and I keep it close. Jimmy has a ring with the same crest on it."

Mason's gaze moved from the necklace to me, and then he leaned in for a kiss. I melted into him as if I were a magnet and a piece of steel. We were irrevocably fixed together in a powerful spell. He held me close as his kisses moved to my neck and back up to my lips.

He stopped for a moment, and I saw him eye the moss-covered shoreline by the forest edge. He glanced back at me, and I found myself nodding. The heat from his body burned like an ember in the water. We made our way to the mossy beach. He gently laid me down on the soft natural carpet.

I was on fire. Every move he made was intense and followed by a kiss. With his fingers and lips, he caressed every inch of my skin. My toes tingled with delight with each press of his lips kiss, and more so with the strokes of his fingertips along my outer thigh. We made love, and it was a perfect moment—a night that would undoubtedly change everything.

My name echoed through the woods as I ran—from someone or something. The voice sounded like Jimmy's but was becoming fainter the farther I sprinted. I reached the beach where I had been with Mason, but he wasn't there. Instead, there was a deer standing on the beach looking at me. I stopped and walked toward it. It didn't flinch as I approached or as I reached out to touch him. His heart beat faster and faster as if he were running.

To my right, and standing next to me was Grandma Marion, my mom's mother. She had passed when I was two, and my memories of her were all but faded. My mom had shown me an old picture once, years later when I couldn't remember what Grandma looked like. She was as I remembered her from the picture, and tears sprung to my eyes when I saw her.

"Grams," I whispered, and she smiled.

"What a woman you have become, Eibhlin."

I smiled at my Gaelic name as her voice carried a heavy Scottish accent, and when she spoke, it was with intent. "You're close to seeing who you really are. I was hoping we would be lost to them, but they have found our family."

I was confused. "Grams, what are talking about? How am I talking to you?"

"Your mind is in a state of peace right now, so it makes it easier," she replied.

I wiped a tear away as I asked, "Jimmy?"

She watched me somberly and didn't say anything. I knew the truth from her expression what I already knew in my heart, but to have confirmation from the other side was another matter entirely.

"You are all that is left, Eibhlin" she said somberly, "but you cannot do it alone. You're not strong enough to fight this, and you need to look at what is in front of you, who is in front of you, to help fight."

I glanced back at the deer, but it was down. Instead, there stood my wolf. He reared over the deer's lifeless body—his fresh kill— and eyed me silently. I looked back at Grams. "How is the wolf going to help?"

She wore a crooked smile that said she knew something but wanted me to figure it out. I turned to look at my wolf again, but now Mason was in front of me. He wasn't staring at me with the same gentle expression he normally did; instead, he was intense, angry. I wanted to talk to him, but he said nothing. He lifted what I thought was a weapon at first, but it was his hand — the fingernails were claws.

His expression softened before he turned toward the water though it was now a field. Bright, green, grassy hills and mountains with scattered giant black rocks on them suddenly surrounded us. I was standing behind him. He let out a wolf's howl. Next to him, the rest of the Cowan family and a little boy, as well as many others, were at his side. I reached for the boy—I didn't want him to go. I was protective of him, but he just smiled.

A tear ran down my cheek as he whispered innocently, "I'll be okay, Mommy."

He followed Mason onto a battlefield where half the army was human, half were wolves. The mysterious dark figure from my other dream seemed to lead the attack from the hill as both sides charged toward a colossal battle of giant wolves.

I screamed no and sat up. It was so real, but there I was, lying on the serene, mossy beach. I peered across the water at Mason's truck. Moonlight glistened off the water, but he wasn't lying next to me. I could hear an animal sniffing, then a strange gurgling and slapping. A moment later, he was next to me again as he laid his arm protectively over me. His body was hot, his pulse rapid.

He fell asleep a couple of moments later, and as I drifted back to sleep, I pondered what I thought I'd heard and my strange dream. Sometimes my dreams revealed current worries or truths, and sometimes they revealed what lay ahead—which one my dream was at that point, I wasn't sure.

~ * ~

The sun was warm through the trees. I opened my eyes to a

deer drinking at the water's edge. I didn't move for fear of scaring her. She stood for a long moment and then ran off. I sat up and scanned the still-sleeping Mason. His ankles and feet were smeared with mud. I wondered if what I'd woken to in the middle of the night had been a dream as well. I wasn't sure. Was my mind playing tricks on me? Maybe he had gotten up to go to the bathroom.

I decided to wash off and take a morning dip. The water was cool, but a relief after the warmth of the sun. I floated, looking up at the sky. There was plenty of blue behind the scattered white clouds. The sun's rays warmed my exposed skin. An amazing feeling of warmth, of tranquility, of freedom. A splash interrupted my moment, and I looked the beach—no Mason. Ripples marked his underwater movement toward me. When he got to me, I wrapped my arms around him as he kissed me.

"I saw something beautiful floating in the water and just had to investigate."

Laughing, I splashed him. "Subtle."

Leaving the water, we made our way to the truck where we promptly got dressed and jumped in. The day was quiet. Peaceful. I didn't want it to end. Mason took me back to the Dawn to get my car.

"Two things," he said as we stopped. "First, there is another live band tonight, so I was thinking you can come, and we can hang out."

I beamed. "Okay, and the second?"

"Well, tomorrow is game day at my house. Maybe you would want to come over and watch."

"Game day, like football?"

He nodded.

"I like football. Sure, that will be fun. What time do you want me to come?"

He shook his head. "No, I'll come get you around noon."

"Mason, I can drive. Do you want me to bring food or something?"

He hesitated a moment and then answered, "No, we, um, tend to eat barbeque."

"So you grill out then?"

"Yeah."

"Okay, well, I'll just bring chips or something?"

"Okay."

"What time then?"

"Around noon is fine."

I smiled as he leaned in, and we kissed. I opened the truck door and jumped out. Lucy was unloading something from her car. "I'm going to see if Lucy needs any help. I'll see you tonight?"

I slammed the door shut, and Mason left. I hadn't seen Lucy much up to that point, other than at the bar or around town. She was always cordial and waved but was never much for conversation. Being the older sister, she was understandably protective of her brother. I went over to her and grabbed another box from the truck. It was terribly heavy. How did Lucy carry two so easily?

"I can get it," she said.

I sucked in a deep breath and heaved the box out of the trunk. "No, I got it."

I followed her inside through the back door of the Dawn. I placed the box on the floor and watched her set both of hers effortlessly on the bar.

"Thanks, she said, turning to look at me. "Did you guys have a good time?"

"Yeah, it's just new, that's all. It wasn't in the plans, but…"

She smiled briefly. "It usually never is, but that's when it can hurt the most." I gave her a curious look as she continued, "I love my brothers very much. But Mason, he gave up a lot."

Ah. I knew where she was going with this. I thought of my conversation with him about him losing his fiancée and how he felt about love. "Are you talking about his fiancée who died?"

Lucy stopped and nodded as she said, "Beth. He loved her more than anything, and after she died, he was never the same. It's like he became a different person and forgot about the part of him that loves."

I completely understood her concerns which were, of course, not the case. "Lucy, I'm not trying to hurt him, if that's what you're getting at. I mean, this totally blindsided me. However, it's like I knew there was something the first time we met. I tried to dismiss it, but it kept happening. And I do understand loss, trust me."

She nodded. "Your brother?"

"Yes, I guess Mason told you."

"I understand, and I hope you find him."

"Did you need help with anything else?"

"No, I'm fine but thanks. Isaac is good for saying we need something and then not being there to unload it."

She was guarded, but I couldn't say I disliked her. She was protecting her brother. If Jimmy had been there, he would have had the same conversation with Mason. I got in my car and headed home to a nice hot shower. When I got out of the shower, I heard my phone ringing. I didn't recognize the number, but I answered.

"Ms. Bennett?" a male asked.

Not recognizing the voice, I hesitated. "Yes."

"This is Sergeant Wills of the California State Police. I received a message you called. What can I help you with?"

I told him what I could but said I preferred to meet with him in person. He agreed, and we decided to meet in Mount Shasta on Monday morning.

I hung up and sat for a moment. Maybe this would be over. Maybe at last, I could breathe.

~ * ~

Sunday morning came, and I was still groggy from the night before. I knew I had to get things together for tomorrow morning when I meet with Sergeant Wills, but I had to leave in two hours for Mason's to watch the game. I ran several clippings and articles through the scanner and then copied a small portion of the evidence to show Willis. If he indicated it was enough, then I would bring the rest.

I drove up the Cowans' long driveway. It was so peaceful as it wound into the forest. As I pulled in to park, Lizzy came out of the house. She smiled and waved. I got out of my car and walked toward the porch as she stepped down to greet me.

"Evaline! So happy you are here. Come on. Everybody is in back."

I lifted my two bags and said, "I brought chips."

She took my hand, and we went around to the back of the house. The large muddy field had four very muddy brothers playing football. I smiled to myself. So, this was "the game." Heavy metal music blared from the speakers on the porch. Lucy was there, sitting by the fire pit. Around the pit were chairs and a small heap of wood pieces to burn. I crossed to Lucy and placed the bags on a portable table.

Lucy stood. "Hey, Evaline."

"Hey. It's nice over here by the fire."

She didn't even have to say anything as Mason quickly noticed me. I smiled at him, and as he waved back, distracted, Aaron came from the side and tackled him. They crashed to the ground as Jonas and Isaac came up from behind them.

Jonas extended his hand to Mason. "Hey, no distractions from the hot chick on the sidelines, big brother."

Mason took his hand and yanked himself up. His brothers chuckled. They came over to us, and Mason's green eyes found me as he took in a deep breath.

"Game time, eh?" I asked with a grin.

"Yeah, well, I was afraid if I told you this is what I meant, you wouldn't have come."

"Chips!" Jonas exclaimed as he opened one of the bags and started eating.

I glanced at Isaac and Aaron. "Hi, guys."

They said hello.

"We're going to play for a bit and then eat, okay?" Mason asked.

"That's fine. I'm good."

As they went back on the field, I turned to Lucy. "Why aren't you playing?"

"Well, we figured you would be more comfortable on the sidelines, so I thought Lizzie and I would keep you company. Lizzie doesn't like to play."

I shook my head. "Don't you think six players are better than four?"

"Evaline, they play rough."

I stood and took my jacket off. "Come on, Lucy. I don't break that easily."

She paused a moment and smiled as she removed her jacket. We waltzed out onto the field, and all four brothers turned, eyebrows raised.

Mason regarded me with both concern and surprise. "What are you doing?"

I took the football from him. "I want to play."

He seemed stunned for a moment, but recovered quickly, glancing at Isaac, then back to me. "We play pretty hard. Maybe you—"

I snorted. "I grew up with an older brother who was captain of his varsity football team. I used to play with the guys every Sunday."

Jonas piped up, "But you can get hurt."

"If you can catch me."

"Oh, a challenge!" he mused.

"This is not a good idea," Aaron uttered to Isaac.

They seemed to look at Isaac as if he called all shots. He gave me with a slight grin. Finally, he answered, "Mason, Lucy, Jonas, you start on offense."

I tossed the ball back to Mason.

As everyone else took their positions on the field, I could hear Jonas ask, "Is it a penalty if Mason kisses his opponent?"

I laughed.

"Hike!" Jonas yelled, backing up and hurling the ball to

Mason. I jumped but missed it. He caught it, fumbled so I grabbed it and darted for the goal line.

"Fumble! Mason, get her," Jonas shouted.

I reached the goal but as soon as I did, I ended up on my back—though gently, as though lifted and set down gently by a strong wind.

When I saw who tackled me, Mason grinned down from his position on top of me. "Nice run."

"Nice tackle," I shot back.

"Touchdown good!" Lizzy hollered with delight from the porch.

Mason got up and helped me as Isaac came over, took my hand, then led me to our side of the field.

"No fraternizing with our opponents," he said, amused.

"Yes, sir," I replied, giving him a little salute.

We huddled, and he said, "I'm handing the ball to you, Evaline, and you run with it as fast as you can. Aaron and I have your back."

I nodded, and we got to our positions.

"Hike!" bellowed Isaac then he handed the ball to me.

I bolted down field as fast I could. Isaac and Aaron took out Lucy and Jonas, but Mason was fast on my tail. Again, it was like a strong wind swept me up, and I ended up on top of Mason this time.

"First down. Good job, Evaline," Isaac said as he approached us.

"Hey, who tackled who?" mused Jonas.

"Two minutes left in first quarter!" Lizzy screamed.

Mason and I scrambled to our feet and assumed our positions.

"Hike!" Isaac handed the ball to Aaron. Blocked by Mason and Jonas, Aaron tossed the ball back to Isaac, who then slammed into Lucy. Without hesitation, she took him down hard. I couldn't believe it. He was huge, and she knocked him off his feet like nothing. They jumped to their feet and shook it off.

"Second quarter now," yelled Lizzy.

"First down," Isaac said. "Hike!"

I scrambled to get away from Mason who was as fast as lightning. Isaac threw the ball to me, but Mason jumped, caught it, and took off down field.

"Interception! Come on, Mason! Run your ass to the goal!" Jonas waved his arms.

I started after Mason, but Isaac and Aaron both tackled him just before he reached the goal. He was still on his back when I reached him. I held my hand out, and he pulled up.

"Are you okay?" he asked.

"Yes, except for the interception," I replied, grinning.

I couldn't help but think they were holding back, as if they were afraid of breaking me, but it was fun, and the rest of the game was much the same. Lizzy kept score and time, and Jonas and Aaron squabbled over calls. Isaac would break them up, and we'd do it again. The fourth quarter was coming to an end, and the game was in final play. My team was down by three points, so we needed a touchdown to win.

"I'll fake the throw to you, Aaron, and then take off and run it through myself," Isaac said in the huddle.

"Bro, it's really far. Maybe you should throw it to me midway," Aaron suggested.

I shook my head. "No, give it to me. They won't expect it. Aaron, since Isaac will be tackled as he throws, you're the only one who'll be able to keep them at bay so I can run it."

He tilted his head at Isaac, who agreed. Isaac glanced at Aaron and said, "Keep them away from her, and I'll get up as soon as I can. It won't take them long to figure it out."

Isaac feigned his throw to Aaron, then took off running. Mason and Jonas saw it and went for Isaac while Lucy darted after Aaron who was running downfield. I bolted toward the goal just as Mason and Jonas tackled Isaac, and he pitched the ball to me. I caught it with ease, but Lucy had switched directions and was coming after me. Mason was after us in a flash, and I expected to be hit from behind, but I wasn't. I heard Isaac and Aaron yelling, "Go! Go!" as I reached the end zone and threw my hands up in victory.

"Touchdown! Woot!" yelled Aaron as he and Isaac ran to me.

"Yes!" echoed Lizzy from the porch.

Isaac and Aaron smiled.

"Good job!" Isaac said.

I tried to see where Lucy had gone and realized Mason had flattened her. Isaac and Aaron followed me as I walked over to them. She was under Mason, and as he stood, I slapped his arm. "You could have hurt her."

He grinned as Lucy hopped up.

"I'm good, Evaline," she said, a bemused smile on her face.

There was a brief, awkward moment as I realized I was missing something, something it seemed only the Cowans alone knew.

She put her arm around me, and we started for the house. "Come on. Let's go get cleaned up. I'm hungry."

We stopped at the porch. I had mud everywhere. There was a

89

process to being cleaned up. Lizzy grabbed the hose and sprayed the heavier mud off us. Afterward, we headed inside to take quick showers so there would be enough hot water for everyone. I got out of the shower and glanced at Lucy who was standing by the door with clothes for me to wear while my own clothes were drying.

"I think we're around the same size. Size six, right?" she asked.

She placed them on the counter and closed the door as she exited the bathroom. I could hear the Cowans outside, and I peeked through the blinds and saw Jonas preparing food, and Isaac, Aaron, and Lizzy sitting around the fire. I gasped as Mason carried a small couch over his shoulder, like it was nothing, to the fire. I shook it off and got dressed. When I walked out of the house, he was sitting on the same couch. I joined him.

"Medium well, right?" Jonas asked, and I nodded. "Hope steak is all right."

"Yes, that's fine, thanks," I answered, reaching to get some chips, but one bag was already gone, and I glanced over at Jonas, who was happily chowing on the second. "Jeez, Jonas, hungry much?" I teased.

"Oh, sorry. Yes, I was. Did you want some?" he asked, offering me the bag.

"No, it's fine. You go ahead," I said, sliding back next to Mason, who wrapped his arm around me. His body was warm—almost hot—as I leaned into him.

"I hope you had a good time today," he said.

"I would have still come."

"What do you mean?"

"If you'd told me I would be watching you and not a game on TV. I would have still come."

He smiled but said nothing.

"So, Evaline, been meaning to ask you—and I hope it's not too forward—but your brother... Mason says he's missing?" Isaac asked.

I wasn't offended or angry, but I hadn't talked about Jimmy with anyone other than family and with Mason, so it took me a minute to gather my thoughts. "Yeah, he is. I don't talk much about him because if I do, then the reality hits me, and it means he really is gone."

"What was he like?" Lucy asked.

I smiled as I thought of my brother. "Jimmy was amazing. He was good at everything he did. Went to college, then law school—even had a job with a firm before he graduated. They really wanted him. Thing is, this firm is one of the biggest in Sacramento. Many of their clients were high profile, into some bad stuff. I think he saw something or found out something and became a threat. Anyway, things got a bit scary when I started digging into his disappearance, but I must find out what happened. I owe him that much."

"Yeah, I can understand that," Isaac said.

Aaron handed me a beer as Jonas put his own beer up to toast. "To Jimmy," he said.

"To Jimmy," I repeated as I took a drink, and everyone else echoed me.

Jonas pulled my steak off the grate and handed it to me. I took it as Lizzy handed me a fork and knife.

"See if that's good," he said.

I cut into it and it was perfect. "It's good, thanks."

He placed six medium-sized steaks on the grate. I started to cut and eat mine as he flipped the steaks over for only a moment and then placed each on a plate and passed them to everyone. I gaped. The steaks weren't even on the grate two minutes.

We were quiet as we ate. I glanced at Mason's steak and the juice seeping from each slice of his knife. He happily ate the red pieces. I glanced at the others and realized all of them, including Lizzy, had pools of red juice on their plates. I took another bite of mine and shot Mason a look. He stopped chewing for a moment.

"Are we freaking you out?" he asked.

Everyone stopped and looked from me to him.

I shook my head. "Not at all. Eat up."

He flashed Isaac a quick look, but I could tell he was still concerned as we went back to eating. I took another bite of my steak as the fire crackled.

Eight

Monday morning came, and I told Kristy—and only Kristy—where I was going. Mount Shasta was the next town over, and the drive gave me time to think. I didn't want to tell Mason. Knowing he wouldn't want me to go alone, I still was reluctant to get him involved, so I swore her to secrecy. Trusting Sergeant Wills didn't exactly feel just right either, but this whole thing needed to be over with, and at that moment, Sergeant Wills was the best possible solution.

Still, my gut told me to be cautious.

I slowed on Main Street and spotted the diner on the corner. Sergeant Wills thought it would be better to meet in a more relaxed atmosphere instead of at the local police station especially given my slight apprehension concerning the local police. I parked, walked into the café, my gaze settling on a man sitting in the corner drinking coffee. He wore a plain, blue denim button-down shirt and jeans, and a black jacket hung over the chair's back. A notebook and a cup of coffee rested on the table in front of him. He eyed me as I walked toward him.

"Ms. Bennett?" he asked in a low voice.

"Yes." After he gestured for me to sit, I asked the server for some water, then I promptly told the officer about Jimmy and his disappearance as well as what I knew about Campbell. He took everything down silently, but he wasn't asking me any questions up to that point.

"Okay, ma'am. Now, this Mr. Spanditto, you believe he is the one responsible for your brother's death?"

My stomach started to knot. Glancing across the café, I blinked, startled. Jimmy stood in the corner, looking at me and shaking his head. I glanced back at Wills and realized what he said. "Sergeant Wills, I don't believe I said my brother was dead."

He eyed me for a moment. "Well, he's been missing for quite a spell. Usually when people are gone this long, they're presumed dead."

I said nothing, but something just didn't feel right. My phone vibrated, and a text came in from Mason. My heart skipped a beat as I read the words: *Trap. Get out now. Back exit.*

I chuckled nervously, and Wills stopped writing.

"Something funny, Ms. Bennett?"

I shook my head. "Oh, it's nothing, just my crazy cousin. She can't cook to save her life. Sergeant Wills, there are a couple more things I need to tell you, but I'm afraid my morning coffee is catching up to me. Excuse me." The waitress was walking by, so I asked her, "Where is your restroom?" She told me, and I got up. "I'll be right back, and then I need to tell you the rest."

As fast as I could while appearing calm, I headed for the back. Right before the bathroom door was the door for the kitchen, and I slipped in quickly. A grill cook saw me and lifted his brows.

"I need a back way out of here."

He didn't say a word, just pointed. I swiftly exited only to find Mason, in his truck, waiting for me. With a screech, a white cargo van raced up the alley toward us.

"Evaline, get in!"

Bolting, I slid to a stop at the side then jumped into the truck. As soon as I did, Mason stepped on the gas, and we were off. The van followed us. "How did you know I was here?"

Mason glanced at me but said nothing. Kristy was the only person it could have been.

I suddenly remembered. "My car! We have to get my car!"

"Relax, Aaron has your car. He's headed back to Dunsmuir. Eva, what were you thinking?"

I stared at him in disbelief. "Are you kidding me? I had a plan, Mason Cowan, which didn't include you getting involved! My issue, remember?"

He smiled. "You are so cute when you're pissed off, you know that?"

Sitting back in defeat, I said, "So how did you know it was a trap?"

"We saw the van drop off the guy you were meeting. What cop arrives in a van driven by someone else? So Aaron left in your car, and I waited for you."

I sighed. "He hot-wired it, didn't he?"

Mason glanced at me. "Sorry. We'll fix it. I promise."

I heard a car revving. Behind us, the van was gaining on us. "Mason!"

"I know." He floored it. "Put your seat belt on."

I did as he asked and nervously watched the van get closer until it was right beside us. It bumped us, but luckily Mason's truck landed back on four tires, and the van skidded. He glanced at the van and veered the truck toward it, attempting to run it off the road. The van wavered and backed off. I thought it was going to ram us from behind, but instead it sped up on my side.

As it did, the rear door opened and revealed a guy with a gun. "Mason!"

He saw, and before the guy could fire, he hit the brakes, the shot missing us. "Get down!"

I did. Mason jerked the wheel to the right. The guys from the van shot again then smashed into us. The truck spun to the right. Swearing under his breath, Mason held on tight to the steering wheel as he fought to keep the truck under control. We bumped up onto the berm, which bordered the ditch on the side of the road. Not even a moment later, we hit a large dip where the berm was worn away by the edge of the ditch. I shrieked as the world flipped.

My eyelids fluttered open, something hard against my back. Where the hell was I? Hearing voices, and then what I thought were cries—the sound was so distant. I breathed hard; my heart thudded, and everything was foggy.

"Pretty stupid, sis. You have to watch who you trust. You'd be surprised how big this is." Jimmy's voice was loud and clear as if he were right beside me.

"Jimmy, I need to find you. You don't deserve what happened to you."

"Eva, you know where I am. For once, it's a place I don't want you with me. You are all that's left of our family, and they know it."

I winced. "Who? Who are you talking about? Campbell? Spanditto?"

"No, they were only the beginning. It's not at all what I thought."

I could clearly hear footsteps as he continued, "You need to stay close to him."

This time, I knew who he was talking about—Mason. "Is he what I think he is?"

Silence for a moment, then Jimmy gently answered, "What does your gut tell you?"

When the fog cleared, he was gone. I blinked as I realized I was leaning against Mason's truck, which had miraculously landed right side up. Sitting forward and peering at the truck, I noted it was dented pretty well and the roof was caved in a bit, but otherwise still seemed drivable. I turned away as Mason knelt in front of me. Worry lines edged his lips. My eyes focused on the blood from a bullet wound in his left arm. He seemed unfazed by it.

"Evaline, are you okay? Tell me you're okay." His fingertips gently stroked my cheek.

I nodded I was all right and touched his hand "Your arm, Mason. They shot you?"

He glanced at his arm but focused on me again. "It's fine. I'll heal." He helped me up, and I studied him for a moment.

His head tilted. "What's wrong?"

I glanced around and saw the van but none of the men who had been following us. "Where are they?"

"Ran off."

Why had he hesitated before he responded? I took a longer look at the smashed van lying upside down several feet away, half in the bushes. On the passenger side, there was a gaping hole where the door had been.

He helped me into the truck, then we headed back to Dunsmuir. I was silent as I tried to take everything in—Sergeant Wills, the van, the chase and accident, and Jimmy's warning. A text from Kristy pulled me out of my thoughts, and I had to read it twice to understand the words. "We need to go back."

Mason's brows lifted.

"Laine is at Mercy Medical. There was an accident or something. Kristy just texted me."

He spun the wheel. "We'll go back another way. Mercy Medical is on the other side of Mount Shasta."

I couldn't help but wonder if someone had deliberately tried to hurt Laine because of me. Quickly grabbing a towel from the floor, I shook it out then wrapped it around Mason's arm. Searching the floor, I found a box of tissues, taking one of the remaining two to put on the cut on my forehead. How I would ever forgive myself if something happened to Laine?

~ * ~

Kristy and Lizzy were sitting in the waiting room when we walked in. Kristy saw me and immediately got up, Lizzy right behind her. She stopped short and had a look of confusion across her face.

"Eva, what happened!?" Kristy asked.

"I'm fine. We had a little accident. Is Laine okay?"

She paused a moment before answering. "He was riding his bike, and someone ran him off the road or something. I guess someone was driving by and saw his bike." She hugged me as tears streamed down her face. "Eva, they said his leg is smashed; he could lose it."

What could I say? I knew it was because of me. As we embraced for a long moment, for the first time I pondered leaving

Dunsmuir again, but this time, it wouldn't be for a new job or to try something new. It would be to save what was left of my family.

Mason and Lizzy stayed with us, and eventually a doctor came into the waiting room.

"Miss Bennett?" He was looking between Kristy and me, and I quickly answered.

"Yes. Please tell us, how he is."

Sitting down gently on the chair, he spoke. "I am Dr. Rich. He's stable now, and we were able to save his leg. However, he will have to remain in intensive care for the time being. He has two cracked ribs, a bad sprain in his left wrist, and a serious concussion. I can't say enough how extremely lucky he was."

"When can we see him?" Kristy asked.

Dr. Rich glanced at the file he had in his hands. "Well, you can see him now, but we had to give him something for the pain, so he'll be out for a while."

"Thank you," I said, and he turned and left.

Mason and Lizzy stayed in the waiting room while Kristy and I went in. The sight of someone who is utterly carefree, confined to a bed with wires, needles, braces, and an IV can be disheartening to say the least. He was bruised and battered but alive. Kristy sat by his bedside and put her hand on his.

I couldn't stand it anymore. "Kristy, I'm so sorry. This is my fault."

"Evaline, you didn't do this. You—"

"No, I did. That cop I was meeting this morning in Mount Shasta? He was one of the bad people. If Mason hadn't been there... Well, I don't know."

Puzzled, she looked at me. "Eva, I didn't tell him. I—"

"Mason tends to know things particularly when there is danger. Anyway, they chased us, and we wrecked. I'm afraid because I didn't stay or give them the evidence, that they—"

Kristy shook her head. "Eva, no. This isn't on you, and Laine would tell you the same thing. But we need to find someone who isn't dirty, who isn't connected to them, and tell them everything. If it is Campbell and this Spanditto guy, they need to be stopped."

A little while later, Kristy and I went back into the waiting room to see Jonas had joined Mason and Lizzy. Kristy brought him up-to-date on Laine's condition, and I sat next to Mason, still thinking of leaving Dunsmuir. I knew he could sense I had mixed feelings—he always sensed my thoughts.

"Evaline, this wasn't your fault. You don't know if it's even related."

"You can't tell me it's a coincidence. Mason, they tried to kill us." He winced. Did he know something I didn't? "What does that mean?"

He hesitated before saying, "Not sure if killing us was the plan."

I blinked. "What? Why would you think that?"

"They weren't trying to hurt you; they were going to take you. Of course, I wasn't going to let that happen, and that's when they took a shot and I... ran them off."

My mouth gaped. "Jesus, Mason." I needed air so I got to my feet. "I'll be right back. I need to go to the restroom."

I hurried down the hall to the restroom. I stood there for a long moment, looking into the mirror. For a moment, I resolved to leave Dunsmuir and, in doing so, keep my family out of harm's way. But, in leaving, I would lose Mason. My heart skipped a beat at the thought. Was it something I would be strong enough to do? Did I want to do that? I splashed water on my face and checked the scrape above my temple. When I exited, two men were standing outside the door. They saw me, and one took a step toward me. I didn't move.

"Ms. Bennett. We missed you this afternoon due to unforeseen interference by a meddling boyfriend. They can be a real pain in the ass, ya know?"

I recognized the man who was speaking as my attacker from the Blue Dawn weeks ago, but I didn't know the other man who had a beard. He had a wild look in his eyes as if his brown eyes were glowing.

My attacker continued, "It would be in your best interest, and the interest of what's left of your family and friends, to come with us quietly. Now."

"I don't think so."

This made him smile as he glanced back at the bearded man, who was also smiling. My stomach tightened in anticipation. There was an IV stand to my right, next to a gurney sitting against the wall, and a door to the stairwell a few feet to my left, but I didn't take my gaze off him while taking inventory. I couldn't yell as I was too far from the waiting room for anyone to hear. My attacker took a step toward me, and I moved to my right and grabbed the IV stand. He was close enough I could smell his breath.

"Now what told me you would say that? Never go without a fight, right?" he said unruffled.

His brow twitched and his fingers flexed as if he was about to make a move, so I smiled and played it cool. I was never going to give them the satisfaction of knowing I was terrified. This could be it—it could all end with this confrontation. I only had a single thought, as my adrenaline surged through me.

I leaned toward him and whispered, "Never."

Abruptly, my knee came forward and hit him square in the crotch, and at the same time, I swung my arm around with the IV stand and smashed it into the bearded man, knocking him down. A second later, I darted for the stairs. My adrenaline ran high as I could hear them yelling above me in pursuit. I made it to the parking lot and hid behind the corner of the ambulance bay outside the emergency room. They burst out the door and looked around. I pulled out my cell and texted Mason.

When I scanned the area, the men were gone. I was cautious not to walk out in the open as I couldn't see where they were. I eyed the door, thinking I could slip back upstairs, but that idea was shattered when I saw my attacker not far from the door. The bearded man was nowhere to be seen.

The coolness of the damp night tickled my skin. The clouds broke up, revealing the stars and the pale moonlight. The parking lot was relatively quiet save for a few people going to and from their cars. It was then the hairs stood up on the back of my neck as I heard a low growl and then felt hot breath blowing on me. I slowly turned around and there, standing directly in front of me like a bad dream, was the biggest wolf I had ever seen. It clearly wasn't the wolf in my dreams nor was this any ordinary wolf.

I reached into my memories of popular culture and the documented cases of lycanthropy I'd read about in my psychology classes and tried to wrap my head around what it really was— impossible. Something society deemed a myth now stood in front of me.

I had seen one before, only a while ago at the warehouse, when the guard attacked me, but that time it was the gray wolf from my dreams, and it had been a glimpse before it disappeared. This wolf wasn't leaving—and it was massive. The wolf's colossal head was nearly my height and took my breath away. The moonlight shimmering through the clouds caused its eyes to glow, which made it look not only magical but very frightening.

I started to move back when its eyes locked on me as it slowly took another step driving me back toward my attacker. Inching bit by bit, I shifted, the giant becoming more agitated by the minute. It bared its teeth and increased its advance. I didn't have anywhere to go but out in the open.

My attacker turned, saw me then strode toward me. "You're gonna pay for that one. They said to bring you in, but they didn't say the shape you had to be in."

The wolf growled at my attacker, who surprisingly spoke as if it was his friend. "No! She has to pay for that!"

The wolf snapped at him. My attacker backed off. Was I seeing and hearing this right? The wolf responded to him. More than that, it seemed to be in charge. How could that be? The wolf cautiously stood at the edge of the bushes by the building, careful not to be seen. My attacker came toward me again but soon stopped as we heard the door open. A security guard exited.

He glanced around and moved toward me. "Ma'am, is everything all right?"

I shook my head and ran to him. "No, this man is bothering me."

The guard took out his nightstick and told me to move behind him.

My attacker stood there with contempt twisting his lips. "Hey cop wannabe, I suggest you turn around and go back inside like you didn't see anything. This has nothing to do with you."

The guard reached down, but before he could grab his walkie-talkie, the pepper-black wolf lunged out from the bushes and lashed at him with its claws. The guard shrieked and started beating it with a stick. I bolted then realized I was heading for the woods.

Then, with no warning, I was struck. The blunt force of the vehicle colliding with me sent me spiraling onto the grass. The wind was knocked out of me so I couldn't move. Gasping, I lay motionless for what seemed like an eternity, looking up at the moon which was now visible. Heavy steps thudded in the grass, and I turned my head and saw my attacker. Then…Mason's voice. I was in and out, but know I heard my name, and my attacker stopped and glanced at the woods and then back at Mason.

I tried to cling to Mason's voice. I opened my eyes again as I heard a low growl and saw the black wolf. When my lids slid closed, I was back in my apartment in Sacramento, slouched on the couch, talking to Jimmy. Our last conversation before he disappeared.

I hadn't thought about that moment in a while, but it seemed like yesterday. He had asked me a peculiar question about what I remembered about Grandma Murphy, our mom's mother.

My lids flickered open and closed, and right before I answered, I saw Mason standing in front of me. I could hear growling and a strange ripping sound, mixed with the sound of clapping hands.

The last thing I remember seeing was there, standing between me and the black wolf, was my light gray wolf. The wolf in my dreams, the same wolf which had saved me at the warehouse—the wolf I *longed* to see.

My wolf lunged at the black wolf, and then it all went black.

~ * ~

Someone was rubbing my forehead with a wet towel. There was the low rumble of a television in another room but nothing else. My eyelids fluttered open to a white ceiling with large wooden beams. I could smell the familiar scent of pine. Lucy sat next to me on the bed and continued to wipe my forehead with the cool towel. I sat up as she smiled at me.

"You're awake. We were beginning to worry, thought maybe you were hit too hard."

I blinked at her with confusion. The events in the parking lot were sketchy at best but there were a few things I did remember. "How long was I out?"

She peered at the cut on my forehead. "A couple hours."

"Is Mason all right?"

She looked down and squeezed the water from the towel. "He's fine and is very worried about you. He keeps coming in and out every five minutes to see if you are awake."

I sighed and then remembered more. "Oh! Laine! He—"

Lucy gently touched my shoulder. "He's okay and is doing much better. The doctor told Kristy Laine would be out of the hospital in a week or two at most. Lizzy and Jonas are with her now at the hospital."

"Kristy doesn't know anything about what happened, right?"

Lucy shook her head.

I put my hand to my forehead, thinking of my words carefully. "Um, the wolf that attacked me..." Had no idea how to finish the question because I didn't know what she knew but that was quickly answered.

"Wolf?" She had half-amused expression. "Evaline, you were hit by a car in the parking lot. Hit you pretty good too." She patted the wet cloth above my eye.

A car? I knew it wasn't a dream though. I shook my head. "It wasn't a car, Lucy. I know what I saw, and I've seen it before." Silence. "What about the guy who attacked me? And I thought I heard Mason."

"Yes, Mason got to you just in time. Was that the same guy

from the restaurant a couple weeks ago?"

I nodded.

"Mason went after him, but he got away." She eyed me with curiosity. "Do you know what the guy wanted from you?"

I paused a moment trying to think of the best answer. "I think so, but I don't want anyone else involved."

Her expression went from curious to calm. "So fearless, Evaline. Sometimes we need help to solve our problems, and sometimes it comes from an unlikely source."

"Lucy, please."

She stopped and tilted her head. "You aren't the least bit freaked about a guy trying to kill you?"

"Actually Lucy, I'm terrified. I didn't want Mason or you or Kristy or anyone involved in this. Obviously, there's more to it than me having collected evidence about someone. And now, I not only have psychotic mercenary killers after me but a werewolf—a full-fledged, big fucking werewolf!"

I stopped, recognizing what I said sounded positively ridiculous, and took in a breath. Lucy sat there, listening but never flinching. She appeared amused by my mini-meltdown. This was of course aside from the bursts of laughter I heard from the other room, presumably from Mason and his brothers. "Sorry."

She couldn't help but laugh herself as I shook my head. She put her hand on me gently and gave me a reassuring look. "It's okay. Just relax. You've been through a lot."

I soon realized where I was. The room was rustic with framed scenes of European hunting parties and the Scottish Highlands. An old cedar chest sat at the foot of the bed. A rendering of a woman hung on the wall and above the door was an old king sword. "This is Mason's room."

Lucy smiled as she got up and headed for the door. "Take your time. You should get more rest, but I made some coffee if you are up to it."

"I need to talk to Mason," I blurted out.

"I know. Isaac and Aaron are waiting to head to the hospital. It'll give you and Mason some alone time."

"Thanks, Lucy."

She smiled and left. My body ached as if I had gone ten rounds with someone twice my size. I was a bit woozy as I stood then slowly managed myself to the window. I heard the door close.

After I walked to the door, I turned the knob then peered outside. The TV was off, and I didn't see anyone. Once outside the bedroom, the house opened to a central grand room. It seemed looking from the rooms that lined the upstairs isle way, they all faced to that one big room, which appeared to be the main living room.

The walls were adorned with a few big game animals and old portraits. Above the massive stone fireplace was a large, mounted twelve-point buck head. Its lifeless eyes stared forward, serving as a memento for the hunter who brought him down. To the right of the mount was a portrait of three women, five men, and a child. They were dressed in European tradition but from an era long gone.

The men wore Scottish kilts and a simple variation of the traditional hat. They had on fur stockings, which were wrapped up to their knees. A fur pouch adorned the front of their sashes and a sword embellished their sides. The women were draped in long dresses, and two of the three had shawls around their shoulders. The third woman had her long hair loose, and the child was dressed like the men but with no sword or hat.

The portrait was beautifully painted. Below the painting was one word: MacCòmhain. I was so occupied with the portrait, while I didn't see Mason standing directly behind me, I sensed his familiar presence and turned to face him.

He quirked up his lips. "I'm glad you are all right. You had me worried."

I smiled and shook my head gently. "I'm fine. Thank you for getting there when you did. You always seem to be there when I need you."

"I always will be."

My gaze went back to the portrait. "Who are they?"

He came up next to me while looking at the portrait as if it was a distant memory. "Ancestors of ours from a long time ago."

Fascinated, I pointed to the word on the bottom.

"That is ancient Gaelic for MacCowan. Obviously, we use just Cowan now."

"I think I like MacCowan better."

He grinned, but I could see he was holding something back.

I moved to the front of the room, looking up at the massive deer above the fireplace. "Yours?"

He shook his head as he followed me. "My father's last big kill before he died. It kinda has sentimental value, if you know what I mean."

I did understand what he meant. Much too well with the passing of my own father so unexpectedly. Mason's sad expression told me he was lost in a memory. I found myself looking past him, to the front door and the sword hanging above it on a wooden plaque with the MacCowan family crest below it. The same as the tattoos on all the brothers' arms.

I had noticed Lizzy had a necklace with the crest on it. "Is that what he killed it with?" I asked, gesturing to the sword.

Mason laughed. "Ah no, that was my great-great-great-grandfather's."

To have such a family history! I clasped my pendant.

He looked away again. I wanted him right then, but I could see he was breathing heavy. "Tell me what's wrong."

His shoulders twitched. "I'm having a tough time resisting right now."

"Resisting what?"

He faced me. "You."

"So why are you resisting?"

"It's probably not a great idea with you being... hit by, um, the car."

"You won't break me, Mason."

He rubbed the back of his neck. "Not a good idea right now, Evaline. You took a hard hit to the head."

Okay, now I was frustrated. But I had been with him enough to know when he was firm on a decision though, so I backed off. At this point I hadn't even asked what happened in the parking lot. I had my suspicions about how he'd gotten there so fast and was right there when I needed him, but it was such an implausible theory I kept it to myself. "So what color was it?"

His brow lifted. "What?"

Before I answered, I considered him intently. "The car that hit me."

It was clear he was avoiding something. I knew what I had seen, but my sense of reality was still shouting werewolves didn't exist.

He sighed and finally answered, "Uh, blue I think."

My lips twisted. "I know it wasn't a car, Mason, but that's fine. I just don't understand why you can't tell me this secret."

Agitated, he moved away. "What secret, Evaline? You're the one with the secrets, and now they've caught up to you."

"They are my secrets to keep. Can you please take me back to the hospital?"

He reluctantly agreed and went in to grab his keys.

~ * ~

The following days were a blur of going back and forth to the hospital, trying to maintain the household, keeping Kristy calm, a string of headaches from the stress and injuries, and of course, my constant Cowan escorts. Usually it was Mason by my side, but at other times, I sensed one of them around me, keeping me safe. He was my sanity, my reason to keep it together. Our meals at the Blue Dawn were welcoming, but the moments I yearned for were the ones out at Alban Loch with Mason. It was the one place I was free of everything.

As Laine got better every day, Jonas was a regular visitor. Jonas and Laine had been best friends for nearly five years. They discussed building a new bike trail on the rear of the Cowan property so they wouldn't get into trouble. I thought Laine was going to keel over right there when the doctor made it clear there was to be absolutely no bike riding or mudding on backwoods trails until the cast came off, which wasn't for several weeks. The look on his face was priceless.

There was; however, no news from my pursuers. Not even a phone call. Two weeks later, Laine finally came home, in a cast and on crutches. For a short time, life was normal.

Kristy went back to work, and I was a frequent visitor at the Blue Dawn several times a week. Friday nights were the best. The Dawn was usually hopping, the brothers sitting at their usual booth, watching the scene. Isaac, continually in control, would sometimes slip out the back door—with a different beauty each time. I never recognized the girls, and they would come back an hour later and sit back down. By the time he returned, he was different. More lighthearted.

AJ and Jonas had their trysts, but none of the brothers had a steady girl—no wives, no fiancées, no girlfriends, no female companions other than for a night. Neither Lizzy nor Lucy had any boyfriends I knew about either. It was a peculiar thing considering how such an amazingly attractive family had no spouses or any significant others—other than each other.

One night, Lucy was bartending, Jonas and AJ were in the kitchen, and Kristy and Lizzy were waiting tables. Mason, Isaac, and I sat quietly in the booth. Mason got up to grab another keg from the back for the front bar. Isaac was across from me, gripping his beer. He was not shy about saying what was on his mind. Then again neither was I. Perhaps that was why he and I got along so well. Despite my presence being more familiar now as opposed to when I first met the Cowans, Isaac still was a bit guarded. My head pounded in pain as another tension headache was imminent, so I put my fingers to my temple to rub it.

Isaac watched me curiously. "Headache again?"

I winced as I tried to ignore the throbbing pain searing in my head right now. "It's nothing. They go away after a short while."

"So, Mason says you are pretty good with numbers?"

"Finance degree. I'm okay at it. Numbers come easy for me."

"You know how to do accounting?"

"Well, yes, but I don't have a CPA license."

"But you know the basics?"

"Sure, why do you ask?"

He paused a moment and then answered, "Future reference."

I sighed as his next question caught me off guard.

"Is there any word yet on your brother?"

I hadn't thought much about what to do with the evidence, and I hadn't dreamed in over a week. I shook my head. "Other than it's no longer an active case because of the lack of evidence, nothing."

"Wouldn't that be a reason to take what you have to the authorities?"

"Yeah, well, I tried that. Didn't turn out too well."

He leaned toward me. "Laine wasn't your fault. You know that, right?"

"Wouldn't have happened if I had just gone with the cop."

"But then you would be with Jimmy, and I would have to watch my brother go through it all over again. A fucking lump of misery was what he was when Beth died."

His bluntness made me blink. "He doesn't talk about her much, even when I ask him."

He put his beer down. "She was headstrong like you. This is the part he loved about her. But she thought of everyone except herself," —he looked me directly in the eye— "and she just wouldn't listen when we told her to stay away from the danger."

I knew he was trying to get me to back off. "Isaac, I get it. I really do. However, when someone hurts my family or those I care about, they're going down. I didn't want Mason involved."

Isaac snorted. "Now, you know the chances of Mason standing down while you put yourself in danger are next to nil. Don't be naïve, Evaline."

"I love him, Isaac," I said with no hesitation, "and the thought of someone hurting him because of me…" I didn't have to finish my sentence.

"I don't doubt you do," he said without reluctance.

Mason came back with a fresh beer and flashed me a smile as I took a drink of my own, glancing at Isaac who shook his head.

Later that night, while I tried to sleep, his words echoed in my head. It was a sleepless night, and I tossed and turned. I sat up and glanced at the clock which read 3:03 a.m. Really? Sighing, I rose and went to the bathroom. I opened the medicine cabinet and tried to find something to help me sleep and saw some Tylenol PM. Grabbing the bottle, I closed the door on the cabinet, and my stomach fell. In the mirror, standing behind me, was Jimmy. I whipped around, dropping the pill bottle, but he wasn't there. Panting, I stood there for a long time, still sensing him. In that instance the pill bottle rose from the floor and gently hovered in front of me.

I snatched it. "Jimmy? Are you here?" No answer. "Jimmy, if it's you, please say something."

Again nothing. I waited for a moment before making my way back to my bed. I knew Jimmy was near. I'd had the same sensation when we'd played hide and seek as children—I could always find him. I wanted to see him again—terribly. I lay back in bed, looking at the ceiling. As the presence lingered, I closed my eyes and took in a deep breath. Slowly, I said his name again. It was only a moment later a cool breeze blew gently against my skin.

"Hey, sis," he whispered.

I found comfort in his voice but at the same time, it was wrong. Grams had always said if someone was lost, we had to help them find the way again—even if it was Heaven they were lost from. Dreams were one thing, but I now knew he either couldn't or hadn't moved on for a reason. "Jimmy, how did you do that?"

He chuckled. "Sorry, Eva. I'm getting the hang of this. I think the longer you're dead, the better you get."

I shook my head. "You were able to move something, and I could see you briefly. What else can you do? Can you take over someone else's body?"

"Like possession? I don't know. It's complicated. I'm still pretty new at it, but I can't manage to do it for more than a minute."

"You should be at peace. I'll be fine. You need to move on."

He paused for a moment then said, "At peace? Oh Eva, how can I when there is so much danger surrounding you? You sound like Mom."

I stopped breathing for a moment. "You saw Mom?"

"Yeah. Oh, she's so beautiful. Dad's with her. They keep trying to call me to them, but I don't wanna go yet."

My heart ached again with the pain and sadness of losing them. I missed both my parents deeply, and I was envious Jimmy had seen them even if he had to die to do it. It was difficult to hold back the tears. "You should go to them, Jimmy. They—"

"No. I'm not leaving you, Evaline. Not yet. There's danger

ahead… danger." His voice faded.

"Jimmy, what's wrong? I can barely hear you." I didn't want him to go. I wanted to talk to him all night. What danger did he mean? Campbell?

Jimmy's voice came in and out. "Evaline, please. You need to…" Then he was gone.

I called him, but he didn't answer. When Jimmy went, the air in the room warmed. He said I was in danger. I knew this, but did he know if Campbell was planning something?

My thoughts were heavy with both sorrow and anxiety. The question had changed from what to do, to when to do it. I needed to find someone I could trust to give the evidence to; someone who could help.

Nine

I peered out my bedroom window. The breeze was cooler than it had been, ushering in October. Colorful medleys of leaves blew across the yard and fell from their branches. A cloudy morning, and I could smell the pending rain in the air. I closed the window and slipped down the stairs and into the kitchen. Surprisingly, Laine was seated at the table, his leg elevated on a kitchen chair. Kristy sat across from him rummaging through a college catalog.

"Did you decide?" I asked.

She put the book aside. "Yeah, I think I'm going to take it slow, but maybe I'll take a class or two in the spring. Still working it out." She tugged on her ear. "Um, Evaline. Was Mason over last night?"

I shook my head. "No. He had to make a run to Redding last night. Why?"

She glanced at Laine. "Well, I thought I heard you talking to someone."

A sigh passed through me as I knew they needed to know. I couldn't keep them safe if they didn't know what and why things were happening. "You heard right." After sucking in a breath, I let it out then said, "I was talking to Jimmy." Their mouths gaped. "It's happened twice since I have been able to hear him and talk to him, but I can't see him, or at least not for more than a glimpse."

Kristy sat up. "A glimpse? Are you kidding me?"

"Did he say what happened to him or where he is?" Laine asked.

"No. He was trying to tell me something, but he kept fading in and out. All I could get is there's danger ahead." Lifting a hand, I stopped Kristy as she was about to say something. "Let me get this out. You both deserve to know what's happening. Do you remember that I told you when I knew something for sure, I would tell you?" Nods. "Well here it is."

I told them Jimmy had a mysterious client at the law firm and how he had two datebooks, and I'd investigated his disappearance after the police stopped pursuing it. I told them what I found out about Campbell and my suspicions of his involvement, and I told them about Harvey Collins and my visit to his wife.

Both Laine and Kristy listened intently, and I could read their concern in their faces—they were scared.

"I called the police, and I went to Mount Shasta to meet the officer. Somehow, they knew or found out, and he wasn't who he said he was." I frowned. "Mason found out and texted me to get out of there. We were on our way back when they caught up to us and ran his truck off the road. That's why when I got to the hospital, I was banged up."

Neither said a thing, so I continued, "Kristy and I were at that warehouse, and Jonas was right. There is something in the pit. I think," —I had to pause a moment— "I think it's something dead, and I think it's human."

Laine's expression displayed both shock and disbelief. "You mean Jimmy might be in the pit?" He eyed me with curiosity as both he and Kristy sat back in their chairs. Worry darkened Kristy's features.

I shrugged. "I don't know for sure."

She finally spoke. "But, Eva, what are the chances that pit is owned by this Spanditto? And the timing—"

"The pit is owned by the very same corporation, and it was purchased in January. Jimmy disappeared in March. I'm sorry I kept it from you, but I figured if you didn't know, you would be safer. I shouldn't have come back, but I wanted to see you guys again, and I thought maybe the harassing would stop, but it didn't. They found me, and now you're both in danger."

Laine immediately sat forward. "Fuck those people, Evaline. We're family, and we can handle this as one. This," —he indicated his leg— "is not your fault, and I would never blame you. We owe it to Jimmy to put him to rest."

Kristy touched my hand. "You can't do this alone. We're here."

I loved them so much for their support but still felt I'd condemned them to the same fate as Jimmy. Suddenly, a wave of nausea hit me, and my head pounded. I ran upstairs to the bathroom.

A few minutes later, I rinsed my mouth out with water. Hunched over the sink, I wondered why I was feeling so awful. There was a knock at the bathroom door. "Yeah?"

The door opened, and Kristy peeked her head in. "Are you okay? Is it another headache?"

I nodded as I splashed more water on my face. "It's gone. I

threw up too. I must be fighting something off."

Kristy touched my forehead. "You're warm. Maybe you should go to the doctor."

I shook my head. "No, it's fine. They never last long. It's just stress." I sucked in air as the headache passed and could smell a faint, sweet smell. "Did you have something sweet?"

She eyed me with surprise. "Um, I had Kahlua last night."

I could smell it as if it were in a glass in front of my nose. "What time do you work tonight?"

"Nine till two. The band will be there. You're coming, right?"

"Yeah, I told Mason I would. I think I'm going to lie down a bit. I feel terrible."

"Okay, well, let me know if you need help. Jonas is coming over to hang out with Laine, and I might take a ride to that college and check it out."

"Kristy, don't go yet; just wait until I can get this evidence to the police. Never go anywhere alone, okay?"

Her lips pursed. "All right. I can do that."

After she closed the door, and I finished cleaning up, I decided I would talk to Mason that night and ask him to drive me to the state police. I figured I was safest with him.

~ * ~

The Blue Dawn was booming by ten o'clock. At the heckling of Jonas, I decided to bring Laine, to get him out of the house. We walked in, and there at the end of the bar were the brothers including Mason. He turned and smiled at me as I went to him.

Jonas lit up and put a beer mug to the air as Laine hobbled on crutches over to the bar. "Whew! What up, bro? This here is what you need."

I couldn't help but laugh. Isaac stood behind the bar and pulled out some shot glasses and a bottle of whiskey. Lucy tended bar on the other side, and she made her way to us. Aaron sat next to Mason, and Jonas stood on the other side. Kristy was as was Lizzy. They came over when we walked in.

Mason turned to me. "You all right?"

"I'm good."

But he continued to look at me curiously.

"What?"

"I don't know," he said. "Something's different."

I thought a moment. "Well, we had a family talk about the whole mess with Campbell and Jimmy."

"And?" he asked intently.

"And I need you to drive me to the state police. Think you can do that?"

A smiled crossed his lips. "I can do that. So now you are okay with help?"

I shrugged, as he leaned to kiss me.

Aaron cleared his throat. "Ahem. Not to interrupt a moment, but can we toast now?"

The group burst into laughter. Jonas waved for Kristy to join us, and we lifted our shot glasses.

Isaac went first. "To healing."

Everyone agreed, and we drank. Lucy, Lizzy, and Kristy went back to working as Isaac cleaned up behind the bar. Aaron sat next to Mason, drinking a beer and talking to Jonas and Laine. The room was filled with the smell of beer, sweat, smoke, and Coca-Cola. The aromas were overbearing at times. Pamela, one of the waitresses, walked behind Isaac, and Jonas watched with a big grin.

"She wants you so bad." Jonas winked at his brother.

Isaac said nothing but smirked.

She came back a moment later. "Hey, Evaline."

"Hi, Pam. Looks like a good night."

She agreed and went to her table with a tray of drinks.

Kristy came over. "It's my break, going out for a quick smoke."

I jumped up. "I'll come with you. I need some air anyway." I turned to Mason. "Be right back."

He nodded, and Kristy smiled as I followed her out the rear door. There was a security light extending from the roof, which lit a small area with a picnic table and a trash can. We sat on the table with our feet on the bench and gazing out into the dark woods. Moonlight filled some dark gaps with light, and other than the music from inside, there was silence. Kristy lit up her cigarette

"I thought you quit?"

"Recent reoccurrence. I guess with Mom, and now this shit with Campbell."

I knew the pain well.

She bent her head to me. "Eva, can I ask you something?"

"Yes."

"The Jimmy situation aside, are you happy here?"

That was something I hadn't thought much about. *Happiness* was a word which seemed so distant with everything that had been happening lately. However, I could honestly say I was happy with some aspects but not all. The sensation of being incomplete, because I couldn't find Jimmy, but the strong sense of danger I knew I was in left me with an uncertainty, and the pressure to protect what little family I had left at all costs weighed on me.

Then there was Mason—my sense of safety and, strangely enough, power. My strange attraction to him complicated everything. It wasn't something I intended, but I firmly believed everything happened for a reason. The reason was the riddle.

Finally, I answered the best way I could. "I am happy here with you and Laine, but I'm not content. I don't think I can be until I know what happened to Jimmy."

She sighed. "I just—I just don't want you to leave."

I shook my head. "I'm not leaving unless the danger gets too close to you and Laine."

Her expression looked troubled as I continued, "Kristy, you two are all I have left. I will not let them take you away too, and if I have to leave to keep you safe, then I go."

She was about to say something in protest, but there was strange thud. We both looked toward the old fence that separated the break area from the parking lot. She got up and peered out into the dark. An arm reached from around the fence and grabbed her—it happened so fast, neither of us had time to think.

I shot up but froze as a man appeared holding Kristy tight by her throat. Her terrified eyes locked with mine. He said nothing as he stared at me. I recognized him. The man who had attacked me. He had a crazed look, something wild, and his dark eyes glowed. His face seemed distorted, but I concentrated on Kristy. When he finally spoke, I noticed his elongated canine teeth. He resembled something from a Lon Chaney flick.

"This wouldn't have had to happen if you would have just backed off to begin with. If you do not give us this supposed evidence you have, you will see how very serious we are. Watch and learn."

My heart sank. Before he could move though, another man clutched me from behind. I kicked and yelled. "You kill her, you'll never find what I have, and you'll all go down!"

The man stopped moving. He'd pricked Kristy's throat with his knife, but now he kept still. His head tilted.

The man who was holding me in an iron grip spoke up. "Tell Campbell we have her and take that one out back and finish it."

I screamed as he covered my mouth with his hand, my gaze never leaving Kristy as the man dragged her out of sight. I fought with everything I had as he yanked me toward the parking lot. Without warning, he froze then lifted his head, sniffing the air. There, standing in front of us, was Mason, Isaac, Jonas, and Aaron. All four had the same rage-filled look, and Mason's gaze never left me and the guy holding me.

"How nice, the MacCowans came out to play."

The brothers didn't even flinch. It was the first time I had heard Mason's family called by their ancestral name by someone other than themselves. Everyone knew them as the Cowans. How did these men know them? Worse yet, did the brothers know who these men were?

Isaac had a hold on Mason, who was ready to pounce on my attacker. Isaac spoke with firmness, but he was cool and collected as he said, "Little too far west, boys, don't you think?"

In the next moment all my suspicions, all those telltale dreams, everything Jimmy and Grandma had been trying to tell me about what Mason really was—all of it was confirmed. It wasn't just him—it was all four of the brothers.

I stared at Mason, who was fixated on my attacker—who appeared to be changing as well. Their eyes glowed bright, and their bodies heaved unnaturally. The thing was, it didn't matter what any of them were. Certainly didn't matter what Mason was either.

Right then, all that mattered was getting to Kristy. I gritted my teeth then slammed my head back. The crack of breaking bone sounded like a gun shot. He screeched in pain, and his grip loosened. With a wrench of my body, I broke free of his grasp.

Mason and his brothers lunged at him even as I scrambled away.

Yelling for Kristy, I bolted toward the woods. At the edge, I slowed as I caught sight of her lying on the ground. Behind her was the same pepper-black wolf from the hospital parking lot.

"Don't move," Lucy's voice cut through my thoughts. She came literally out of nowhere, and now she had her hand on my arm, holding me back.

I did what she told me to and froze, and the big wolf stopped as four equally large wolves advanced on it. One of the four turned to me, gazing at me for a long moment—my gray wolf. That's when the reality of who the wolf was finally washed over me. Every breath told me it was impossible, but my heart knew the truth. The black wolf snorted, bared his teeth, and fled as the others took off after him in pursuit. In a blink, my wolf was gone.

I watched them disappear into the forest anxiously, but shook it off and ran to Kristy, who was motionless in a pool of blood. *No! No! No!* I kept screaming in my head as I knelt beside her and pulled her to me. She gasped and made gurgling sounds.

Lucy and I put our hands to her throat to try to slow the bleeding. "Kristy, you stay with me, please don't leave... Don't you leave me too."

Lucy was trying to soothe Kristy the best she could.

"Lucy, we need to get her into the car.

She shook her head. "No, the ambulance is here."

I observed in disbelief at the ambulance almost upon us. How did it get here so fast?

~ * ~

An hour later, I stood alone in the hospital waiting room, looking out the window at the moonlight blanketing the forest. Without turning around, I sensed Mason's presence as he came into the room and walked right for me.

I spun directly into his arms, and he held me for a long moment. "Are you all right? I don't know what I would have done if..."

"I'm fine. Really. Thank you for showing up when you did."

He watched me for a long moment. It was now or never. The funny thing was, I wasn't scared. Not in the least. My unwavering love for him remained intact, regardless. Mason's expression was both one of worry and anticipation. He released me and stepped back to gaze out the window.

"I have this one recurring dream," I murmured. "In this dream, I'm running from something. It's a monster of some sort that clearly wants to hurt me. Each time I'm running away from it, I find my way to the edge of the forest, but whatever it is, it always stops chasing me when I reach the edge. It's afraid of what I meet up with there."

Mason was guarded as he whispered, "What do you meet with there?"

I took a moment to study his concerned expression before answering, "A wolf. It's frequently the same big, beautiful, light gray wolf with piercing green eyes. And when I turn to face the monster, it's not a monster but a human. The wolf always lunges at the figure... and then I wake up."

Mason was motionless in front of me, his gaze intent on mine.

"The wolf always makes me feel safe—the very same feeling of security I have with you. Why is that, Mason?" I wanted him to say it.

He shook his head but still said nothing.

"Mason, I deserve the truth. Tell me. Tell me now."

His chin lifted. "What do you want me to say, Evaline?"

I wasn't backing down. "It wasn't the presence of the wolf that gave you away. It was the eyes—those same green absolutely wild eyes, and the same eyes I am positively in love with."

Those eyes widened for a moment before he stepped back and stared out toward the forest again.

"It doesn't matter what you are. I still feel the same about you."

He sighed. "Evaline, you just don't get it."

I leaned toward him. "What's not to get?"

He frowned. "I *am* the monster, the monster from all the fairy tales and the one that hides in closets and underneath children's beds."

"No, you're not. Mason, I wasn't running from you. Don't *you* get it?" I clasped her shoulders, giving him a slight shake. "The monster in my dream is human. I think I was meant to come back here. I think I was meant to meet you, and I think… we are supposed to be together."

His tight expression eased, a calmness spreading through him as he realized I wasn't scared of him.

"So, I saw it's you and your brothers. What about Lizzy and Lucy? Are they as well?"

He nodded.

"Are you immortal?"

He glanced at me and then back toward the mountains. "Not exactly." He took a couple steps closer to the windows. "We age but not like humans. It's about one year for every century in human years. It's hard to tell."

"When were you born?" I asked, unable to rein in my curiosity.

He rubbed the back of his neck. "I was born in 1762 in Lancaster, Pennsylvania. I was twenty-one when I was turned. We left the east in 1901 with the push west, and we've been bouncing around from area to area every so many years. We live on the outer fringes of society, so we can lie low without people suspecting anything."

I was surprised. "So, you weren't born one?"

Mason shook his head. "It's complicated."

"Then you don't hunt humans?"

He looked me directly in the eye. "I didn't say that."

I can't say chills didn't go down my spine when he said that. My mind searched his every word to find some knowledge about what he was saying.

"We are all we have, Evaline. We are the closest a family can be, and if anyone was to jeopardize that unity or is a threat, it's usually not a question. We protect the pack at all costs."

I had to think how to word the next question since the subject of Beth was a fragile one. "When Isaac and I spoke about Beth the other day, he mentioned a danger, and she wouldn't listen when you told her to stay away. Was the danger you?"

"No. Beth was supposed to be my human future, my normalcy in those days. When the attack happened, she was caught in the middle of a nasty dogfight, and they killed her to prove a point. When they did, my decision to not look back at what happened and continue going forward was made easy."

I could see it was a painful memory, and a strange sensation of distant sorrow overcame me for a moment.

Mason took a step toward me, and when he spoke, it was very firm. "The fact you know puts you in extreme danger, Evaline. No one outside the family, except one, knows. And he's on a level beyond most. The point is we don't know what to do here."

I could see the major concern on his face as he continued, "My love for you complicates it—or at least, that's what the dilemma is."

"So, you are deciding whether to turn me or kill me?"

"It's more problematic than that." His eyes were sad as he placed his palm gently on my cheek. "I could never damn you to this, Evaline, and even if I wanted to, the chances of you surviving are next to nil."

I touched his hand and pulled it to me. "The only way you could damn me is by us being apart. Is it your brothers?"

He squeezed my hand. "Not really. It's me. I want you so bad, it hurts. I'm afraid I'll do something wrong, and you won't survive."

I was a bit puzzled at that. "Mason, I don't understand. Are you afraid you'll hurt me?"

"No, I want you—*all* the time. The thing is, we have strong sex drives, more intense than humans do. Sometimes it makes it difficult to control."

"Well, we'll have to be careful. Out of curiosity, what would happen if you tried to turn me?"

Fire lit his eyes. "Lucy and Lizzy are two out of only five females we have seen since the late eighteenth century. I guess the female body can't take it. Isaac knows more about it than me, but I don't want to find out."

"You would think because we have babies and our bodies change, there would be more she-wolves."

"I know. It would make more sense, but this change may be too drastic. I don't know," Mason answered.

"Are they going to hurt me?"

"No. You are not in danger from us."

Pondering his words, I gazed up at the half-moon. I sensed

something else. "Mason, I have to see this out. I'm seeing Jimmy in my dreams; he's not at rest. I know he is dead, but I deserve to know why and by whose hand or order, and that warehouse outside town is involved somehow. That night you saved me from the guard, Kristy and I *were* there checking it out. I was in the pit, and I think—I think I saw something. And I think Jonas sensed something that day when he and Laine were there."

Mason was silent, likely thinking about what I said.

"Is it possible you can smell something when a human can't?"

"Like what?"

"Like death?"

He took a moment to answer. "Well, we have heightened senses and yes, we can smell things a human can't."

I pursed my lips together and considered his expression. I think he knew what I would ask. I needed to know. I needed to know *for sure*. "Did Jonas smell something in the pit?"

Mason shook his head; lines rimmed the edges of his lips. "Evaline, you may not like what you find in the pit. These people are bad news."

I placed my hand on his cheek this time. "This is why I wanted you out of it. Now they know about you. One by one, my family and friends are being taken away, and I don't think I could take it if something happened to you. Hard to kill or not, you are out."

He frowned. "Nice try, Evaline, but not this time. Others of my kind are involved, and that fact keeps me in the game and close to you."

I sighed. Not going to win this one. We walked to the other waiting room, near the ICU. Lucy, Lizzy, and Laine, his leg elevated, sat quietly in the chairs against the wall, and Mason next to me as I finished giving my statement to the deputy. Figures Campbell wouldn't be taking my statement himself. I just couldn't sit still. I was so very anxious.

The deputy made a couple notes. "Okay so, Ms. Bennett, just to verify, you're not sure what it was. Do you think maybe it could've been a bear?"

I shrugged. Of course, I couldn't tell him what it really was. A bear attack was more believable than a giant wolf. "I'm not sure, it was dark. Maybe."

"Okay, if we have any other questions, we'll be in touch."

I was still covered with Kristy's blood, and the smell was suffocating. I kept playing the attack in my mind—the man calling Mason's family MacCowan, the teeth and growling, finding Kristy in a pool of blood, then my subsequent conversation with Mason. All of it was overwhelming.

My gaze turned toward the door as Isaac, Jonas, and AJ entered the waiting room. They acknowledged everyone, and then they glanced from me to Mason. If I sensed the tension, I'm sure Mason did too. I could tell they wanted to talk so I stood and stepped toward Lizzy and Laine

"Lizzy, why don't you and Laine go get something to eat?" I suggested. "They said it was going to be awhile, anyway."

She rose and then got a reluctant Laine up from his seat.

"Kristy and I both need you strong," I told him. "Get something to eat, okay?"

He finally agreed, and they left. I stood there for a long moment pondering how to begin, but Isaac beat me to it.

"How is she?"

"We don't know yet. They're still trying to save her life."

He glanced at Lucy, who was sitting quietly in one the chairs. "Was she bitten?"

Lucy shook her head. "No, she wasn't."

I listened, but still had to know. "So, she won't—"

"No," Isaac said, interrupting me. "It would have to be a bite."

"Did you know who they were?"

Mason shook his head. "No, we didn't."

I glanced between him and Isaac but didn't move. "Then how... how did they know your ancestral name."

No one knew where to start, but after a moment, Isaac spoke up. "Certain... circles know us by our true name. Everyone else knows the shortened version."

"Isaac, they were going to take me, not kill me, and they mentioned Campbell by name. None of this makes sense. I thought he wanted me dead because of what I know, and now suddenly he wants me alive?"

He shook his head. "I don't know what it means, Evaline, and I don't know what this is about, but I do know this: whatever it is, you're in over your head."

Rubbing my temples, I paced. "You think I don't know that?"

Mason faced me. "I think maybe I need to drive you to the state police station now. That way they can't find out."

Thinking about his words, I took another couple steps then stopped. *Now?*

"We've had this conversation," he said. "You can't handle this by yourself."

"Mason, please. It's not that. We can't go now, not with Kristy in this condition. These people killed my brother." I glanced at the others and then back at Mason. "You still have yours. If something happened... And it doesn't matter what you are, and since they are what you are, it apparently doesn't matter to them either. I just couldn't bear it if something happened to any of you."

Frustration washed over his face as he took a step back.

"Well no offense, Evaline," Aaron said, "normally we wouldn't care about any of this. But seeing as how you and our brother have this weird connection, keeping us out of whatever is going on is out of the question."

"Well, what if I change my mind and don't want your help?" I asked, then pressed my lips together.

Mason smirked, and the others seemed amused. "It doesn't work like that, baby."

I wasn't getting anywhere. "What do you mean?"

He glanced at Isaac then back at me with the same gentle look he always had—and the doctor and a nurse entered the room.

The doctor acknowledged me. "Ms. Bennett?"

Ignoring Mason for the moment, I said to Lucy, "Lucy, can you please text Lizzy and tell her and Laine to come up?"

"Already done."

I sat, Mason at my side, and the doctor found a seat across from me.

"She lost a lot of blood," he said. "We were able to stop the bleeding; however, we had to give her more to compensate. She was on the brink of bleeding out, and had you not got to her when you did..."

"So, she is going to be okay?"

He tugged on the collar of his lab coat. "She's alive, but she's not out of the woods yet."

Laine and Lizzy came in, as the doctor continued, "I can't tell you how lucky she is to have survived so much blood loss. We are doing everything we can, but she remains in critical condition for right now."

Laine glanced at me and then back at the doctor. "When can we see her?"

He shook his head. "Not right now. It's too soon, and she is not conscious. I will send the nurse out when we get her more stabilized." He got up then and left with the nurse.

Laine was clearly struggling with the prospect of losing his sister, the pain evident on his face. And I was the reason my family was in anguish.

Ten

My head was pounding, and I sat up in bed, soaked in sweat. I panted as I put my hands to my temples in a vain attempt to ease the pain. Dim moonlight shimmered through the window. The strange sensation made my body shudder. Rising, I walked to the bathroom. There, I took four ibuprofen and splashed water onto my face, watching the water go down the drain as my breathing slowed. I could sense Mason behind me, and I couldn't help but smile as I spun to see him standing in the doorway.

Mason, Lizzy, Lucy, and the brothers were taking turns watching me, Laine, and the house, as they were convinced there would be another attack. I couldn't say I didn't feel safe with six werewolves standing guard.

Mason looked at me with concern. "You okay?"

I winced at the pain. My head was splitting in two but then, my headache eased.

"Evaline, maybe you should go see the doctor."

I shook my head. "It's just anxiety. I'll be okay."

He had a strange look as he watched me—as if he sniffed the air.

"What's wrong? Do you smell something?"

"It's very faint, but it's the distinct smell of our kind."

I went to the window and gazed out. "Do you think they came back?"

He shook his head, like he was still trying to figure it out. "No, it's closer than that." His gaze fell on me, and I wanted to laugh at the thought.

I lifted a brow. "Well, don't look at me. You probably smell yourself on me."

He seemed content with that as we left the bathroom.

We had a plan. The day after tomorrow, on Monday, Mason and Lucy would drive me to the State Police in Redding. We decided not to go to Mount Shasta since it was where I had called before. Laine would go to the Blue Dawn, so Jonas and Isaac could watch him. Lizzy was at the hospital with Kristy, and AJ would follow us in his truck.

"What if they don't leave me alone?" I asked Mason. "What if, even after I hand it over and the police agree to investigate or at least do something, then what? I'm sure werewolves could give a shit about human laws."

"They aren't on their own, Evaline," he said. "They're working with someone—someone very human. Otherwise, this would have been over. All we can do is turn over the evidence and see what happens next." He put his hand on my cheek. "I won't let anything happen to you. Do you understand?"

I leaned forward. "I know you won't."

He smelled unbelievably good and just like that, my headache was gone. He leaned in for a kiss and its intoxicating aura completely enveloped me. Within moments, his kiss turned into a lovemaking session. Outlandishly intense, it was like we were no longer two people but one. Passion consumed me as Mason moved slow and in unison with my own body. It was a strange sensation compared to when we'd made love at Alban Loch. This time, the passion and intensity remained ever constant, as though we shared one long orgasm at the same time, leaving us both utterly exhausted. We were still sleeping when there was a knock at my bedroom door.

"Evaline?" Laine's voice was a whisper.

I was absolutely spent. Sunlight streamed into the room, but I didn't want to move. "Yeah?"

The door creaked open as he peered into the room. "Are you guys getting up?"

I twisted my body up a bit, holding the sheet to my body. "Well, yeah, but isn't it a little early?"

"Evaline, it's twelve thirty."

What? I rolled over and peered at the clock which read 12:29 p.m. and sighed as I glanced back at Laine. "Didn't sleep well. Um, I'll be down in a minute okay?"

He nodded and closed the door. I sat there for a moment, thinking about what I was feeling. Not a headache. I was tired, but that wasn't quite it either. My stomach turned strangely, and I put my hand to my mouth and ran to the bathroom. I hated being sick. The nausea passed as I stood in the bathroom doorway watching Mason coming toward me.

"Are you okay? Did you puke?"

"Yeah. It's gotta be the flu or something. I just feel weird. Do you realize it's twelve thirty?"

He glanced over at the clock and then back to me. "We must

have been tired."

I smiled. "No doubt our nightly activities left us exhausted."

Mason grinned too. "Yeah, that was something."

After we dressed, we made our way downstairs, to the kitchen, and Laine yelled from the couch, "Something came for Kristy this morning, and I left the coffee on for you guys."

We sat at the table quietly, and I glanced at the envelope for Kristy and put it into my pocket.

Lines edged the corners of Mason's mouth. I took a sip of my coffee while he perused the sports section. "Mason, I'm okay. It's just a flu or something."

"Maybe," is all he said with a skeptical look on his face.

I was sure what was weighing on his mind. "You didn't bite me, did you?"

He shook his head. "No, I didn't. I'm careful with you, Evaline. Besides, I think you'd be dead if I had."

"Well, I mean, there must be someone who has survived a bite."

"Yes, some do, but it's mostly men, and even then, not all make it. I told you, it's rare for a woman to survive it."

He had explained to me some myths were true—bad tempers, extreme strength and speed, and an unwavering sense of loyalty to fellow pack members, but he also told me not all wolves were in a pack. Apparently, there was what Isaac called "rogues," wolves who chose to be alone. One was no more dangerous than a pack.

Most stayed away from humans, which didn't sound too difficult because werewolves kept their numbers low. It was easier to blend in that way. But Mason said there were packs and individuals which still wouldn't think twice about taking out a human who happened to be in the wrong place at the wrong time. Silver seemed to be the one thing that was a mystery. When I asked him about it, he said none of them had ever seen or heard of a werewolf being killed by a silver bullet.

Mason said something to me as he finished his cup of coffee and placed the cup in the sink, but I was focused on the front page of the newspaper: "SEARCH CONTINUES FOR ANIMAL RESPONSIBLE FOR RECENT ATTACKS."

I sat back and studied Mason for a moment. "The other werewolves maybe?"

"Likely. Says three hikers went missing about twelve miles north of town, and another pair of campers were found mauled just west of here, in the forest. They suspect a bear or a mountain lion."

I rose. "Well, I need to go to the drugstore and get Laine's meds and dressing for his wound, and I need more ibuprofen."

Not long after, we pulled up to the curb in front of the drugstore in Mason's truck. He stayed in the truck as I collected everything we needed. As the pharmacist placed Laine's prescriptions on the counter, I asked him if he knew about any flu going around. As I listed my symptoms, he eyed me for a moment and then walked down an aisle, me following behind. He handed me a box, and I couldn't help chuckling. "Oh, I don't think that's it."

"It's better to be safe than sorry. This particular one is the most accurate."

He walked to the other side of the counter and rung the box up with the prescription. Impossible. Wouldn't that be the topper to an already complicated situation? I paid for my items and left. I just needed to get through tonight and then maybe tomorrow, it would be over—just maybe. We headed to the hospital. I needed to see Kristy even if it was only for a short while.

She was resting when we got there, the only sounds being the evenly timed bleeps from the monitors. She would have a breathing tube in until the throat healed.

Placing my hand on hers, I still couldn't believe what happened. I had heard even people in comas and under sedation could hear who and what was around them. The guilt was overwhelming. It was my fault she was here. Flashes of me scrambling to her in the parking lot, as she lay in a pool of blood kept replaying in my head, as if I were stuck in a bad dream. Mason's secret, Laine's accident, and my decision to go to the State Police weighed heavily on my mind as well.

Still holding Kristy's hand tight, I whispered to her, "Kristy, please forgive me. I'm so sorry. I was trying to protect you and Laine, and I failed. They got you because of me."

I paused and took in a breath. She still lay there motionless, the breathing machine making soft noises. "Mason had a secret. They all did. Thing is, it doesn't matter. He's the one I want. Since this happened, neither Mason nor his brothers have let me out of their sight." I smiled at the thought and then continued, "In fact, Mason is in the waiting room right now, and Lizzy has visited you every day. You are so lucky to have a friend like her. Oh, and something came for you." I pulled out an envelope and regarded Kristy. "I'm gonna read it to you." I opened the envelope from Shasta College and the letter aloud.

Dear Miss Mullins,

We are pleased to inform you that you have been accepted to Shasta College for the spring semester. Please contact the administration office below for information on orientation and registration. We look forward to serving your educational needs for your future. Congratulations!

Couldn't help but well up as I read it. "Oh, Kristy, you got in. Congrats! I'm so proud of you. Whatever you need, I'll do it." I sighed. "We'll figure it out when you're better." After putting the letter away, I stood.

Leaning over, I kissed her gently on the forehead. "Come back to us, Kristy." Pulling away, I had to leave the room. This needed to end tomorrow.

~ * ~

I was on the edge of the tub, debating whether to even take the test. *This is ridiculous. There is no way.* I followed the test steps and placed the test stick on the counter. One minute, then two, then three, and it was still negative, no second line. To cover the evidence, I put the cap on it and shoved it in the wrapper and then into my pocket. I would throw it away later where no one would find it and freak out. I took a breath and stepped out of the bathroom.

Mason was sitting at the kitchen table when I checked the soup I was making. "That smells awesome."

I smiled at him just as Jonas followed Laine into the kitchen. I glanced at the time and handed a glass of water and two pills to Laine, who quickly downed them.

"This pain just sucks. I just…I just wanna sleep," he said.

I could see he was in pain. "Why don't you go ahead and sleep? The doc said you need your rest. Your appetite will be better tomorrow."

He pursed his lips before asking, "Do you think Campbell and the others will leave you alone after tomorrow?"

"I hope so, Laine. Our family deserves a break, ya know?"

It was important to not allow Laine to know what was after me in addition to Campbell. Until Kristy was awake and alert enough to talk about what attacked her, I wasn't sure how that conversation would go.

He eyed me for a long moment, and a scowl crossed his face. "I think we should go after them."

I glanced at Mason, who was looking from me to Laine. I

turned to Laine. "We are."

He shook his head. "I don't mean with evidence, Eva. We need to go balls to the wall and kick some ass."

Jonas grinned. "Fuck yeah! That's what I'm talking about."

"Calm down, both of you. Laine, this is not up to you. We have to be careful." I glanced at Jonas. "And I don't need to remind you why it's not a good idea."

He sighed and rolled his eyes. Mason stood, eyeing his brother. "Stop being so impulsive." Then, as if, they could read each other's thoughts, he said, "Only if we need to."

Jonas remained quiet, and Laine just shook his head.

My cousin's disappointment piqued. "Laine, I almost lost you and Kristy to these people. There's a lot more at stake than we thought. Just let me do it my way."

"Since when is diplomacy your way?"

My eyes widened.

"Evaline, you have never been one to give up. Do you remember when we were kids and the Stein brothers were picking on Kristy and me? Rick Stein towered over you by nearly two feet and outweighed you by an easy one hundred and fifty pounds, and you still knocked him on his ass like he was nothing."

"That was different. We aren't talking childhood bullies. These are people who we suspect have killed at least two people we know of."

He shook his head. "Whatever. Did you know that the Stein brothers never bothered us again? Or what about Lauren Getts? That bitch didn't know who she was fucking with."

"Enough. Laine, let it go okay? Please just trust me."

He paused a second and finally shook his head. "Fine. I just don't understand what you're protecting."

I glanced at Mason, then back at Laine. "Just go upstairs and get some rest."

He disappeared upstairs.

Jonas was smirking when I turned to him. "What?"

He smiled as he replied, "So, you were a bad mother—"

"Jonas. Just make sure you come back after you drop Laine off at the hospital to stay with Kristy and Lizzy. We want to leave at least by nine o'clock tomorrow morning."

"No problem."

The afternoon turned into evening. The television blared from the living room as I stirred the soup again and tasted it. As I added more salt and pepper, I knew Mason was near. Glancing at the doorway, I saw him standing there.

"Hey." Gesturing with the spoon, I said, "Come here. I need an opinion."

He came to my side, and I lifted the spoon to his lips.

After eating the soup, he licked his lips and smiled. "Amazing as always."

I grinned, but my smile slipped from my face, and he became serious. Neither of us said anything for a long moment until I finally broke the silence. "What?"

"I don't say much. You do what you want, and I say nothing, but please know I will always be there."

"Yes, I know. Even when I choose not to tell you where I'm going, you still seem to find your way to me." Continuing as I sighed, "I know it won't do me any good to tell you to stay out of this, and I have accepted that. Is it a wolf thing?"

He shook his head, dead serious. "No, it's a love thing."

I smiled and pulled him to me, and he held me close. I whispered, "It's just I know how dangerous these people are. I just couldn't bear losing you or your family because of this. I told you, they already took Jimmy from me." I stepped away. "Do you understand? You still have your brothers."

He was breathing heavily, and I could see the wild in his eyes. The same animal shimmer I had seen in his eyes before. "I will protect what's mine, no matter the cost."

Relief, fear, and the same intense wanting overcame me. Despite Mason being so powerful, wolves were not immortal. According to him, they were just very difficult to kill. He regarded me with the same intensity for a long moment before glancing at the living room then back at me.

I smiled. I knew what he was thinking. "Right now?"

This was what a heightened sex drive did—not that I minded. I wanted it more and more myself. I thought about it more than ever. It was an extraordinary sensation of both passion and power combined. It was a primal sense, which electrified when he held me close to him. I didn't hesitate, reaching behind me to turn the stove off as he followed me upstairs to my room.

~ * ~

Standing at the edge of the forest, I peered into the darkness. Distant growls echoed around me, and all I smelled was death and the overwhelming scent of decay. Despite seeing nothing, I was anxious even as a strong sense of security overcame me. I turned and was now amid a wolf pack. Even in their animal forms, I knew it was the Cowans. As I moved again, standing directly in front of me was

Campbell.

Motionless. Fear welled in his eyes. "You can't hide. We will get you one way or another." He started to back away, as if staring at a monster.

Mason was suddenly right next to me. "Steady. Never take your eyes off him. When he thinks he's safe, that's when you pounce."

I panted as I did what Mason said.

"She is not ready," Isaac said from my other side, in human form.

Mason's voice broke through the silence. "Evaline, focus!"

I focused back on Campbell, who had disappeared into the darkness. An overwhelming thirst came over me as I dropped to the ground and began to hunt. The howls from the pack intensified as I loped faster and faster. Two huge paws stomped the ground as I ran. They were my paws, and I was stalking the monster. My focus was on my prey, and my heart pounded fiercely. I was in a clearing before long and could hear bagpipes in the distance. Back in human form, I saw many figures, both human and wolf, on top of a ridge. I couldn't see faces, but they were calling to me, beckoning for me to come. I took a step and someone grabbed my arm.

Jimmy held on to me. "No, Evaline. Your place is here. No matter what they say or what they do, don't give in."

I faced him fully. "Jimmy, why did they take you?"

"They want us back. They want all of us back in Alba."

Out of the corner of my eye, I saw Campbell bolt, and in a flash, was after him again but stopped abruptly at the mystery figure with no face, now several feet away from me. Not' Campbell, but the same faceless figure I dreamt about before. Who could this be if not Campbell? Before I could finish my thought, I hit the ground in agony, gripping my head in pain. From everywhere, hands came at me, pulling me in two different directions. I screamed.

I woke up, drenched in sweat.

Mason was next to me, trying to shake me awake. My head ached, and I gasped.

"Evaline, are you all right? You were having a nightmare," he said in a loud, sharp tone.

I inched my body up and tried to catch my breath.

"What was it about?" he asked, a concerned expression on his face.

"Just intense."

My stomach turned again, and my head still pounded as if I'd pulled the pain from my dream into reality. It was overwhelming, and I put my hands to my temples, then jumped from the bed and hurried into the bathroom.

I was on the floor next to the toilet when he entered and knelt next to me. "You need to call the doctor about the headaches. They're getting worse."

"It's the stress. I didn't have migraines like this before. I'll be fine."

"What was the dream about?" he asked.

How could I tell him? I didn't know what it meant. Sometimes the dreams were puzzles that needed to be pieced together; other times, they were messages. I didn't know what this one was. I couldn't tell him how primal I felt, how savage, how free. Didn't make any sense.

"It was just Jimmy helping me to get away from Campbell again. Like I said—pretty intense."

"It's gotta mean something, Evaline."

I shook my head as he helped me up. Daylight streamed into the bathroom through the window.

We got dressed and headed downstairs. Jonas was asleep on the couch. Today was the day everything would change; Campbell would lose his grip on me.

We sat at the kitchen table, nibbling on a coffee cake. I watched Mason as he took small bites.

"So, can you eat anything you want?" I asked, curious.

"Just about. Of course, we eat more meat than most humans."

"The meat—it has to be raw?"

He grinned. "No, not necessarily, although the bloodier, the better."

I winced at the thought of bloody meat, which made him laugh as I asked, "What do you hunt?"

He watched me for a moment before answering, "Game animals mostly."

"You said before you hunt humans. I just—"

"No, I didn't say that. I said we protect our family at all costs, and if it means killing someone who gets too close or jeopardizes the family, well, then…"

I knew what it meant. "And you can change at any time?"

"Yes, once you link to your inner wolf, you can at will. But until then, you are at the mercy of the moon."

I pondered his words for the moment. Everything was so intriguing. "Is it only the night of the full moon?"

"It varies. Can last two to five days surrounding the actual full moon."

I blinked. "So, if you haven't joined to the wolf inside and you are at the mercy of the moon, you can change and not know it for two to five days?"

"As I said, that's why it's important for a newborn wolf to couple with its human part before the human completely disappears. If the connection isn't made within the first cycle, when the wolf takes over, the person will have no recollection of what happened, and that can be dangerous."

A shiver went down my spine, and I wanted to change the subject. "So, is Lucy coming over?"

"I'm not sure." He immediately pulled out his phone and texted her. A moment later, a ding on his phone indicated her response. "She's at the Dawn. We'll go pick her up and go from there."

We needed to get going.

Mason woke Jonas. The three of us walked out. Jonas was with me in my car, and Mason followed in his truck. The plan was Jonas would take my car to their house while Mason, Lucy, and I drove to Redding in Mason's truck. No one could follow me if I wasn't on the road or at my house.

As we drove to the Blue Dawn, Jonas said, "This car is sweet."

"Thank you."

"Runs well for how old it is. You probably won't need a complete restoration."

I liked talking about my car. Made me think of my dad.

Jonas took in a breath. "So, Mason has been schooling you on us, huh?"

Amused, I glanced at him. "Yeah, he answers my questions if that's what you mean."

Jonas grinned. "You mean he hasn't shown you?"

"Well, I did see all of you..."

He shook his head. "I mean the actual change. You only saw us in our hunting forms."

My eyes narrowed. "You have another form?"

"There are three forms we can take: human, hunting, which is less intimidating than the third form, one we don't use too often. Our bipedal form."

I blinked. "Bipedal form? Why not?"

He grinned as I checked the rearview mirror and noticed Mason was no longer behind us. Before I could even say anything, Jonas stopped smiling and anxiously glanced back. "Evaline, step on it. Get us to the Blue Dawn now."

I did as he said. "Jonas, where is Mason? What's happening?"

He didn't say anything, and only at the last second did I see the huge truck as it struck us. My car shook violently as if we had hit a wall head on. I had no time to react as the car rolled repeatedly. When the car finally stopped, it had landed on the roof. I frantically looked over at Jonas, but he was nowhere to be seen.

"Jonas! Jonas!" I shouted his name as I managed to unhook the seat belt and fell into a heap on what was left of my roof, which was destroyed.

We had been struck on the passenger side, so I feared the worst. It didn't take long before several pairs of legs headed toward the car, and I heard voices, but they sounded so distant. My heart sank as a police car crept closer. I knew who it was.

Taking deep breath and closing my eyes, I thought, *Mason, I love you, and I am so sorry.*

As if he were there, I heard him say, *No*, and then I heard faint shrieks from what sounded like Isaac and the others. The voices stopped as fast as they'd started as two men peered into the car.

"She's alive."

The last thing I heard was, "Bring her now, before the MacCowans come."

And then everything went black.

Eleven

My name was being called by several voices; including Mason, as if I were lost, and they were looking for me. It was an odd sensation, but when I heard them—and I didn't know how I knew—the familiar voices belonged to Mason, Isaac, Lucy, and the other Cowans crying out all at once. Mason's voice trembled with sadness and anger. I wanted to ease it but didn't know how.

My thoughts focused on his face, and when I called out to him to ease his pain, he answered me, "Evaline, where are you?"

Realizing the conversation was in my head, I perceived other voices, not so distant but rather closer to me. I started to stir.

Someone said, "Be quiet. She's waking up. Go tell Mr. Minyawi she's awake."

I opened my eyes to see a metal ceiling and a fan blowing a soft breeze. My head pounded—not from the accident. The very same strange ache I had been experiencing over the last several days, appeared again but this time, the throbbing became worse as I put my hand to my head. Trying to focus on my surroundings, I shifted my body, so I could survey my surroundings. It seemed to be an office of sorts where there were two desks with old, dusty paperwork and boxes stacked on them. Random file cabinets and piles of loose papers and files cluttered the musty room. The smell of old musty papers, like wet newspaper was very strong.

I was on an old, musty couch, and across from me, two men were standing by the door, watching me. They resembled delivery boys rather than criminals. I sensed immediately they were human, as their eyes lacked the shimmer that Mason and the others had, and these men had a strange scent, not pine or the fresh aroma of a rain.

A moment later, the door opened, and three men walked into the room. The man, who came in first, wore a black suit. His hair was in a ponytail, and he was clean-shaven. The second man was Campbell, still in his sheriff's uniform. The third man was a black man with long, black hair streaked with gray he wore in dreads, which he kept pulled back. He wore a dark gray suit with a bright blue shirt. I eyed this man experiencing a strange familiarity but couldn't place where I had seen him. As far as I knew, I had never laid eyes on him. I could tell he was a man of importance just by how Campbell and the others existed around him. I also knew he wasn't human. He had the same energy the Cowans had. He and the man with the black suit were the same.

He stopped abruptly as he approached me and glared at the two men standing by the door. His voice was calm but still conveyed rage. "Idiots. You do realize she's like a beacon, and they probably know exactly where she is."

One of the men stepped forward and peered at me. "How were we supposed to know? Campbell told us to bring her here."

The man in the gray suit snapped, "I suggest you place everyone on heightened alert. *Now*."

They jumped and exited quickly.

I didn't understand what he meant, and now the man in the black suit was looking at me as if he'd never seen a woman before. How was I a beacon? The man in gray motioned to him, who put a chair in front of me, and he sat and studied me for a moment. I glanced from him to Campbell and back again. Finally, the man in the gray suit spoke—with a strange accent I couldn't place.

"Miss Bennett, my name is Mr. Viktor Minyawi. I oversee North American operations for the Spanditto Corporation. You have been a handful. You have cost us precious time, not to mention money."

As he spoke, Campbell grinned.

"Miss Bennett, are you paying attention?" Minyawi asked.

I stared at him but said nothing as he continued.

"Where is this evidence you supposedly have?"

Ignoring his question, I narrowed my eyes. I had questions of my own. Without hesitation, I asked, "Where is my brother?"

He sat back and sighed for a moment. "I see."

Campbell chuckled, and I flashed him a hard look when he asked, "How's the family?"

Anger welled inside me, but I calmly answered, "How's the lip?"

He took a menacing step forward and reached for something in his jacket, but Minyawi put his hand up. I didn't move as Campbell froze in place by the man's gesture.

"I suggest you don't make her angry, Sheriff," Minyawi stated.

I looked from Campbell to Minyawi, waiting.

He finally returned his attention to me. "Your brother made a bad decision. I would ask that you don't make the same mistake."

"Why because he saw something? Jimmy wouldn't have said anything. You were his client."

Viktor then stood. "Stand up, Miss Bennett, please."

I took a breath and did as he asked. He stepped forward and was less than a foot from me. Closing his eyes, his head tipped slightly back as if he was smelling something. He opened his eyes and peered into mine. His had the same glimmer as the Cowan's, and he was lost in thought as he studied me.

As the pain in my head began to intensify again, I gasped faster and sweat beads rolled down my face.

After a moment, Minyawi smiled. "A bonus for sure but an unfortunate one given the circumstances."

"You've got to be kidding, Viktor," the man in the black suit said with a strong Scottish accent.

Viktor took a step back and flashed him a look. "Not so much, Leathan. Nevertheless, it doesn't change our business. It will be dark soon and we need to move. After it's done, have them attempt to throw her into the pit with her brother, then you can instruct the bulldozers they have the okay to fill it in."

Leathan's eyes narrowed, and his expression appeared irritated. "Attempt?"

Viktor said nothing but simply grinned in my direction.

Glaring at him, Leathan continued, "You know it's against the diktats. This wasn't the plan."

Viktor flashed him a displeased look. "Calm yourself. Robert is now involved. It's out of our hands. However, it appears to have just gotten interesting…"

No further protests came from Leathan as he regarded me with uncertainty.

It was obvious Viktor had enough power to keep the others in line. I pondered a moment on his words. Attempt? He said to have them attempt to throw me in the pit. What did he know that no one else does?

He spoke with confidence as he turned to me. "Your brother wasn't killed for something he saw; he was killed because he refused an offer, and it is something that is only offered once. The offer was an answer to an ancient decree which began in 1774. After your brother made his decision, his fate was set, but yours was yet to be determined—this left you, as the last descendant of the last of the lost families. Since there was no one else, we were going to take you. We didn't, however, expect you to go on a personal investigation and make things difficult for us. With your friends and your father's relatives, it was more trouble than it was worth. Despite your utter importance to something much older than this current business, your fate has been the topic of debate as of late and appears to have taken a turn for the worse. However, I am anxious to see how it ends."

I had no idea what he meant, but the pain spread to my entire body, and every bone, muscle, and nerve twitched. Despite me being in visible discomfort, he calmly took an envelope out of his coat and placed it in the inside of my jean jacket pocket.

Ever so gently, he whispered, *"Fur yer een an' theirs."*

I couldn't stand the pain and collapsed on the couch in agony. No one moved except Campbell, who took a couple steps toward me in confusion.

Campbell turned to Viktor. "What did you do?"

Viktor merely glanced at Leathan and then at me one last time before exiting the room.

Leathan nodded and then regarded Campbell. "Take care of this now. And tie up any loose ends including location of that file. Make sure you take her to the pit first." He studied me for a long moment and turned back to Campbell as he continued, "This time, don't screw up, or it will be you at the bottom of the pit."

Campbell's lips thinned before he said, "When can I go home as well?"

Leathan glared. "So anxious you Campbells are. When your debt is paid in full, then you can go home." He glanced at me one more time and then Campbell. "Finish it." With that, he left.

Campbell swore under his breath as the pain in my head started to subside, and I was able to catch my wind.

"Here it is, Evaline," he said, stepping toward me, "if you do not reveal where the evidence is, we'll finish off both your cousins and maybe your boyfriend. Do you want to be responsible for getting them killed?"

I sat on the couch gasping, worrying the pain would return but managed to get the words out. "You are deplorable—a disease with no cure, a monster."

He smiled and leaned to get in my face. "But this monster will be rewarded well at the end. Maybe I should have gone a step further in Sacramento. We could have had some fun together."

I laughed. "You are a vulgar, disgusting little gangster wannabe, and you make me want to vomit. Your day is coming, Campbell, mark my words."

He took a step back and yelled, "Alan!"

I clutched my head again; the pain intensified like my head was splitting in two.

A moment later, both delivery boys came into the room. One of them took a step toward me. "What's wrong with her?"

"Who knows?" Campbell replied. "It's not our problem. Come here."

"You and Bylar take her to the pit and do what you have to, to find out where the evidence is. When she gives it up, kill her." He spoke low, as if he didn't want me to hear, but strangely enough, it was crystal clear, as if he were right next to me.

Alan asked, "And if she doesn't tell?"

"I think you know the answer. This whole thing needs to be done so we can get back on track with the shipments."

Alan agreed, and they picked me up from the couch.

My entire body tensed. I wanted to jump out of my skin. When we walked outside, the brisk air relieved my sweaty skin. The pain came and went, subsiding, as they shoved me toward the pit.

As I walked, I peered through the trees, wondering if help was out there. I wanted to run. Would this pain go away if I did? I began thinking of Mason and Jimmy. *Oh Jimmy, I am sorry I failed! I will be with you soon.*

That was everything that brought me to now. Everything I did, everyone I met or spoken to now led up to this moment—the moment of truth. By Campbell's order, I would die just as Jimmy had.

I stood at the edge of the pit and took a profound gasp. I could smell it. It was undeniable and overpowering. I never realized how distinct the smell of death was until this instant.

Jimmy stood next to me. "You shouldn't be here, Eva. You know you can get out at any time?"

I turned to him. "Jimmy, please don't leave me. Please stay."

He smiled. "I'm always with you, sis."

I glanced back into the pit which had been filled in save for a large hole directly below me. "You're in there, aren't you?"

"We all are. You must fight back. Now."

As my eyes opened, I noticed something shiny sticking out from underneath a rock—a small golden dove. I had seen the dove before. It was Amanda Collins's. She told her husband had an identical one. A quick shove broke my focus, and I turned around.

"Where is it?" Alan yelled.

I looked back at him just as the full moon emerged from behind a cloud. "It's in a safe place where the state police can find it."

Bylar hit me hard across the face. I staggered but didn't fall back. The anger welled in me as I gazed at the sky through my hair and locked on the moon. My mouth watered, my anxiety peaked, and my heart thudded.

I was screaming in pain inside of my head, and I wanted to let it out. Despite my ear-splitting yelps, I could still hear Mason, but like a blanket, my swelling anger muffled his voice. I cocked my head to look at the men, and adrenaline surged.

I shoved each of them with strength that came from somewhere within me which I wasn't aware of. For a moment, I wasn't in control, and before I knew it, I was on the other side of the pit which was at least forty feet wide. In the next instant, I leaped over the fence and heard Alan and Bylar start after me.

My skin tingled as I ran faster than I thought I ever could through the thick forest. The damp forest clung to my body with every stride. The trees themselves blurred, and I wanted to go faster and faster.

There was a light fog in the approaching clearing, and the moonlight glistened through the fog, shimmering in-between the canopy of trees as I sensed my pursuers getting closer. I was breathing hard and fast as pain shot from my head to my feet continuously. The familiar smells of old pine and earth were overwhelming, and with every step, the nighttime sounds of the forest became as overwhelming as the smells.

Overwhelmed by the sensations, I fell to the ground. I couldn't take the pain anymore. I dug my fingers into the ground, the damp earth squeezing through my fingers. Clutching my head did nothing to stop the pain. Rustling in the woods told me my pursuers were close, too close. I peered through a bush and saw them. As I briefly watched them, I suddenly got so terribly thirsty; a different kind of thirst than anything I had ever experienced. Perhaps water would help this odd thirst? I heard a trickle of it somewhere, but I needed to get away—far, far away from them.

It was then I heard Mason, his brothers, Lucy, and even Lizzy. They were calling me, and I sensed them closing in. I wanted to answer Mason but there was a weird sensation drawing me deeper into the forest. This feeling was so strong, it was as if I was fighting for my own body.

I ran my tongue over protruding fangs and a row of razor sharp teeth. A strange tingling rattled through my fingers as I pulled my hands toward my face to see. I was astonished to find them strong, powerful weapons with long, black claws protruding from my fingertips. How could this be? I hadn't been bitten. This must have been what Viktor was talking about. He could see I was turning; he could smell it. An overpowering aroma washed over me and I still felt the terrible thirst. The smell must have been Alan and Bylar as I knew they were close by. I didn't want to hurt anyone, but whatever was fighting for my body wanted blood. I was finding it difficult to stay quiet when my head screamed in agony.

My body was on fire, yet I was not sweating—and I continued to get thirstier and thirstier. I finally managed to get up and run toward the sound of the water. I fell at the foot of the stream, my whole body in searing pain. It was as if my body was being stretched and contorted, but I looked down and there was just me, unchanged. An owl hooted in the distance, and I immediately narrowed in on the tree where he was perched.

How did I know where the owl was when the tree was several yards away? The owl left the branch in pursuit of prey below, and I could hear the flap of its wings as it glided through the air and then the tiny screech from the field mouse as the owl swiftly picked it up with its talons. A bullfrog up stream found a rock to sit on. A deer was quietly feeding on a bush of berries somewhere nearby. These sounds cried at me from every direction.

Again, I gripped my head as agony pierced my very soul, and then, like balm, two hands grabbed me, and the pain stopped. I smacked into the ground as someone tackled me from behind. My pursuers had found me.

Bylar flipped me over and pressed his cold hands around my neck. Adrenaline surged through me, and when I shoved Bylar from on top of me, he went flying and landed against a tree several feet away.

I was going in and out of consciousness, but I managed to get to my feet. Alan stood in front of me stunned but was aiming a pistol at me. I don't remember striking Alan, but he sprawled in a pool of blood. My nails were like razor blades had pierced them as fresh blood dripped from my fingertips onto the forest floor. Blood flamed through my veins like lava pumping through me. Pressure built, leading to an inevitable eruption. With every heavy breath I took, my entire body heaved. The sound of a heartbeat thundered in my mind, but this time, it wasn't mine. My unwavering focus was on Bylar, whom I had thrown against the tree. He lay rigid on the ground, and he gazed up at me with terrified eyes as I crouched to pounce. All I could smell was the metallic, tasty tang of blood.

Images kept flashing through my head randomly: The field with Jimmy, Kristy, and Laine as we got ready to play baseball. Watching through the back window at Kristy and Laine as Dad pulled the car away the day we moved to Sacramento. My conversations with Isaac. Jimmy coming home so excited after he found out he got his first job. Kristy laying in a pool of blood. Mom's small figure in her bed—the last time I saw her.

Campbell walking up to my car. Dad's funeral. Mason standing in the doorway with a smile. Grams giving me a cookie with a smile. Dad and I sitting in the garage working on the Cougar. Alban Loch.

Am I dead? Did Campbell win? People say your life flashes before your eyes right before you die. 'I thought of what Mason said—most females couldn't take the change. Maybe I changed and didn't make it. I wasn't ready to quit! I wanted to wake up. I could hear a voice, a sweet voice, calling me.

"Evaline, wake up."

In my fog, my mother smiled at me, and I blinked.'

"Evaline, can you hear me?"

I opened my eyes. Not my mother. Lucy's voice cut through my thoughts.

"Evaline?" she said my name again.

Mason's room again, as the familiar pine smell and old wood filled my nose. Sitting up, I was exhausted. It was like I'd been asleep for days.

Lucy seemed relieved. "Evaline, take it easy. You're not used to it yet."

Glancing out the window then back to her, "What happened? Did I..." the right words just wouldn't come out, but she understood.

"No, not all the way. Do you remember anything?"

I shook my head.

"We found you and brought you back."

"I do remember hearing your voices, Mason's and Isaac's especially."

"We were looking for you. Pack members have a telepathic link. It's how we know where we all are or if one of us is in trouble. That's how we found you."

Everything she was saying seemed so surreal.

Remembering what Campbell had threatened to do to Laine and Kristy, I asked. "Are Laine and Kristy all right? Did anything...?"

"They are fine. Lizzy is with them both at the hospital."

Relief came over me when I knew they were both safe. That is when I noticed she was holding something in her hands, but I couldn't see what it was.

"Hey," Lucy said as she held out the pregnancy test I'd forgotten to throw away.

"Yeah, well, it's negative so I don't think that's why I changed."

Lucy gave me a sympathetic look as she kept the stick extended. "Take another look."

Taking the test from her, I looked at it in disbelief. There it was—what hadn't been there before—a second line. The sketchy memory of my conversation with Viktor began to come back to me—he knew. He could smell it, just as he knew I would turn.

Lucy as she smiled excitedly. I couldn't help but grin myself. Despite the circumstances, it was exciting news.

She gripped my hand gently.

I turned to her. "Does he know?"

"Yes, they do, and we're all worried about you. Mason especially. He lay next to you almost all night."

A smile crossed my lips as I thought of him staying with me. So many questions surrounded me; what-ifs were everywhere.

"I don't understand why I changed."

"Well, get yourself together and whenever you are ready, come out and we'll talk."

She slipped out the door.

For a few moments, I took in the fact that I was now different. Something that, up until a week ago, I'd thought was a myth. The thing is, the most puzzling aspect of this change to me, was somehow I sensed I was completely loved and wanted. Remembering Viktor had slipped something into my coat pocket, I glanced around for my jacket, which was dirty but otherwise intact. I hoped the envelope was still there since I had no recollection of the latter part of the night.

I got out of bed hardly noticing the huge shirt I was wearing. A simple sniff revealed it was Mason's. Reaching into the inside pocket of my jacket, I was relieved to see the envelope still there. I opened it and pulled out what was very aged paper. On it, there was a pyramid of Scottish family crests. There was the MacCowan family, and I gasped when I saw one which was even more familiar to me than theirs.

Clasping the pendant around my neck, I glanced from the pendant to the paper—my family crest was part of this pyramid of crests. I didn't recognize any of the others, but two had lines through them, and the third had the word *Home* over it. Five crests under one larger crest. What did it mean?

Viktor's words about an ancient search for the lost families and how Jimmy had refused an offer kept running through my mind. I put on my jeans and took the paper to the other room with me. It was time to find out some answers.

They were all there—Jonas and Mason sat at the kitchen table, while Isaac stood, leaning against the sink. Aaron was leaning on the fridge and Lucy was next to the kitchen counter. Taking a breath, Mason's worried expression indicated his anticipation; his worry, his fear of me blaming him, his anxiety about me being in danger. Glancing at Isaac and Aaron, who smiled back, I eyed Jonas with surprise. *Jonas!* Relieved he was all right, I was curious what had happened to him. I took my coffee with the cream, which was right next to Lucy.

Quietly uttering a thank you to Lucy, I took a seat at the table. No one said a word for at least thirty seconds, which seemed like an eternity.

Indicating Jonas first, I was the first to speak. "I am so happy you are okay. What happened?"

"I was, uh, thrown from the car when the roof collapsed, and then I landed twenty feet away, woke up an hour later with a headache."

My gaze now fell on Mason. "I'm okay. The wolf thing, it's new but I'll deal." I placed my hand on his as he breathed a sigh of relief.

He spoke after a long moment. "I'm so sorry, Eva. I wasn't careful enough."

I could see where this was going, so I stopped him before he could finish. "Mason, you didn't bite me or scratch me. I'm not angry at you—I could never be angry at you. I'm right where I want to be—with you. No matter what." I sat back a moment, trying to find the right words. "Did you know it would turn me?"

"No, I didn't. I never imagined in a million years it could happen. I mean not from that. I—"

"You didn't turn because you're pregnant, Evaline," Isaac interjected. "Others of our kind have gotten humans pregnant before, and they didn't turn. This was something else."

Confused, Mason shook his head.

"Well, if she wasn't bitten or scratched and it's not the baby, then how did she turn?" Aaron asked.

"I've only heard of it happening once or twice, and it's the main reason I've ordered all of you not to get attached."

"What? I changed through sex?"

Isaac shook his head and looked pointedly at Mason.

Mason's brow turned up as he first blinked at Isaac and then he said to me, "Evaline, remember I told you about the big sex drive thing. If it were just sex that turned people, we'd have a huge population of fellow pack members. You changed because I love you."

I lifted a brow at Isaac, who confirmed it. "You shifted because of passion through love. Like I said, it's rare because most women can't take the change so we are always careful."

"Well, I guess you never saw me coming."

Jonas smiled. "Nah, you belong here. You were kinda badass before, remember?"

I had to laugh. "Yeah, real badass. Why do I feel like I was hit by a truck? Oh wait, I was. But why can't I remember what happened last night?"

"What is the last thing you do remember?" Isaac asked.

I pulled out any memories I had from the night before, which were clear up to being led out of the warehouse.

"There was a black guy named Viktor Minyawi, who said he was the head of North American operations, and I was basically a pain in the ass. He said Jimmy wasn't killed for what he saw but rather because he refused an offer they made him." Pursing my lips, I regarded Isaac then continued, "He said it was an offer which is only asked once. Then he talked about an ancient search for lost families that started in the 1700s, and I guess it's continuing." I paused a moment remembering some of the events of the previous night but not all. They listened intently as I continued. "I was standing at the pit, and they were going to kill me, and I closed my eyes. Jimmy was there. He said *they* were in the pit. Maybe it hurts more finding out I was right all along as opposed to not knowing at all. This is why I didn't want any of you involved. I didn't want anyone else to get hurt or killed because of me, and they still managed to almost take away what I have left. Kristy, Laine," —I glanced at Jonas— "you."

"Eva, there is a lot of death in that pit. It's overwhelming when you stand over it."

I knew what he meant now that I'd been there as a... nonhuman.

Mason's tone was firm as he said, "Well, you won't have to go through it again."

"Campbell got away. He was there, and he ordered them to kill me."

Isaac stared at me, hard. "What else happened?"

I reached into my pocket and pulled out the envelope. "Before they took me to the pit, Minyawi put this in my jacket pocket without the others seeing. He and one other guy were like us, and he whispered, '*Fur yer een* an' theirs' in my ear."

Mason exchanged a look with his brothers.

"That's ancient Gaelic," Lucy said. She glanced at Isaac who was puzzled as she continued, "It means 'for your eyes and theirs.'"

I handed the paper to Isaac, who opened it as the others moved or craned their necks to see. At the top of the pyramid was the family crest for McGregor. It became apparent by their puzzled looks, no one understood completely the connection between the family crests.

Lucy spoke first. "That's us." She indicated the MacCowan family crest on the pyramid.

"Your crest isn't the only one on there I recognize," I said as I pulled out my necklace.

Mason remembered right away. "Your grandmother's pendant."

Isaac examined it and then at the paper; the dragon with a sword in a shield and the family name: Murphy.

Their gazes then fell on me.

"Evaline, what did you say your grandmother's last name was again?" Mason asked.

"Murphy."

"Well, there was a line through Murphy like these others, and then it looks like they erased it."

"There were things Minyawi said. I think he knew they couldn't kill me. He knew I was turning as soon as he saw me, and he got real close, like he could smell it, and I think he knew I was pregnant."

Jonas turned to me. "Did you recognize the other guy with him?"

"No, but he had a Scottish accent, and they mentioned someone named Robert was now calling the shots. He's the one who told them to take me out to the pit."

Isaac folded the paper and handed it back to me, seemingly lost in his thoughts.

Lucy eyed Isaac. "This is the least of our worries. She has to get through the next couple of nights."

I glanced from Isaac to Mason. "I remember the pain. I was in excruciating agony. I remember standing above the pit, and they were asking me about where the evidence was, and when I didn't answer, they hit me."

Mason's expression went from concerned to angry in a split second.

"It's fine," I assured him, "but I remember getting pissed, and that's when I started feeling something inside me wanted to rip them to shreds. I remember shoving them, and the next thing I knew, I was on the other side of the pit, and then I ran. The pain was unbelievable. I knew I was changing when I saw my hands. It was like my body was—"

"Fighting with itself?" Lucy asked.

The anxiety welled in me but a sense of relief as she knew what I was talking about. She indicated for me to continue.

"I kept going in and out, but they caught up to me at the stream." I stopped. The memory was broken like a missing puzzle piece to a larger picture—an image of Alan in a pool of blood and a terrified Bylar looking at me. "I think I, um... I think I killed them."

I'd struggled with just saying the words. As much as I had been through, as many times as I had sworn to protect my family at all costs, I had never taken a life. I turned to Isaac. "Why am I only remembering bits and pieces?"

Isaac considered the question a moment before answering. "Unless you tap into the wolf, once it takes over, you won't remember because you aren't driving. You have to make the connection."

I thought for a moment on something Mason had said before. "Until then, I'm at the mercy of the moon, right?"

Mason nodded.

"So, I'm still in danger from changing?"

"Yes, because when we found you, you hadn't completed. You were kinda in a transitional form. You're particularly vicious in this form because your body is fighting with itself," he said.

"Vicious? Did I hurt you? Tell me I didn't hurt any of you."

Jonas chuckled. "Nothing we can't handle."

"But what about Kristy and Laine?"

"They're fine. We'll figure out what to do later. Right now, they think you're just crashing here for a couple days."

"And Campbell? He has to know by now his guys are dead, and I didn't talk."

Aaron winced. "Don't worry about that. He's not your problem right now. You need to concentrate and connect to the wolf by tonight, Eva, or you will change again and not know what's happening."

I sucked in a deep breath to calm my nerves. "But how? How do you tap into it?"

"The trigger," Jonas said. "It's what we call it. You need to find it, and it's different for everyone. It's what you concentrate during the process."

Mason said, "It's something you can relate to with your wolf, a common thought or it could be a person."

"What is yours?"

"My trigger is loss. I think of what I lost because of what we faced and became."

I couldn't help but want to hold him at that moment.

Turning to Jonas, who answered, "My trigger is my mom. I think of her and what they did to her."

It was beginning to make sense. I looked at it in disbelief. The "trigger", as they called it, was something that got you angry and then, of course, prompted the wolf to come out.

Rotating back to Mason, I asked. "What happened to you on the highway yesterday, anyway? One minute you were behind us, and the next minute you were gone."

"A logging truck pulled out as soon as you passed it, and they had me there for what seemed like forever. By the time I got around it, I found the car and Jonas unconscious."

Thoughts of my beloved Cougar flashed through my mind as I realized it was likely destroyed in the accident.

Mason noticed. "What's wrong?"

"It's just my car. It was the one thing my dad and I did together." I shot Mason a look. "It's fine. I guess it's just a car."

"Maybe we can fix it?" Jonas suggested.

"Jonas, we were hit by a three-ton Mack dump truck. I think it's safe to say my Cougar didn't survive."

He shrugged, but Isaac said, "Never say never, Eva."

Leaning up against the kitchen sink, I indicated shyly. "I'm hungry."

Mason stood. "Did you want something in particular? We have food here."

Isaac mused, "Yeah, if you count Jonas's shit food as real food."

Jonas laughed, and Aaron patted Jonas on the head playfully. Jonas swatted Aaron's hand away.

Lucy placed her coffee cup next to mine and asked, "Is there anything in particular you're in the mood for?"

"I don't know. I just feel like I could eat a cow right now."

Jonas, still laughing, said, "Really? Cause there's a farm down the street... we can—"

Lucy slapped his arm. "Dork, you know what she meant."

I couldn't help but laugh as it now appeared that phrase may not be just a figure of speech anymore.

Turning to Lucy, I asked. "Maybe we could order a pizza or something."

She smiled. "Coming right up." She picked up the phone, and I motioned for Mason to follow me into his room.

Twelve

Mason held me close, and I found myself not wanting him to let go. He pulled away just far enough to place his hand on my belly. It was a tender moment, and he had a look of complete contentment. I placed my hand on his and gazed up at him.

"I told you I'm meant to be here, but I think it's partly to show you can still have what you gave up so long ago."

Still touching my belly, he answered, "Maybe. Or I'm meant to have happiness within my grasp and still lose it because I'm damned."

I placed both my hands on his face. "Baby, you are not evil. It was circumstance that changed you, not a personal choice."

He turned toward the window. Mason hadn't told me much about the days right after he was turned. He certainly hadn't divulged any details about when and how it had happened. The only thing he would say was he's protecting his family and had to make a choice—even if the choice, at least in his eyes, was damning his soul.

"We used to go to church every Sunday. The minster knew all of us and saw us grow up. It was our town; where we would live, get married, have children, work, and die. That's what people did back then. It's what I wanted."

He turned to me as he continued, "After it happened, Isaac went to the church to see the minster and seek advice. He didn't know what to do. At first, the minister was sympathetic, but then he told Isaac the only way for us to redeem ourselves in front of God was to die by our own hands, or we would be judged. When Isaac told us what happened, we knew we would never be allowed in God's house again because in the eyes of the church we were damned. So, we left and never went into another church."

I came to his side. "Mason, that was a time when if people didn't understand something, it must be evil. God didn't abandon you, and I know this because he brought me to you."

Mason studied me for a long moment.

I finally whispered, "Just trust me, okay?"

He agreed and held me close.

The afternoon wore on, and I texted Laine to see how he was holding up and how Kristy was doing. I was happy when both Laine and Lizzy called to say Kristy was finally awake, but it would be awhile before she could speak. Lizzy said Kristy was trying to say something but she couldn't because of the breathing tube. Lizzy assured her everyone was fine. What would I say to Kristy when she could speak? It was a conversation for another day.

Jonas left to go relieve Lizzy at the hospital. An intense fear overcame me as I watched him drive away. Assuming Campbell would be out for blood and given what, I could remember from the previous night, I had to accept he at least suspected what we were.

We were eating pizza in the kitchen eating pizza. I thought of Jimmy's words by the pit. "Alba…" I whispered, as Isaac walked into the room and placed a thick book on the table.

His head reared back. "What did you say?"

"Alba. It's something I heard last night in a dream. Do you know what it means?"

"*Alba* is an ancient Gaelic word for Scotland. You said you heard it in a dream?" Isaac asked.

I paused a moment as I studied his expression on what I was about to tell him. "My brother visits me sometimes in my dreams, normally to warn me or tell me what's coming. I saw him again last night, by the pit, and he said, 'They wanted to take us to Alba.' I'm sure my grandma emigrated from Scotland because she had an accent, but my mom was born here. I don't understand."

Isaac quickly answered, "I don't know, but your dreams sound more like visions to me. There's someone coming over—someone I trust implicitly—to meet you. I want you to tell him about these visions. He has experience with them. He's coming over to check you out. I'm nervous about whether the change will affect the baby."

My mouth open, I gaped at him as Mason came into the room. "Affect the baby?" I choked. "You mean the change could hurt it?"

"We don't know. This is new. And I think he can help us. He'll be here soon. Just relax."

Mason sat next to me. I stared at the book laying there and asked, "What is that?"

"The books from the Blue Dawn; we're losing money somewhere, and I need to figure out why."

I focused on Isaac. "Did you want me to take a look?

"Oh yeah, finance degree. I forgot about that. Yeah, maybe you can help."

After pulling the book to me, I opened it then I closed it again.

"I'll need the books from the last two years as well so I can do some comparisons, all right?"

He quickly exited the room.

Mason chuckled as he turned to me. "You know you just sealed your fate as the family accountant."

I laughed. "It's not a problem." I tilted my head. "This person coming to see me Isaac is talking about... Is he the one you were talking about, the only other person who knows?"

Mason bobbed his head once.

"You said he was 'above most.' What did you mean?"

"Sam is a Shasta Indian elder and medicine man. He understands what we are and has helped us in more ways than you can imagine. He will hopefully have some answers about how the change affects the baby and how we can help you."

Just then, Aaron and Lucy came back into the house, wrapped in blankets, their ankles and legs muddy.

"It's tonight, Isaac. They're coming tonight," Aaron said.

"How do you know for sure?" Isaac asked.

"We caught two of our kind snooping around, and they took off when we gave chase. They know she's here," Lucy answered.

"Then we need to be ready when they do," Mason stated.

Isaac nodded, his voice firm as he said, "Aaron called Jonas to come home but tell Lizzy to stay put to watch Laine and Kristy. Lucy, you'll watch Evaline, and we'll fight."

Mason lifted his chin. "I'll stay with her."

Isaac shook his head. "No, you're fast. We need you with us. Lucy will stay with Evaline."

Mason's worried expression indicated he clearly wasn't happy.

"She'll be fine, Brother," Isaac said, his voice reassuring.

"Baby, I'll be all right." I placed a hand on Mason's arm. "I don't want you to see me deal with this, not yet, okay? Just go with Isaac tonight, please?"

I couldn't say what Isaac's concerns were—or my own for that matter. If I didn't survive the change, Mason would not be there to see another woman he loved die. As if projecting the pain, he experienced centuries ago, a moment of complete sorrow and pain overcame me. I couldn't let him go through the pain of loss again.

"Evaline, start concentrating on your trigger," Isaac suggested.

With that, they left the room, leaving me and Mason. Exhausted, I lay on the couch, and the next thing I knew, Mason's voice woke me.

"Evaline, Sam is here. Wake up."

Mason was sitting on the couch next to me, and Isaac and the others stood by the fireplace, and standing directly in front of me, watching me was an old Indian man. He had on faded blue jeans and a long-sleeve shirt with bright colors and beading that appeared to be Native American. His black and gray hair was tied back in a ponytail.

"Evaline, this is Sam, a medicine man for the Shasta people. He is our oldest and most trusted human friend."

Mason gestured at me. "Sam, this is Evaline."

Sam didn't say anything but studied me for a minute before nodding and chuckling as Jonas pulled a chair up for him to sit in front of me. I glanced at the window and noticed the sun was going down.

"How long was I asleep?" I asked Mason in a whisper.

"About an hour."

Sam sat across from me, again not saying anything but watching me. He finally held his hands out, open, as if waiting for something to be placed in them.

Without a thought, I placed my hands in his, and he clamped them gently, just holding them in his for a long moment. The connection was strange but real. I was completely calm in that moment. My breathing was deep and regulated.

He closed his eyes and chanted in a language I didn't recognize. Isaac and the others hovered behind Sam, watching with curious expressions. Mason kept quiet'. I studied Sam as he chanted. If each wrinkle in his skin could tell a story, I wondered how long the book would be. After a few minutes, he opened his eyes but didn't let my hands go.

"She is your blood, Isaac," Sam whispered.

"Well yeah, Sam, she is now," answered Isaac.

Sam shook his head and turned to Isaac. "No, her blood comes from the same line as your own. It is an ancient blood. Both of your families come from one of the nine sons of the moon."

"One of the nine sons? What is that?" I asked.

"It's an old Shasta story. Explains where we came from—at least, that is what Sam thinks," Isaac indicated.

I looked at Sam. "Please, tell me the story."

"When Old Man created the earth, both the sun and moon had nine sons each. The nine sons of the sun threatened to burn up the earth, so Coyote came and found eight of the nine brothers and killed them so they would not burn up the earth. Before he could find the ninth, there was a great coldness upon the earth. The nine sons of the moon threatened to freeze the earth, so Coyote went to find them. It was then the spirit of the wolf came and had sons of his own. They only ran at night but still had their human skin. It is said the wolf spirit comes from one of the moon sons. When Coyote came to kill the sons of the moon, he saw the children of the wolf spirit and how cold they were. He killed eight of the moon's sons and looked upon the ninth. Coyote admired the children of the wolf spirit because he saw himself in them. He made a bargain with the remaining moon son. Coyote would spare him, the wolf spirit, and his own sons if he agreed to not have cold without warmth. The ninth moon son agreed. Coyote brought the ninth son of the sun and the sons of the moon together to give fur to these children of the wolf spirit." Sam paused a moment.

I could only stare at him as he continued.

"Your families both come from the same wolf spirit, but not all can change, only selected ones." Sam's gaze fell on me once again, and he still held my hand. "Daughters are few but play a very important role in the giving of life." He released my hands and touched my stomach. "New generations born, not bitten, must be to inherit the earth from their fathers."

Smiling, I glanced at Mason. He leaned forward clearly interested in this last part.

Isaac asked, "Sam, will the change affect the child?"

"A woman's body naturally protects the growing life inside her. This is no different. She will protect herself and the life of the unborn, and her body knows this."

Sam pulled back, and a tinge of pain glimmered in my head, but I ignored it as I sat back in the couch. I glanced at Isaac and then at Mason. "If I survive the change."

Sam gave me a reassuring look. "You are a daughter of the wolf spirit, and he smiles on you. He will give you the strength to survive the change, and you will be able to run with your brothers and sisters." He stood and strode for the door. As he placed a hand on the knob, he turned to me again. "Your grandfather, the moon, will be smiling on you tonight. Mind him and your father, and you will live."

Isaac extended his hand as Sam shook it.

"Thank you, Sam," Isaac said.

Sam leaned to him and whispered, "She must link to the wolf within this cycle, or she will run without a soul."

Isaac nodded, and Sam left.

No one said anything for a long moment, and again there was pain from my head indicating a headache was imminent but it went away.

I lifted a brow at Isaac. "What did he mean 'without a soul'?"

After a moment, he answered, "He said what we told you. If

you don't connect with the wolf, you'll run wild and not know what you're doing. You'll go into a rage, and it's hard to reel you back. If you don't find your trigger within this lunar cycle, it's nearly impossible to find it in the next. The wolf is more dominant the second time around if you haven't made the linking."

He turned to Aaron. "Let me know when you see them."

Aaron pulled his T-shirt off and unbuttoned his jeans. His eyes had the unmistakable glimmer as he turned and left out the front door.

The sun went down not long after Sam left, and with it, my head ached again and another knifing pain from my chest occurred. The television blared as Lucy and Mason sat there with me. They both tensed as if preparing for something to happen. A moment later, Aaron came in and Isaac joined us from the kitchen. My body's nerve endings pulsed as they had last night. I sat up but said nothing.

Aaron looked at Isaac and indicated it was happening. They were here.

Isaac turned to us. "Game time. Everybody look sharp."

My breathing began to change from long breaths to short ones, and Mason shot me a concerned look.

Everyone kept their gazes on me. I was the one person in the room not concerned with me but with them—what they were going to do, how they were going to fight for me.

I got to my feet. "I'm not feeling too good."

Mason and Lucy shot to their feet as I turned to Isaac.

"Isaac, please? Don't risk everybody's life for me. Let's just go far away," I pleaded, but his expression remained the same.

He came near me and gently cupped my cheek and I was shaking. "We protect our family, Evaline. That now includes you."

It would be futile to argue. Mason joined Isaac as I finally gave in.

Isaac dropped his hand and viewed me for a long moment before turning to Mason. "It won't be long." He nodded at me. "Keep your focus."

Isaac and Aaron left. I clutched Mason to me, and he held me close. My body ached, and the headache was now constant. Through the panting, I whispered in his ear, "What if... what if I can't connect with it? What if I hurt someone?"

Mason reared back slightly. "You won't. We won't let that happen, and if you don't make the connection tonight, we'll try again." He gazed into my eyes for a moment and took in a breath—he gave me the same look Isaac had a few moments ago. What were they seeing? He leaned and kissed me, flashed Lucy a quick nod, and was gone.

She closed the door behind him and turned to me, but I spoke first. "Why was he looking at me that way? Isaac did the same thing."

Smiling, she indicated the mirror on the far wall. "Take a look."

After crossing the room, I stood in front of the mirror and couldn't believe it. My eyes gleamed brightly—the same glimmer I had seen in their eyes, the same glimmer which unmistakably indicated what we are, was now looking back at me from the mirror. Lucy stood behind me as I studied myself for a moment.

"Why aren't yours as bright?" I asked.

"Because you are about to change. It's the main sign. That along with the headaches, body aches, breathing—"

"And weird thirst," I finished. "What is the thirst?"

"It's how the wolf inside us feels hunger. It draws us to the forest; it drives us to find prey, beckons us to hunt and only stops when you feed."

I sucked in a deep breath. I knew what that meant. "Is that why I have to link with my wolf?"

She went to the window, then turned to look over her shoulder at me. "Yes. It's why you must find your trigger. The thirst takes over, and you can't tell what you're hunting." Her eyes glazed over as if she was in a distant memory as she continued, "We didn't have anyone to help us when we turned. Isaac is our brother, our leader, but he was as new as the rest of us. We had to learn on our own."

In an instant, as if her memories projected into my head, a flash of images came into my mind showing what happened if they didn't find their triggers: a group of militia finding three mauled villagers; two boys playing in a field making a discovery of a dead body; hunters finding mutilated deer and a bear; crying from somewhere. I blinked, and the images stopped.

"We're trying to save you from the pain. Sometimes, the wolf memories surface, and you realize what you did. You have to find your trigger, Evaline."

The pain hit me at once, far more intense than last night. I fell to the ground in agony, my head splitting. My entire body quivered with an indescribable ache.

Lucy rushed to me, placing one hand on my head and shoulder.

"Evaline! Evaline, look at me!"

Despite my ear-splitting yells, I tried to focus on Lucy's voice. I could see her from the floor where I was.

"Evaline, stay with me. Keep focused. You can do this. Find it! Find what drives you."

Her voice was beginning to sound distant. No matter how much I focused, she sounded far away. Screaming, I flipped onto my back, holding my head.

My back arched. Was I being broken in half? When I scanned the room, everything was different—like someone held a red magnifying glass over my eyes. I saw every dust particle; smelled the old socks underneath a bed; heard the tatter of the small spider walking its web in the corner. Again, the battle for my body was happening.

"Evaline! Look at me!" Lucy shouted, but it was a muffled voice, and I knew the wolf wanted to come out—I couldn't hold it; the wolf was coming whether I wanted it to or not.

I managed to look at Lucy. "Outside, take me outside" was all I can get out.

The outside cool air tingled on my skin, but I was yelping in pain on the ground. Lucy was sitting next to me, holding my shoulder and talking, but I couldn't hear her. Instead, there were dozens of beats, like drums echoing through the forest—heartbeats. The thirst was back.

I remembered Lucy's words: "It beckons you to the forest."

My tongue slid over large, sharp teeth. I looked down, and my body wasn't mine. *No! No!* Growls were so close—and then I realized the growls were my own. *No! I need to stand! No! No!*

Lucy backed away and got to her feet. My pain seemed to subside for a moment but returned as I tried to stand. I reeled in pain when the transformation took hold. My clothes were on the ground as I stood on four legs for the first time—no longer human, but a wolf.

I shook my head wildly, then suddenly stopped as I stared right at Lucy. Eyes wide, she cautiously took a step back. Right then I knew I hadn't made my connection. Evaline was no more, and instead a newborn werewolf, powerful, completely unchecked, and wild, faced Lucy. I drew back my lips.

Lucy crouched slightly. Did she worry I would come at her? As utter agony ripped through my body, I yelped, the sound echoing throughout the forest. I let out a vicious growl and leaped toward the forest in a full gallop.

Lucy wasn't far behind. Quick flashes of trees and a stream kept coming into my mind, but I was so very thirsty and all I could think of was quenching this thirst. Another flash of two werewolves about to pounce hit me. Where did that come from?

Several humans with big guns surrounded something. A familiar voice rang out in my thoughts to find me. I think it was Isaac, but I wasn't sure. Another flash of a fight and then I stopped for a minute as gunshots rang out not far away. Lifting my nose to the air, I scented something in the wind. Two separate smells—one was similar but not familiar which told me perhaps another wolf, but the second scent was undoubtedly more inviting: prey.

Several quick blinks of a dogfight came to me but not consistent. Then, another flash of another time and place of the Cowans when they had been shot before, back in the early days, when they'd first turned. It stung like hell, but once the others dug the bullets out, they would heal within a day or two. The quick healing helped.

Then another of something called a *Lycan an t-Sealgair*. Now a man, not known to me, but surrounded by the Cowans. Mr. Cowan, Mason's father? He was telling his family the legend of a *Lycan an t-Sealgair*, which was Gaelic for "werewolf hunter."

This was followed by what appeared to be the mid-nineteenth century when the Cowans came across an actual hunter. Of course, they didn't know what he was at first as their father only told of them in his tales but this man was no story. He knew everything about werewolves—including how to kill them. As the story played out, he almost killed Aaron, but Mason and Jonas got to him first and killed him swiftly.

Lizzy located his case and found a journal and weapons of pure silver and vials of wolfsbane. According to the hunter's journal, wolfsbane was used to repel the wolf and induce it to go back to its human form, so was easier to kill. That had been their first encounter with a hunter but certainly wouldn't be their last.

Where were these images coming from? So quick. So scattered. They seemed to not be related. Then they stopped when the delicious aroma of prey filled my nostrils. It was close.

My focus narrowed in on a bush several feet away. In an instant I leaped toward the bush and found my prey. He screamed. A gun lay next to him. He reached for it, but I his fear smelled...delicious.

I bit down, and the man stopped struggling. Not more than a moment later I felt a sting on my shoulder as I turned from the dead man below me to another standing behind me with a syringe. I started shaking. A familiar wolf came at me. Before he could near, he was blindsided by another unfamiliar wolf; the other similar scent I picked up earlier.

Quivering violently, I yelped in pain. What was happening? Was my body shifting again? That's what it felt like. The familiar wolf arrowed through the air and slammed against a tree, but then rolled back and shook it off and faced off against the other wolf. Both bared their teeth and growled viciously, ready to attack.

The wolf that faced off against the familiar wolf, was big and equally ready to strike. I couldn't help as I bayed in pain. The familiar wolf seemed to regard me with concern, but the other wolf decided to take advantage of this lapse and lunged at her with full force, catching her neck in his powerful jaws and began tearing at it with his claws. Flashes kept coming of this attack as I think it was Lucy the wolf attacked.

She yelped in agony as she turned her neck around and got a hold of his paw. She bit down as he yapped and released her, rolling back ready to attack again. The other wolf and Lucy clawed and bit each other, facing off on their hind legs.

She leaped and bit his face and ears, and he sprang at her neck and lower jaw. He was strong as he swiped with his huge paw and knocked her over. Then, out of nowhere, two more wolves lunged at him from the darkness, taking him by surprise. The wolf must've realized he was outnumbered and decided to fight another day, as he gained his composure and ran with the other two wolves chasing after him.

While I couldn't move or talk or even growl, heard. A familiar voice rang out close to me. A voice I knew well. Mason. "Evaline, wake up."

My eyelids opened but not by me. Isaac examined me. He glanced away for a moment then grabbed the syringe laying on the ground. He put it to his nose and made a face. "Wolfsbane, and a lot of it. We need to need to get her home before they come back."

Nodding at Lucy, he placed his hand on her jaw. "Are you okay?"

Still in wolf form, she licked his hand so he would know she was fine. I heard slapping sounds, and someone picked me up. I was gliding through the forest at an unnatural speed and then everything went black.

Thirteen

I woke up in Mason's room again. I know I changed last night. Trying to sit up, my head felt heavy. There were incoherent images from the night before but I didn't remember anything specifically after being in the living room. I do remember telling Lucy I wanted outside—then it was a bunch of weird images. I don't think it was a dream or a vision, but perhaps a faint memory.

Trying to remember more, I grew angrier with myself as I wasn't sure if I made the connection or not. I hated not knowing exactly everything that happened the night before or what I had done. I was pretty sure I had hurt someone but what if I had hurt one of *them*?

I moved to the edge of the bed gingerly and put my hands to my head. A rather nagging headache loomed, but it wasn't like the others. I honestly could sleep all day, but I could hear the television in the living room, and I could smell everyone was in there—the anticipation as they waited for me to wake up was palpable.

"She's awake," Aaron muttered from the other room.

These heightened senses were going to take some getting used to. Mason's shirt hung loosely on me and covered the fact that I had no pants on. My jeans were nowhere. Groggily I went to the door and opened it. Everyone smiled at me, but no one said a word. Mason, relieved I was awake, bade me to come and sit next to him.

He handed me a coffee cup. "Figured you'd want some."

I smiled as I took a drink. So good. I turned to Mason. "I'm sorry. I tried to fight it but it was really strong. I don't know if I connected or not."

Mason's voice was soothing. "Baby, it's fine. You didn't connect but we'll just try again."

I turned to Lucy. "What happened last night? I didn't hurt you, did I?"

She shook her head. "No, you didn't, but you did successfully change—obviously you didn't find your trigger though. You were a little scary."

I sighed and looked at Isaac. "I think I killed someone. There's weird images from last night. I think some guy tried to hurt me, but I don't remember everything."

Isaac regarded me with sympathy and then flashed Mason a look. Did it mean I had killed someone? No one answered as I realized one member of the family was missing. "Where's Jonas?"

"At the hospital," Aaron replied. "Kristy is awake."

"Lizzy, do you know how she is? Is she talking?"

"She's good. She can't talk yet, but she can write. We got her a whiteboard, and she asked if you were okay. I told her we're fine, but I know she wants to see you. I told her you weren't feeling well and you'll be around in a few days when you were better. Laine was harder to convince. He knows something is up."

"Isaac, they did attack last night, right? Campbell?" I asked.

"They attacked but Campbell wasn't with them. I guarantee they'll come again."

"Well, maybe we should go to the state police right now."

"I don't think they care much about that right now, baby," Mason interjected. "When we got to you last night, they'd injected you with wolfsbane."

"Wolfsbane?"

"It's an herb used to suppress the wolf, so you'll go back to human form. That way you're easier to handle or kill," he answered.

Regarding Mason, I asked, "So, what do we do? Just wait here for another attack?"

"I don't think we need to wait long. There's someone coming." Lizzy stepped away from the window as Aaron got up and peered from behind the curtains to the front of the house.

"Two black vans and a police car," Aaron confirmed.

Isaac turned off the television and looked at Mason. He spoke firmly as he grabbed a jacket from the couch. "Take Evaline to Alban Loch. Stay there and wait for us." He passed the jacket to Mason, who gave it to me.

I put it on, and Mason picked up a pair of Lucy's shoes and handed them to me as we headed for the back door. I glanced back and watched Isaac and the others go out the front door.

Mason held my hand tightly as we ran through the forest. It was beginning to rain as the cool drops hit my head. The air was cold; winter wasn't far away. We reached the lake and stopped by the water's edge. I saw flashes of the others, but I shook it off.

"I keep seeing Isaac with Campbell, talking," I finally said.

Mason turned to me. "Members of the same pack are telepathically linked. We can project thoughts and images to each other so we know where we are. That's how we found you the other night and last night. The link is the strongest while in wolf form. Isaac prefers us to not use it in human form, but sometimes it can't be helped. We've been using it for so long, it's now second nature. Right now, Isaac is talking to Campbell. There are around two dozen men with guns and about ten other wolves. Things are getting tense."

I thought for a moment about my conversation with Jonas only a few days ago in my car before we were hit. "You mean he hasn't shown you yet?" kept running through my mind. Mason was watching me curiously.

"Show me," I said carefully.

"Show you what?" Mason retorted.

"Show me how we change, Mason."

A surprised Mason asked, "So going through it isn't enough? Now you want to see it?"

I shook my head. "I've never seen it, baby. I want you to show me. Show me what we do. I need to see what happens."

He gently held my head, leaned down, and kissed me. Then he caressed my head and released me, and I took a couple steps back.

Mason took off his shoes and removed his clothes, and I feasted my eyes on his perfect body. Every inch was more beautiful than the next. His eyes were bright, glimmering, and dilated. He closed his eyes and breathed heavily, and when he opened them, they were wild. He made a slight pained sound, but recovered, and I watched in amazement as his body contorted and changed.

The strange slapping sounds I heard the night in the hospital parking lot made sense now as I realized it had been bone and muscle contorting until he fully shifted into my big, beautiful, light gray wolf. Without fear I stared at the massive wolf in front of me.

He watched me cautiously but unflinchingly as I came to his side then touched his head and ran my hand through his thick fur. He was magical as though he was from somewhere in my wildest dreams. If I could have frozen that moment, I would have. In this form, he resembled a large wolf, but upon closer examination, it was very apparent he was something else. Something more than a simple wolf. The eyes are what indicates this, and his eyes weren't entirely wolf-like. They resembled more human distinction, but they weren't as human eyes were. There was a glimmer about them. The same glimmer all wolves have.

Our tender moment was suddenly interrupted by a bloodcurdling howl as scenes entered my thoughts like a television with flickering reception. Mason shifted back to his human form. The flashes, as incoherent as they were, showed me a chase with the Cowans as the prey.

Isaac's confident voice echoed through my mind, telling Mason to keep running as Campbell dispatched men and wolves to come after us. Mason threw on his clothes and took my hand. We took off but stopped abruptly as we came to a clearing in the thicket. Something was wrong.

He held me close as we smelled the unmistakable scent of danger. They were already here. Mason's eyes glimmered brighter, and I knew he was prepared to shift again to defend us. We sensed our family getting closer as Isaac and the others called to us.

Mason shifted in the same instant as three huge wolves leaped from a tree and lunged at him. The four of them crashed together in a heap several feet away, crushing every stick, stone, and bush in their path. I wanted to help but how? *I am useless without a moon!* The Cowans were still too far to help Mason, and he kept yelling thoughts for me to run. But every bone, every muscle, every nerve in my body wanted to stay with him—but strangely enough, when Isaac shouted with him, the combination acted like a switch, and I bolted. I ran fast but had no idea where I was going.

Continuing until I reached a stream, I hid underneath a sinking tree root next to the water's edge. I couldn't sense anything anymore or hear Mason and the others. I sat there, underneath the root, totally untouched by daylight. Trying to listen for them again, I closed my eyes and concentrated on their faces. Almost immediately, scenes started coming, this time uninterrupted.

Isaac and the others had reached Mason, but there a nasty fight was going on as the pending danger of more wolves and men with guns following the path from the house. In the bushes, there was a man who had a dart gun, and he aimed at one of the Cowans.

No! I screamed out in my thoughts.

It wasn't long before I realized both Lucy and Isaac, who were clearly the biggest wolves, were now lying on the ground, motionless, in human form. The darts had to be wolfsbane.

"We need to kill the brothers now. Start with Isaac. He's the alpha. Mason will be next because of his connection to the girl," Campbell yelled as four wolves aimed for the weakened Isaac.

"No!" I cried out again.

Only Mason, Lizzy, and Aaron were still able to fight. The Cowans were outnumbered and something inside me welled—anger, no—rage. As Campbell's smug voice cut through the scene as he leaned down to Isaac, who was awake but couldn't move, rage swelled within me.

"Looks like I get bonus points for bringing down the infamous MacCowan clan, as well as bringing in the last of the Murphy clan. Newly turned, she shouldn't be hard to find."

The tension brimmed on Isaac's face as Campbell continued, "Of course, the females will be taken back," he said. "They're too valuable to kill. Maybe they'll let me have *her*." He grinned as he eyed Lucy.

My anger was at a point where I was on fire. Sweat poured down my face, and I panted. Something snapped inside me, and I fell to my knees, grabbing my head. The pain was extreme as if I was being ripped apart from the inside. Was the change happening with no moon?

I focused back to Mason and the Cowans. I can't let them die! I won't let them die! I won't! My own thoughts went from sounding like my voice to a muffled growl—the wolf was coming out.

Looking down, my body wasn't my own. The headache stopped, and my thoughts and focus were the Cowans—no, my thoughts and focus were on my family. Crawling out from under the tree root, I stood up—on two legs but farther from the ground than usual. I was in "bipedal form" as Lucy called it. I let out a low growl and using my powerful legs, I moved from the ground to the trees and back down again, each step bringing me closer to saving my family.

I concentrated on their faces to see what is happening. Lizzy fell next as two men, one armed with a gun and the other with a syringe, managed to stick her. She threw a last swipe at her attackers as she went to the ground and changed back in human form. *No!* Aaron and Mason are still fighting ferociously, but the darts keep missing them. As I stepped on a boulder to look down on the fight, Mason's and Lucy's words to me keep playing in my mind.

"*Newborn werewolves are particularly vicious and dangerous.*"

I stood, watching at the fight below from the top of a large rocky cliff and let out a long, deep but low growl. Campbell froze. It was amusing to watch him panic as he realized he missed one of us. The others ceased fighting and looked around. Mason and Aaron froze, and I heard Mason's golden voice pierce through my thoughts.

"Evaline?" he asked.

I answered him in thought, "*I'm right here, baby.*"

Leaping from the boulder, a good twenty-five feet up, I landed on my feet and let out a roar that echoed through the mountains. Everyone needed to know I would protect my family and I was powerful—the wolf, and I were now one and fully connected.

The human with the dart gun took aim but missed as my reflexes were unbelievably fast. Two wolves charged at me, but I deflected one with a claw, and he went flying across the clearing. The second I caught, and as if the anger inside me has a mind of its own, I squeezed its head hard with my powerful arms. It yelped and thrashed wildly until it stopped squirming. Its lifeless corpse dropped to the ground. More wolves had joined the fight as they reached the clearing. Three more attacked me from the side, but Mason grabbed one. Now in bipedal form as well, he charged the other wolves. Aaron shifted to bipedal form and lunged at the third which attacked me.

We were supernaturally faster in bipedal form. As the attacking wolves shifted to their bipedal forms, the human attackers started running back to the house. I narrowed in on Campbell, who was standing in the middle of the clearing. Starting toward him, I halted when a familiar black-pepper-colored wolf stood in front of me. He was bigger than me, and with a quick swipe of his powerful arm, he knocked me onto my back. I hadn't seen it coming.

Mason let out an angry growl as he lunged for the wolf. Two more tackled Mason, pushing him back. The black-pepper wolf took a step toward me, and I recognized the scent—the man who had attacked me at the Blue Dawn and the hospital. I rolled onto my knees just as his head darted at me. Surging to my feet, I leaped out of the way of his large and muscular arms and landed behind him.

Before he could turn around, I hopped on his shoulders and bit his neck as hard as I could. Shrieking and roaring in pain, he reached back and pulled me off. I hit the ground but rolled and popped to my feet in an offensive stance, ready to attack. He growled at me and charged.

I leaped again, but this time he caught my ankle and swung me into a tree hard and I fell in a heap. Dazed, I got up and shook it off. By the time I did, the wolf was there and snapping at me again. Before he could, I jumped onto his back and bit, this time taking out a chunk of skin.

The wolf shrieked in pain, and I got thrown off again. I saw Isaac, who was being approached by a large bipedal wolf. In an instant, I darted toward Isaac, who was still immobilized. The wolf was seconds from swiping his claws at Isaac, which would have killed him. I bounded in front of Isaac and roared in anger. The wolf backed off but didn't give up. I advanced and slashed at him with my claws.

I squealed in pain as something sharp pierced my side—the dark gray wolf had slashed my side with his dominant claws.

I growled and sprung right back at him without hesitation.

From nowhere, Jonas leaped onto the battleground with a snarl and took out two more wolves.

I was in a face-off with the dark gray wolf and in the sights of the wolf who wanted to attack Isaac. The wolf advanced, but Mason swiftly tackled him, and they twisted up with each other, kicking up mud and dirt all around them. The dark gray wolf didn't advance. He just stood there as if he'd already won. A throbbing ache in my shoulder caused me to turn around, and there was Campbell, standing there with a syringe. I swiped my claws at him, nicking his jaw and lip before my claws retracted. *No!* My wolf weakened.

"No, Evaline!" Lucy cried.

I glanced at her as the last of my strength drained. The hair on my body retracted into my skin as did my protruding jaws. My crying turned into a blood-curtailing shriek as the pain from the wolfsbane invading my bloodstream made me want to vomit. Fire coursed through my veins as every inch of my body felt stunned. My body gave one last jerk as my muscles relaxed. It was my own voice I could hear when I collapsed to the ground, now a human once again. Campbell stood directly in front of me.

"Gotcha. They wanted me to bring you back, but you have succeeded in pissing me off for the last time." He snorted.

I managed to get some words out, and I was completely spent. "To where... Bring me where?" was all I could get out.

Campbell paused and then motioned for the dark gray wolf to wait. He kneeled. "You and your brother represented the last of the missing families. We told him what he could be and how much more powerful he could be. We told him he had to come back to Scotland, and he had to convince you to come back as well. All he had to do was agree. Instead, your idiot brother refused our offer, so I had to end him. Then there was the complication of you, and we were coming for you, but then you started snooping around, got more cops involved—and killed. I was ordered to track you down and bring you home but come to find out, you collected this nice little file on me, which of course would make life very difficult for my employers. The thing is, Evaline, I was just going to kill everyone you loved and figured the evidence would die with you. But then you went ahead and complicated everything by getting yourself turned. Had I known that the other night, I would have saved my two guys from being chew toys. Fucking MacCowans! But I guess we can thank you for that one since they were the other lost family we thought were dead. And now you are just a liability." He threw the syringe. "Fucking waste." He stood and motioned for the dark gray wolf to come forward.

Lucy and Lizzy screeched as Isaac tried to crawl to me. Mason roared but was pinned down. The dark gray wolf raised his claws, and I knew it was to deal me a deathblow. Then, out of nowhere, Aaron leaped onto the gray wolf's back and twisted his neck. The wolf's growls of pain echoed through the canyon but they ended with an echoing crack. The gray wolf fell lifeless onto the ground. Aaron had snapped his neck. He jumped off to brawl with another wolf.

"I don't believe it," Campbell uttered under his breath.

He pulled out a gun and took aim at my head. I knew I could die, but I was completely paralyzed. My muscles loosened, and my veins burned as the wolfsbane went through in my body. Unable to move, the wolfsbane was like a brick weighing on my chest. It was now or never and if this was my last breath, he was going to know.

"Mark my words, Campbell," I said with difficulty, "you'll get yours. The right people know where to find it and what I collected, is enough to put you away for life. Or, better yet, maybe your employers will kill you because you're the liability."

He cocked the gun, and just I was about to close my eyes, a shimmery arm reached out and knocked the gun out of Campbell's hand as a glistening leg kicked him to the ground. I looked up in disbelief at Jimmy, standing in ghostly form.

I blinked and strained to focus through the wolfsbane effect. It appeared Campbell's wolves could see him on the ground but they could not see Jimmy, and for a moment, they lost their focus, giving Aaron and Mason an edge in the fight.

Mason's voice cut through my thoughts. *Kill them now!*

Jimmy's voice echoed. With an eerie rasp and hints of his own voice, he asked, "What's wrong, Campbell? You look like you just saw a ghost." He paused, then, "Oh wait, you are." He took a step to Campbell who remained frozen.

"You aren't here! You're fucking dead! We killed you," Campbell shouted.

Jimmy grinned at Campbell and without warning, jumped *into* him. Campbell screamed and flailed wildly. As if having a horrible seizure, I realized Jimmy was tearing Campbell apart from the inside. His eyes began to bleed as he squealed uncontrollably.

"Enough of this!" a familiar voice rang out through the battleground.

Everyone stopped fighting and fell silent, the only sounds being the heavy breathing and squeals coming from Campbell. Mr. Minyawi walked toward Campbell and knelt. He touched Campbell's chest, and Jimmy surged out of Campbell and landed a few feet from me. My brother was fading and managed one last look at me before he disappeared. I turned back at Minyawi, who was rubbing his hands together.

"It's good I travel with provisions," he said, "including salt. It's so good for the pores as well as making pesky little spirits go away."

Viktor Minyawi regarded Campbell's wolves and ordered them back, indicating for two to pick up Campbell, who was now unconscious. The retreating wolves remained in their bipedal forms as they cautiously withdrew. Minyawi considered the dark gray wolf's broken and bloodied body lying dead on the ground.

He whispered under his breath, "His own nephew. So careless, Patrick. Such consequences to follow over one dead wolf."

Mason and Aaron, still in bipedal form, came to me, and Jonas, also in bipedal form, stood by Lizzy, who is still weakened from the wolfsbane.

All eyes were on Viktor as he casually approached Isaac, who at this point had gained some of his strength back as the wolfsbane was starting to subside. He had made his way to where I was on the ground.

Calmly, Viktor eyed Isaac. "This isn't working out the way it was supposed to. Your family is a real problem. Here we thought you were killed the last time we tried to take you home, and now here you are. Here we are. We are tired of the cat and mouse games. I must admit, it was surprising to learn you happened to be here, in this place, as we tracked Evaline home. It kind of makes you think of fate, doesn't it? Campbell was sloppy and doesn't follow instructions, but he is effective for getting, how you say it, under one's skin. It's amusing. You managed to quicken his end of service and of course, his pending reward." He grinned. "You will be sure to see him again."

He glanced at me. "Ah, Evaline. What a magnificent, wild beauty you are. I knew you were going to turn that night. Well done. I must say, I am quite impressed at your perseverance concerning your brother. I have never seen one so strong in the face of danger and death."

He glanced down where the dark gray wolf was lying, now the lifeless body of the man I recognized as my attacker at the Blue Dawn.

Sighing, Viktor eyed me as he continued, "You have remarkable strength, and I look forward to seeing your progress." He returned his attention to Isaac. "Come now, Isaac, be reasonable. We do not wish for any more bloodshed. You wish to save your family? You can. All you have to do is go home. Your pack needs you."

Isaac, unflinching, replied, "My pack is right here, and we *are* home."

Viktor laughed. "Oh, Isaac, still a pup yourself. Home is in Alba, and the McGregors are your pack. It is time for the clan to be one again. Why are you being so difficult?"

"We are MacCowans," Isaac shot back, "and if you or your lapdogs come at my family again, I will bury you."

Viktor laughed again. "No, you are McGregors. MacCowan was merely a cover so the English couldn't track down everyone. So, I am to assume you will not be returning to Alba then?"

Isaac said nothing, but his eyes told Viktor everything. Without their gaze leaving Viktor, Mason and Aaron shifted their bodies as if they prepared to attack if Isaac ordered them to. Instead, Viktor simply frowned, turned, and began to walk out of the clearing.

As he neared the edge, he turned once more. "It is a shame."

Isaac still said nothing, and just eyed him.

After a sigh, Viktor said, "You have no idea what powerful hands you are forcing. So be it. Hell is coming, Isaac, so be prepared. If you will not submit and come home, you will be destroyed."

He retreated, taking Campbell and the other wolves with him.

A long moment after Viktor was gone, Isaac turned to Mason and Aaron, who shifted back to human form.

"Let's go home," Isaac said.

Mason knelt by my side. "Are you okay?"

I felt completely exhausted and managed a whisper, "Just weak."

He swept me up. Lucy's wolfsbane was also beginning to ware off as she had managed to get up on her own and stood next to Aaron. Jonas picked up Lizzy, and the seven of us headed for home. As Mason carried me, I couldn't help but think it was not the end but the beginning of the end of something.

When we reached the house, we got cleaned up. Lizzy and I needed more time before the effects of the wolfsbane passed. Isaac said it would take forty-five minutes, give or take, to get our strength back.

I stood in front of the mirror in Mason's room getting dressed. Thoughts and voices were quiet but from the few thoughts that came across, the pending fight Viktor spoke of was a worry.

Slipping on Lucy's jeans, and a shirt Lizzy let me borrow, I noticed how different I looked: the slight glimmer in my eyes, my flawless skin; my long brownish-red hair shimmered as it lay on my shoulders and down my back, and of course, my now noticeably longer fingernails.

I walked out of the bedroom to find everyone in the living room, just as they had been earlier. Lizzy was lying on the couch, her feet in Lucy's lap. Isaac had parked himself in the big chair. Aaron and Jonas were on the coffee table, and Mason was on the couch, indicating for me to come sit next to him with a smile of relief.

I sat down, but no one said a word. It was like we were deciding what to say. After a long couple of minutes, Jonas finally leaned forward toward me and broke the silence.

"You were a fucking bad ass!" he exclaimed.

Any tension evaporated as we laughed. That morning, I had been the one member of the family that couldn't be counted on because of a non-existent connection, but not now. Not ever again.

"You were amazing. I couldn't believe it," Mason said.

"Neither could Campbell," Aaron added.

Lucy asked, "How did you know how to take that form instead of the hunting form?"

I answered, "I don't know other than I was pissed—really pissed. And I didn't want to hunt; I wanted to kill something."

"So, anger is your trigger?" Aaron asked.

"No. When I was hiding, I wanted to know what was happening, so I focused on Mason, and I connected with his thoughts, like a television channel. After hearing Campbell and what he wanted to do. He was going to kill all of you, and as he spoke, I grew angrier and angrier, into a rage, until I snapped inside and then the intense pain told me I was shifting. I wanted blood, and that was the one form I knew would be the most menacing, and then it just happened."

Pausing, I looked at Mason. "You are my trigger. All of you. Even when Campbell hit me with the wolfsbane, I wouldn't have hesitated to die to save any of you."

"Family," whispered Mason with a smile.

I smiled back, leaned over for a quick kiss, then sat back and glanced over at Isaac. "So, what are we going to do?" I asked as everyone quieted.

"Well, looks like it's not over." His expression was worrisome as he continued, "We have an unseen enemy in Scotland who obviously has a long reach here and for whatever reason, they wanted us there."

"Well, wasn't McGregor at the top of the list Evaline had?" Lucy asked. "It has to have something to do with the names on that list, which included us and Evaline's family."

Isaac agreed. "And Campbell said something about bringing us down and Evaline being the last of the Murphy clan. I don't know. It just doesn't make sense."

"Well, whatever the reason or motive, they're coming, and we need to be ready," Mason said.

Isaac shot a quick look at Aaron. "I agree."

Aaron walked over to pick up his cell phone. "I'll call Caleb." And he disappeared in the kitchen.

That night when I asked Mason who Caleb was, he said Caleb was the leader of a brother pack back east. They had apparently hunted together in the past, but Isaac had become wary of them because they were rough and sometimes, animals weren't the only things on the menu.

I suppose any extra help would be welcomed. We needed to be prepared for anything or anyone.

Fourteen

The combined smells of infection, bleach, and fresh blood flooded my head as I walked down the hallway to Kristy's hospital room. I'd never realized how bad hospitals smelled until I *really* could smell it. Strolling into Kristy's room, I found Laine snoozing in the chair. Kristy was awake and smiled at me immediately, reaching for my hand. Sitting next to her on the bed, I held her hand. She tried to speak, but nothing came out, and I gestured for her to use the board.

She picked up the board and wrote, "Was worried. You okay?"

"I'm fine. I didn't come because I didn't want to get you sick. You look good though. You really do."

Her smile faded as she studied me. Using her eraser, she removed any previous words and began writing again. She indicated the words she wrote on the board. "You look different." Then she wrote me again. "You know it wasn't a bear."

What could I say? She remembered. I couldn't contradict her.

The eraser quickly deleted the words and she wrote again, flipping her board towards me again. It said, "What's going on?"

I reached for her hand again, and after a moment, "Kristy, I need you to trust me, okay? Everything is fine. I'll explain everything when you get out of here, all right?"

Her gaze lightened a little and she wrote something down again. "Promise?" Is all it said.

I gave her a smile for reassurance.

She mouthed, "What?" as I smiled even wider.

"I have the most awesome news," I said.

Grinning, she threw her hands up, as if the anticipation was too much.

I decided to just blurt it out. "I'm pregnant."

Kristy couldn't hold in her excitement. She clapped excitedly, which woke Laine.

"What, what's wrong?" he asked groggily; then he noticed me. "Evaline! Holy shit, I was worried about you."

I hugged him as Kristy, still excited, grabbed his arm and

began trying to tell him with her hands. As amusing as it was to watch her try to explain without her board, he was still so clueless. Finally, she rolled her eyes, frustrated, and picked up her board. She wrote. "Pregnant!" and showed Laine.

His expression went from confused to pissed off. "Who the fuck was it, Kristy? I will kick the guy's ass! You don't—"

I couldn't help but grin in amusement at her frustration. She finally threw her board at him and pointed to me. He looked at me in surprise.

She grabbed my arm and motioned for her board. She started writing. "You aren't leaving, are you?"

I shook my head.

It was a happy moment, but it was clouded by the as-yet-to-be-had conversation about how I was now different. How would I explain it? No one was supposed to know. I was clear to Isaac that Laine and Kristy were also still my family and I couldn't just cut them off. He understood, but it just complicated everything. I would be around to watch them grow old and have families of their own. How strange it was going to be to not age as a human does. If one had been looking for immortality, this was the next best thing.

Of course, I never wanted it. It was Mason I wanted to be with, who just happened to be a werewolf—who happened to age just a bit differently than a human. I was complete with Mason—he was the missing part of my soul. He and I accepted that our intense attraction was due to the fact I was connected to them but so many questions remained.

Viktor had said we were part of a pack known as the McGregors. Then there was the question of Alba. Both of our families came from Scotland and there were other werewolves outside of Scotland as Minyawi was clearly not Scottish. Then there was Campbell. Even Isaac couldn't understand how a human managed to have power with wolves. He wasn't supernatural that I could see, but he was, in every sense of the word, a monster and a human monster was worse than any other kind. A human monster wasn't out to eat you or scare you. A human monster was a psychological nightmare which will tear into your very heart and soul and smile as it watched.

~ * ~

Caleb told Aaron they would get things in order and come as soon as they could, and in the meantime, Isaac was on full guard mode and ordered surveillance of the town in addition to running the Blue Dawn.

There was a special delivery I had to make.

Mason glanced at me and then back to the road. I peeked at the box of evidence in the back seat.

"Do you think they left?" I asked.

"No. At least that wasn't the impression we got from Minyawi. I think another fight is coming no doubt, and I especially need you to be careful."

"Why?"

"Because it's not just you I'm worried about. Evaline, we don't know enough about our kind having babies to know how changing, fighting, or anything else will affect it."

"Mason, regular wolves fight and hunt all the time, and I guarantee the pregnant female doesn't stay home. I'm pregnant, not incapable."

"This is much more complicated than you think."

"How so?"

"Because all of us instinctively want to protect you, and it's gotten more pronounced since last night. I feel like, at the drop of a hat, if someone or something is too close to you, I'll rip into them. It's worrying Isaac."

"Well, that's ridiculous. I can take care of myself."

"But that's it. We are not just like any other family. Baby, it's a whole new thing. You are not human anymore, but you're still thinking like one. We are a family, but it's a pack mentality. Isaac is the oldest, but it's not why he's the leader. He's the leader because he's the strongest."

Something clicked as I listened to him. "Is that why when you said to run in the woods when they attacked, I didn't want to, but when Isaac said to run, I did, no matter how much I wanted to resist?"

"Yes."

I couldn't believe it. "Well that… that just sucks, Mason. It's like my mind isn't my own anymore."

"No, it's not like that. You can say no and refuse, but it's a weird feeling when you do something opposite from what he says—not to mention Isaac's temper when you don't do what he says." He grinned at something.

"What?" I asked.

"This weird urge happens primarily when something is going down, but when it's like everyday stuff, it doesn't work. So, when we were first turned, Isaac was learning how the leader thing worked. Well, one day he looks at Lucy one day and says, 'Jump on one knee and bark.' She turned to Isaac and told him to fuck off. He was so pissed."

I laughed. She was tough and easily held her own. Mason pulled in front of the state police station and turned the truck off.

"Are you sure you don't want me to come in with you? I don't like it you want to go in alone."

"Mason, it's a police station. I think I'll be fine. Besides, it's best you're out of it."

After opening the door, I reached in the back of his truck for the box. As I walked up the steps of the Redding State Police barracks, I thought to myself, Jimmy, this one's for you.

~ * ~

Within days, the warehouse was seized, and the pit excavated. It was grim, but I knew what they would find.

There was a knock at my door weeks later, and it was Detective Roberts. At my behest, the state police had called him in since he had been the detective in charge of the initial investigation with Jimmy. My heart was heavy as I focused on the familiar ring in the evidence bag in his hands. They had found Jimmy. Roberts dropped it in my hands as I held that ring tightly.

"Thank you."

"No, thank you. We owe you an apology. There's an investigation into Officer Campbell, and it's much bigger than just him. There were thirteen other bodies in the pit. We're still examining, but we have identified all of them. We'll release your brother's body tomorrow so you can make arrangements."

"Thank you. Oh one more thing, what is the Spanditto Corporation?"

"Well, we are still looking into it, but so far, we think it's a dummy corporation for smuggling. We're just not sure what." He walked to the door and turned to me. "I am so sorry for your loss."

I shut the door and stood there for a moment, holding Jimmy's ring. I closed my eyes. All of those dreams, those sleepless nights boiled down to Jimmy trying to help. There was one other mystery that remained; the enigmatic dark figure in my dreams; the faceless representation of something I was supposed to see but didn't. Perhaps it will remain the unanswered riddle, which has plagued me these last several months.

~ * ~

We buried Jimmy next to my parents, beneath the black oak tree. Through all of it, the pain, the crying, the funeral—Mason never left my side. Afterward I began to heal. Not that the empty hole in my heart would ever be closed, but I had a new life.

Isaac officially hired me to handle the books and the financial end of the Blue Dawn. Kristy and Laine both healed and returned to normal. I decided to keep my secret from them, not because Isaac told me to. It was the best way to keep them safe. Only a couple nights a week did I stay at the house as it was more innocuous for me to live with the Cowans.

Shortly after the funeral, I was sitting in the living room when the Cowans came into the room. They gathered around with smiles, and I eyed them suspiciously, glancing at Mason.

"There is something outside we need you to see," he said.

He grabbed my hand, and we walked to the porch. There, standing in all its glory and a bright red paint job was my Cougar. The roof was fixed, and the paint was new. I couldn't believe it. My Cougar had been completely restored. I looked at Mason, who was smiling from ear to ear.

"Do you like it?" he asked.

I was speechless and near tears, so I smiled and hugged him tight as an answer.

"It was Aaron and Isaac mainly," he explained.

I pulled away and wiped my tears as Lucy and Lizzy hugged me. I walked to Aaron and Isaac and squeezed both as I whispered, "Thank you."

Aaron opened the hood, revealing a restored engine, which purred. It was a moment I knew made my dad smile. Perfect—a perfect moment in a perfect place, and I was finally happy.

~ * ~

A private flight landed in Sacramento. Several men, dressed in black suits, stepped off the plane and were greeted by a man waiting in a limo. Viktor Minyawi sat across from one of the men and calmly handed him a file.

"They are strong," he said.

The man opened the file, read the contents briefly, and glanced at Viktor. "Alastair isn't happy," he said in a thick Scottish accent. "What was supposed to be a simple extraction ended up bringing down our North American business enterprise. The heat is on, so we have suspended operations for now. He's now dealing with the death of his nephew Patrick; he wants them to suffer consequences."

Viktor took a moment before responding. "It will not be an easy task, Robert. As I said, they are strong."

Robert sat up straighter. "Isaac is a stubborn little bastard. Who would have ever guessed he would be as strong as he is when I bit him? I should have killed all of them that night when their father begged for their lives. And as for Evaline Murphy, Campbell's trying to harass her into backing off since he fucked everything up. Now she's turned, the agreement to leave her be is void."

"What of Kamden?" Viktor asked. "Wasn't that agreement between him and Alastair?"

"Kamden should be happy his niece is still breathing." He handed Viktor a folder and studied him. "You were briefed on the plan?"

Viktor's expression remained unmoving but smug.

Robert continued, "Then you know what must be done, which is why we are here. We cannot afford any more problems."

"Then you shouldn't have left Campbell in charge of this. He is reckless and impulsive," Viktor retorted.

"Campbell is no longer your concern. The MacCowan situation will end," Robert said with authority.

Viktor quietly nodded as he understood. "And what of Leathan?"

"He has new orders, but he will continue to operate with what we need here. You just concentrate on your next move, Viktor."

Viktor grinned. "As you wish."

Robert's gaze was focused up at the half-moon, his eyes gleaming and revealing the unmistakable glimmer of a hungry wolf.

Epilogue

The sun was starting to go down. Jimmy sat next to me as we watched the sun set. We were on the mountaintop we used to go to when our parents brought us here as kids. Every time I watched the sun from there, it was as beautiful as I always imagined it to be close to heaven. Jimmy seemed calm as he sustained his gaze on the setting sun and spoke to me.

"I know I'm gonna miss this."

I watched him as he continued.

"The silence, the smell, the sight." *He seemed deep in thought as he turned to me.* "You know you could have talked to me at any time; you always had it in you."

"No, it still wouldn't have saved you."

He smiled. "You did save me."

There was a moment as reality sunk in. His eyes filled with tears as did mine. "How can I do this without you?"

He looked down as if searching for what to say. "You can, Evaline, and you will. You will always find a way and you will never be alone." *He paused and appeared as if someone were there. He grinned as he turned back to me.* "He will never leave your side, and he will love you until the end. You need to know that."

A smile crossed my lips as a single tear rolled down my cheek when he spoke of Mason.

He glanced at the sun and back to me. "Any message for Mom and Dad?"

I sighed as I wiped the tear away. "Tell them I love them and I miss them so much."

"I will." *He then turned to me.* "Eva, can you do something for me?"

"Anything."

"I want you to live for me. I want you to do everything you wanted to do, everything life can offer."

"I will, I promise."

He looked again at the sun. It was almost down. "The light is *almost gone. I have to go."*

Not wanting the moment to end, I beheld him. He also watched me with sad but peaceful eyes. We were both crying, the tears streaming down our cheeks.

"*I love you, Evaline, and I always will." As he leaned in to kiss my cheek, I closed my eyes.*

A cool raindrop landed on my face as I opened my eyes to see Jimmy's headstone in front of me. The tears were still pouring as I blinked and whispered, "I love you too, Jimmy, forever."

Mason stood beneath the oak twenty feet away. He was giving me time, patiently waiting for me. I wiped the tears away and placed the single white rose on Jimmy's stone. He was right next to our parents and grandparents. They were all there, save one.

I walked to Mason's waiting arms as I embraced my new life and an uncertain future.

About the Author

Nothing captures the attention of M.L. Mastran more than writing a good story with amazing characters and a history arc that made the history books. This is *Albion Moon* in every sense.

On the flip side, M.L. can also journey to another world completely and pull the same elements with fantasy and make the reader yearn for more. Her uncanny ability to blend genres makes her unique to the literary world and an absolute reading joy.

From the first moment you open the page, curiosity will pull you in and keep you engrossed in the story as you take the voyage with the characters to different places and times; to experience the events as they unfold. Whether being told from a one-character perspective or several points of view, her stories will unfold in your mind like a movie playing in your head. This is what pushes M.L to write her stories. It's the thrill of the read and the drive to carry readers away that will make this trip to the literary world of imagination all the sweeter.

M.L. loves to connect with her readers. You can find her at:

Twitter: @MLMastran
Facebook: https://www.facebook.com/MLMastran/

~ * ~

We hope you enjoyed *Albion Moon*, book 1 of the Albion Moon Chronicles. If you did, please write a review, tell your friends, or check out the other offerings from M.L. and the other authors at Champagne Book Group.

Now turn the page for a peek into *Claimed*, the first book in the Claimed series by Andrea R. Cooper.

Claimed
Andrea R. Cooper

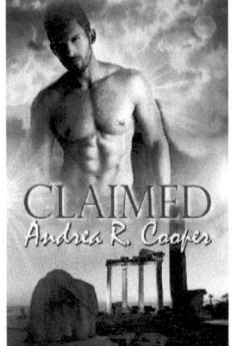

Renee Maxwell lands her dream job as assistant to archaeologist Damon Cubins in wondrous Turkey. However, she starts seeing strange things after finding a unique crystal. For one, hot Damon now looks like the sexy demi-god and underwear model of her dreams. Her feminist ideals are challenged with each bit of banter and seductive look he gives her, but she's not falling for his charm.

Time is of the essence for incubus, Damon Cubins, who must find a one-of-a-kind crystal or turn into a full-fledged demon. He has neither the time nor desire for love, but his new assistant tests his resolve. When he discovers she's got the crystal he needs to save himself, he must make a decision to either romance it from her or walk away. But can he?

One
Renee

Renee scooped out another bucket load from the archeological site and wiped her brow. So far Damon Cubin's saving grace was his extensive knowledge of ancient Phrygian culture, almost like he'd experienced it firsthand. Not to mention, he was the first archeologist to give her a chance as an assistant; for every other excavation, she amounted to nothing more than a volunteer. So, she ought to lay off him, or maybe it was the two hours of constant digging she'd been doing since dawn.

She exhaled, air trickling through her parted lips until her lungs screamed. The breathing exercise did little to unsour her mood.

Sifting through dust and rock was what she craved—the careful, almost artful search to discover a piece of lost history. The tan-colored tent several yards away mocked her, and she gritted her teeth. For God's sake, she was in Turkey, her dream spot to excavate religious artifacts, not babysit a guy who couldn't keep his dick in his pants for more than twenty-four hours.

Days earlier, when he met her and the rest of the team from the airport, he offered them meals and drinks. His easy-going nature and archeological knowledge enamored her. Not only was he living her dream, but the few pictures she'd scoured online didn't do him justice.

Intelligence radiated in his blue eyes, and she swore they peered into her soul. Then he showed his true colors by bringing some random woman he meet at the bar to the dig site to sleep with him. Did he hire Renee for the summer because few could tolerate his arrogance and demands? Demands such as he must strike ground first and they provide daily reports rather than the standard semi-weekly. She kept reminding herself: this was for her own future.

She scooted to another area in the grid, closer to the post mold. Damon believed this edge was once part of a goddess-worshipping temple. Last week, the Turkish government approved their expedition outside of Cappadocia, Turkey, and she was ecstatic when she received Damon's phone call to attend the dig. Now to focus on the archeological side of the job and not worry about her mentor vanishing again.

As the sun brightened the sky, the other team members and volunteers emerged from their tents to the tasks of making breakfast and setting out the tools for the day. The camp lay in a valley surrounded by sloping cliffs on two sides, a river, and sparse trees on the other. Gorgeous. Geological volcanic towers called Fairy Chimneys rose in the distance and pointed the way to Göreme.

In front of her was a roped maze of randomly dug holes for any artifacts. Damon must have already started before the entire team arrived. When she became a rich and famous archeologist, she wouldn't create rules just to prove herself a big shot. Holes littered the area; he must have started before she and the rest of the group arrived last night.

Beside the closest hole, she knelt. Scholars believed the Phrygians worshiped the Great Mother, and in the mountains, she was called Mountain Mother. Finding proof of a goddess revered together with a god in unity gave Renee hope that perhaps men and women could be equal in all nations and religions.

The idea of god as a woman appealed to her more than a stern old man killing everyone who didn't agree with him. Exhilaration surged through her at the possibilities. And yet, Damon had not stirred from his tent. Didn't he care about this dig or only about the female sharing his bed?

Last night, his lantern flickered after everyone, except Renee, went to sleep. Moans drifted from Damon's tent until late. *Who makes love for that long?*

A few paces away, several of the other team members milled about camp while Sarah, the cook on duty, warmed a pot of oatmeal over the fire. Renee's belly grumbled.

Using her flat masonry trowel, she scrapped a layer of dirt. Her handpick, looped through her belt, was available if the ground became too hard. Soon, she would shovel the soil she dug up and run it through the sieve before dumping it into the soil heap. First, she ensured no artifacts hid in the dirt. The sieve would take care of small pieces, but she shifted through the pile for anything larger. Nothing.

Renee inched closer to the hole. A sharp stone dug into her knee, and she cursed under her breath as she tossed it. *Damn it.* She wiped away the drops of blood. Not too deep of a cut. Later, she'd get the first aid kit for a bandage.

She glanced over at Damon's tent. No movement or sound. *Where the hell is he? Still asleep?* Perspiration rolled down her spine, and she straightened, pushing her shoulders back for a few seconds to ease the tension.

Kneeling forward again, she thrust the trowel in a little too deep and struck something hard.

Shit! She eased the tool out, then grabbed one of her small brushes and a dental pick. *Please don't be damaged.* Her hands shook, and she took a breath to steady herself.

She drilled at the hole with the trowel, then wiped away the debris. Something reflected the light, and her pulse raced. She'd never forgive herself if she broke an artifact. Biting her lower lip, she used a smaller dental pick to widen the hole.

As she fished with her fingers, a smooth slip of a surface hit her fingertips, then a rougher one. Excitement zinged through her. *Better than opening presents.* She retrieved a toothbrush from her tool belt and slowly swept away the soil and debris. Now the object looked like a piece of jewelry or a gem. Realizing blood remained on her fingers, she rubbed them on her shorts. Careful to avoid any further harm to the object, she eased the piece out of the hole with her clean hand. The artifact was the size of both of her fists.

"Breakfast is ready," Gary, one of the volunteers said, startling her, and caused her to almost drop her prize.

"Thanks. I'll get some in a bit." No time for food. Hopefully, she hadn't inadvertently cracked the object. Her goal of running her own dig soon would be struck down if she had. Sure, everyone made mistakes, but she'd been careless.

There were too many people around the excavation for her liking, and often half of them didn't know the first thing about how to handle archeological equipment. Yesterday, Damon told them he sent the resistivity detector for repairs after one of the men dropped it when they set up camp.

Renee's fingers wiggled the item to extract it. If she could get a bit more leverage... She dug around the item. The piece released with another tug, and she held it in her hand. *A rock?* Dark quartz with a smooth reflective surface on one side and a chunk of granite embedded in the other. For a moment, her vision darkened as if the stone hypnotized her. Despite blinking rapidly to focus, the tunnel narrowed. Was she passing out? *Don't panic.* She took several deep breaths and relaxed as the blackness faded, and finally her vision cleared. *What the heck just happened?*

Disappointment pierced her heart. Not an artifact at all, but a smoky quartz that had grown out of the granite and would be sent to the midden, the site's area used for disposal, as trash.

Still, the quartz was pretty enough. She could have it cut out of the rock, polished, and crafted into a necklace. With her experience she knew none of the archeologists, including Damon, would care about a piece of quartz. A wave of nausea cascaded through her. She should eat breakfast. Soon.

Once she thrust the crystal into the pocket of her shorts, she speared the dirt with her trowel, careful not to strike too deep. If anything, the necklace would be a souvenir of her time here in Turkey. Cappadocia, once part of ancient Greece until the Ottoman Turks took over, was a country she loved. How she wished the ancient temples stood in all their glory and not heaped in piles of rubble.

Sarah tapped her on the shoulder. "Your oatmeal is getting cold, dear."

Behind Sarah, the others laughed around the tents at the campsite and a few hiked toward Renee with their tools rattling on their belt loops.

"Thanks." She accepted her bowl of oatmeal.

"This heat is ruining my skin." A woman whined to Renee's left.

Damon and his girlfriend emerged from their tent. Her thin figure contrasted with her enormous breasts, making her look as if she would topple over.

Wish I could pull off wearing short shorts like those, but they'd climb up my butt.

"Come back to bed and entertain me some more." The girlfriend pouted.

Damon, dressed in khaki shorts that showed off his golden,

muscled legs didn't answer as he scanned the dig site.

Renee took out her ear buds from her back pocket, and after stuffing them in her ears, cranked the rock music up. *Much better.* Nothing was worth hearing Damon's conversation with his picture-perfect girlfriend.

With her breakfast finished, Renee rose to set the bowl among the others near the cooking fire. Stumbling, she caught herself before she toppled. Did she get up too fast? The dizziness subsided, so she shook off the feeling and after the metal bowl clinked with the others, she returned to her location and bent over her work. Even after two additional full shovels out of the pit, nothing but dirt and more rocks. Not even another crystal.

When a shadow darkened her work area, from her crouched position, she took out her ear buds and glanced up.

"Anything unusual?" Even though Damon's words were casual, annoyance filled his expression.

Her breath caught. Sure, normally she thought of male models when she saw him, even down to the pouty full lips and stubble on his chin. This time, he looked like a god. Like he would make Michelangelo smash his David sculpture and use Damon instead. She swallowed. His skin appeared to capture the light as if in a photo shoot. Even his eyes... Good god, they were a swirling mix of twilight and indigo. A hallucination?

Had she'd been in the sun too long?

"No nothing yet." She nearly drew out the quartz weighing guiltily in her pocket. Except, he'd probably laugh at her. "I'll let you know if I find anything worthwhile."

"Who gave you permission to dig?" His tone was condescending.

How dare he insinuate she went against protocol! "The holes all round—"

"Didn't you read your contract? It specifically says nothing is done outside of my approval." Now he frowned. "Even shovels of dirt *after* they go through the sieve, I must inspect before anything is added to the soil heap."

"I know. You have rights to break ground first, and you have." An undulating movement like a heat wave shimmering on a burning road, glided across the ground between them and she blinked several times to clear the image.

"Have I?" A breeze lifted the edges of his golden hair. "How do you know *I* dug these holes and not local treasure hunters?"

"Since you've been here a week before us, I assumed you did

this."

His brow furrowed. "Don't *assume* again. If you uncover something, anything unusual, bring it to me *immediately*." He shook his head. "I thought I could trust your judgment, but perhaps I was mistaken."

Rather than aiming her trowel at his feet, she stood. Clenching her jaw, she forced the words. "Sorry. You're in charge. It won't happen again." *Your holy highness.*

Without another word, she stomped off toward her tent, her legs nearly buckling. Travis, balding even though he appeared only to be in his late twenties, blocked her path. How had she not noticed his hair loss before? He was one of the site stewards who watched for looters. A volunteer if she remembered correctly.

Her mouth tasted as if it was filled with sand. Was she getting sick?

"Damon's under a lot of pressure." Travis changed the subject. "Probably another layer or two before we reach the assemblage."

Thank goodness he didn't patronize me by giving the definition of an assemblage like the last archeologist she worked with the previous summer. How many times had she told him, 'I know an assemblage is when a group of artifacts are discovered together?' Each time, the man had blinked hard, then grumbled.

Nodding, she waivered. Travis merged between human and gnome-like, similar to the ones Paracelsus, the Swiss alchemist, drew in the sixteenth century. The same pointy elongated ears, squat body, and white beard stretching to his belly. Geez, she was losing it.

When her knees wobbled this time, she lost her balance.

"Easy there. Are you okay?" Travis grasped her elbow, steadying her.

Yes, the heat was definitely getting to her. Need to lie down before she fell. Just great if everyone remembered her because she fainted. "I'm fine, low blood sugar or something."

The oatmeal in her stomach churned. She didn't bother to explain herself further, but stumbled into her tent. The two steps to her cot seemed miles away and beneath her the ground bobbed. Dizzy, she pushed her legs forward. Except they refused to listen to her commands, and she collapsed.

We hoped you enjoyed the excerpt from *Claimed*. This and other terrific books from Champagne Book Group are available at major booksellers and vendors.

~ * ~

For notice of sales and special deals, visit Champagne Book Group at (http://www.champagnebooks.com) and sign up for our newsletter, including chances to get advance copies of releases before the general reader public does.